# Mammoth Secrets

I0670067

## Ashley Elizabeth Ludwig

**Mammoth Secrets**

Contact Information: titleadmin@pelicanbookgroup.com

All scripture quotations, unless otherwise indicated, are taken from the Holy Bible, New International Version(R), NIV(R), Copyright 1973, 1978, 1984, 2011 by Biblica, Inc.™ Used by permission of Zondervan. All rights reserved worldwide. www.zondervan.com

Cover Art by Nicola Martinez

White Rose Publishing, a division of Pelican Ventures, LLC
www.pelicanbookgroup.com PO Box 1738 *Aztec, NM * 87410

White Rose Publishing Circle and Rosebud logo is a trademark of Pelican Ventures, LLC

Publishing History
First White Rose Edition, 2015
Paperback Edition ISBN 978-1-61116-435-0
Electronic Edition ISBN 978-1-61116-434-3
**Published in the United States of America**

## Dedication

To my grandparents, Bob and Vivian Bryan, who've gone to their heavenly home—thank you for the moonlit Spring River, southern summer nights, and providing the home of my heart.

To my Aunt Anna Lou "Boo" Weathers, who believed in my stories long before I believed in them myself.

# Praise

Ashley Ludwig's snappy, contemporary voice meets nostalgic, small-town romance in *Mammoth Secrets*, where the only thing as sweet as the memories saved are those being made. ~ Joanne Bischof, Christy Award Nominated Author of "Be Still My Soul"

# 1

And you will know the truth, and the truth will set you free. ~John 8:32

Lilah Dale mulled her newest menu idea for the family diner, shortcutting through Cherokee Springs Park across the footbridge. "Too spicy. Too exotic. No one'll even try it."

Water rushed over the falls beneath her feet in an endless curtain, where the river curled south through Arkansas.

She passed the red-handled cooler from one hand to the other and glanced at the sun, just rising over the hills.

Eden was opening, and her polar-opposite sister was never late.

If Lilah hurried, she'd make it to town in time to prep before the breakfast crowd arrived. Mentally, she ticked through the same old, same old, day in, day out.

Mr. Hackleberry would want toast and poached eggs. Because it was Saturday, the Emerson clan would be there for mountains of pancakes. Scrambled eggs and sausage for Mr. Steadman, who'd sit at the counter by Papaw like it was his job.

*Lord, what I'd give for a little bit of change...* Passing the visitor center, she cast a longing gaze heavenward, all but tasted the cilantro she'd chopped up yesterday. Her latest kitchen triumph was perfecting chipotle sauce. Change today looked like grilled trout smothered in the stuff. Totally crave-able. Too bad no one would order it.

The lonely truck in the empty lot gave her pause, parked just to the left of a posted "No Camping" sign.

California plates, windows steamed with a night-full of breath, and it didn't look like the driver could afford the two-hundred-dollar ticket.

Taking a mental coin toss between where she needed to go and what she ought to do, Lilah crossed the parking lot to the driver's window, and saw him through the foggy glass. Like an old motor, her heart kicked over.

His jaw hinged open in a snore. A crop of overgrown, red-gold hair obscured his face in shadow, his movie star features looked a day or two past shaving. Handsome in a gut-check way, though she had no right to look and admire. Not now, and maybe not ever again.

Lilah set down her gear and knuckle-rapped on the window, quick-stepping back when the drifter's eyes flew open in a gasp.

"Wha—? Where?" He blinked, sluggish, and a hand scrubbed his stubbled face.

"You lost?" She nodded toward the crumpled map at his side.

The now-awake stranger seemed more rugged. Raw. And utterly male.

"N-no." He cranked the window down and wiped his eyes. "Road weary. Pulled over last night to wait for morning. Guess the falls put me to sleep."

"You can't camp here. They'll ticket you, for sure." She thumbed at the sign. "Park gets more cash that way than from tourists, believe me."

"I'm not—"

"There's a motel across the river, or if you're tight, the campground. It has showers, facilities." She picked up rod and cooler, elbow-pointing the direction. "Good thing I got here first or Rita might've called the cops."

~*~

Across the river, the fierce wail of an approaching train caught their mutual attention.

Jake watched the engine heave its bulk around the curve, *rat-a-tatting* across the tracks. Its rusty cars and cargo stuttered through the trees like a loose movie reel.

He turned for a better look at the girl who'd woken him.

Tall and willowy, with blonde curls that framed her suntanned face, a dusting of freckles on her nose, and an obvious distrust of strangers, by the way she stayed well out of arm's reach from his open window.

He did his best to cast a friendly, non-ax-murderer smile. "Catch anything?"

"Rainbow." She revealed the ample stack of filleted trout. "Good morning for it."

"As delicious as that looks, is there a fast food restaurant or something nearby?"

"In Thayer, just across the state line." She flicked her gaze to the little wooden cross dangling from the rearview mirror, then back to him and grinned. "You could do a lot better than fast food, you know. Try Earl's Kitchen, in town. Good for the soul." Her brows jogged in good humor, and Jake watched her ponytail swish as she disappeared under the bridge.

He should have offered her a ride, said something,

but she hadn't really given him a chance to mention that he wasn't passing through. But waking to the sight of the natural beauty with a cooler full of fish had scrambled his thoughts.

Dragging the crumpled state map from where it bookmarked last night's reading from Exodus, he spied his location. Mammoth was a dot, just on the Arkansas side of Missouri's boot heel. He'd made it after all, though he thought he'd missed it altogether. Blink and you'd drive right by. *Now what, Lord?*

Would Margaret have ever come to a place like this? With no mall, no fancy restaurants? Not a chance. Because his hair blocked his view, he blew through his shaggy bangs. "That's not the haircut of a pastor," her voice scolded in his memory.

Great way to make a good first impression with his new congregation. Accordioning the map, he tossed it to the dash. Wifeless. Homeless, except for the lodgings the Women's Auxiliary League provided for him.

His parent church hadn't given him much background on his new home, just that they needed a fresh start as much as he did—that's why Dad allowed him to abbreviate his name, arrive incognito. Jake Gibson would be known as Jake Gibb until he'd found himself—decided which path to take. Accept his place as heir to his father's mega ministry, or to leave the pulpit all together, with no one the wiser.

"It's better for you, better for everyone until you get back on your feet."

Memory of his father's calm, mega-church pastor's assurance followed him as he drove east, and still churned his gut. A good son, he'd try it Dad's way. For now.

Maybe this was what he needed. He'd deleted himself from all social media, as if he'd never existed, with no old friends, and nothing to fall back on but his teaching and the Lord's good graces. And a town of under one thousand souls? To Margaret and her friends, it probably looked like punishment, hidden away from everything and anyone he'd ever known. And right now? That was fine with him.

Jake opened the driver's door, cringing at the long creak. He hopped out, turned this way and that to stretch his back and to catch the mid-April breeze. The glassy pool of Cherokee Spring beckoned, a broad, flat lake rounded by rocky slopes and patches of grass. Its edges grew thick with sucker plants. But the water! With shades ranging from clear at the shore to midnight blue at the depth, it struck him as a mini Lake Tahoe. No tourists, though, and no one fishing on this brisk spring morning. Just a sad-looking dock with paddleboats tied up on one side, while crumbled cement pilings jutted off on the other like a bridge to nowhere.

No one was fishing up there.

He thrilled briefly, thinking about the mysterious blonde with the cooler full of trout. When his ragged-edged heart healed, he'd only date girls not afraid of baiting a hook.

He jammed hands into his jeans pockets. Since a path wound around the spring, he decided to walk it, take in his new surroundings, and pray the weight of guilt off his shoulders. He wished he'd taken the time to search the internet for the church and the town, instead of trekking across the country like Moses with a map. A church like this was basically a blank slate. But then again, so was he.

Turning away from the stream and lake, Jake hoofed it toward the now-open structure. Inside, a heavyset ranger sat behind her desk, paperback tight in her hand. She greeted him without glancing up. "Welcome to Cherokee Springs State Park," she said in a drawl. "Bathroom's down the exhibit hall and to the right."

"Thanks, but that's not why I'm here." Jake stood in front of her and grinned. "The lake. It's fascinating."

Her romance novel dropped a few degrees as surprise brightened her gray eyes. "The aquifer feeds the whole Ozark river system, but I like the Cherokee legend–says the chief's son died here, looking for water after a long drought. The spring came up right where they buried him. Been bubbling ever since."

"In my experience, most legends come from some slice of truth."

He gathered a map and brochure from the Plexiglas stands and studied a picture of a clear blue aquifer, young weeping willow trees at its edge. "You been here long?"

"I started with the parks service right out of high school. Only job I've ever had." She straightened her name badge, eying the wall frame congratulating her for thirty years of service. "Used to be beautiful." She shook her straight, granite-colored locks, giving him the feeling she meant more than just the park.

"It still is." Jake looked out the window, trying to see it through her eyes. "The bones of the place are good. Thanks for the map, Ms. Hollister."

"Call me Rita. Everyone does." Her grin erased ten years from her dour appearance. Turning the swivel chair toward the sidewalk, lined with scrub-grass and bare earth, she sighed. "Just wait until the wildflowers come out in a couple weeks. But, you're just passin' through. Maybe when you'll be headed back the other way?"

"I'm here to stay, I'm afraid." He held a hand out in greeting. "Name's Jacob-Jake Gibb. I'm—"

"Pastor Gibb?" She gave his hand a hearty pump. "As in Cherokee Springs' new pastor?"

"That's right."

Her gaze went deer-in-the-headlights, caught. "Not to be disrespectful..."

"Believe me." He leaned in, voice lowering into a conspiratorial whisper. "I'm as surprised as you."

They shared a laugh as she hopped off the stool. "Let me be the first to welcome you to Mammoth, Pastor Gibb." She circled around the counter to walk him to the door, standing all of five feet tall, hands parked on her hips. "We've certainly been waiting for you!"

"Sorry it took me so long to get here." He frowned, knowing that he should have arrived in the middle of last week. "I had some business to attend to in California before I came out..."

"Ah, yes, about that, Pastor." She cleared her throat with a noisy rattle.

His stomach dropped a notch or two. Here goes, lowering the boom. The church leaders had decided they didn't want a divorced man leading them. Mouth dry, he flicked a glance to the packed truck, his homelessness spearing deep. "Is there a problem?"

She frowned, a flush rising to her cheeks. "Just some friendly advice. Be careful with too much California talk. Folks 'round here think anyone from west of the Rockies can't be trusted. Not me, a'course." She hooted a laugh.

"I'll take that under advisement." A sudden rumble from his midsection and he palmed his empty stomach. "Sorry. I haven't eaten anything but chips and a soda since last night."

"That's easy enough to fix." She pointed out directions. "Under the bridge, and left on Main Street. Earl's Kitchen's on the right, across from the pharmacy. I'll phone the auxiliary, an' all. Let 'em know you're coming."

"I'd appreciate that." His smile betrayed thoughts of the freckle-faced young woman with the cooler of fish. Brochures in hand, he paused at the door. "Where's that diner?"

She jotted quick directions on a pad and then handed it over. "Earl's is kind of Mammoth's meeting place, especially since our old pastor...well–" Her voice went grave. "Since–"

"Right." He nodded, as if that explained everything.

"Hot Springs Ministries didn't have much of a bio on you. And the ladies league didn't find you on that Facebook."

"Yeah, I try to stay away from social sites." Jake dragged a hand over the back of his neck, sighing. *Should have been ready for this, Lord. I should have—*

"I'm with you, Pastor. If I'm gonna make friends with someone, it's over a cup of coffee."

"No need to worry about me. I, um, my wife..." The words lodged in his throat. *How do I say this?* "Uh, she, she's no longer—"

"Oh, Pastor!" Impossible not to notice the wash of sadness over her pale blue eyes, the tinge of pink at her cheeks—her obvious embarrassment for asking such a personal question.

He cringed. "Actually—" *Just say it, Jake.*

A crackling radio interrupted before he could explain. The rapid firing of code numbers snapped Rita into action. With a squelch, she grabbed her walkie-talkie.

"Duty calls!" She walked him out to the parking lot and waved goodbye as she hefted herself into the little electric golf cart with the spring's logo. "Under the bridge, hang a left to get to that diner."

"Well, then." He backpedaled and climbed in behind the wheel. "Thanks for the directions. And the welcome."

"We should be thanking you!" she called out and buzzed off.

With a final wave, Jake headed to the scatter of buildings that made up the blip of Mammoth, Arkansas.

His new home.

# 2

Lilah stowed her morning's work in the walk-in fridge and punched her card just a few minutes later than planned.

Hallelujah pop filtered through the built-in speakers and spoke of her sister's, holier-than-thou mood.

Through the window that separated the kitchen from the floor, Eden wiped down the last of the booths with her vinegar cleanser. Even the prep table's stainless steel gleamed.

Lilah dragged a fresh apron from the stack and called a hello across the empty restaurant.

"You're late." Eden popped a piece of gum and went to the register. Change rattled into the drawer as she hip-shut it with a bang.

"Sorry." Lilah hustled to the counter and grabbed her whiteboard. With a frown, she wiped off the un-ordered special from yesterday. Strike that. Plenty of people had ordered the French dip. Just not with the layer of melting Swiss or caramelized Vidalia onion. With swoosh and flourish, she scrawled her description of succulent, pico de gallo-covered fish sandwiches with tangy chipotle sauce.

Raymond slunk through the back door, blue bandana tied over his overgrowth of black, curling hair. With a yawn and stretch, he tied a white half-apron over his jeans.

"You're late, too," Eden scolded, adjusted her name badge over a square of lace handkerchief. She changed "Closed" to "Open" with a flip. "I made the coffee."

"Better drink it before the customers come in and complain about too much chicory."

"I know how to make coffee, Lilah." Eden snapped.

Lilah propped the board up over the soda fountain for all to see. And ignore.

Raymond ambled to review her handiwork.

"Don't matter how you word it, Lilah." He spoke in a slow, resonant drawl. "They're gonna order what they always do." He was eighteen now and not a bit the boy she once babysat.

"Can't blame a girl for trying."

The bell announced the breakfast rush.

Eden shot to hostess mode and greeted morning regulars by name with hugs and chatter, until booths and tables filled to capacity. The phone rang, and Eden answered, "Earl's Kitchen! How can we make your day?"

Low, lyrical voices buzzed as one by one Lilah plated orders from the wheel. The rhythm of the work, the repetition, the monotony as coffee sloshed into mugs, bacon sizzled and popped on the griddle, and home fries crisped under the broiler. Just another day.

Save for the drifter.

Those eyes. That smile. No ring on his hand. With an idle rub to her own free finger, she gathered the toast and tossed a few jelly packets on the plate. Looks could deceive.

She slammed the order bell a bit too hard. Scrambled eggs with well-done sausage plated for Mr.

Steadman. Ray emptied the industrial washer at Lilah's back. A quick scan of the tables showed no new faces. Maybe he'd gone to that fast food joint across state line after all. Just the same old, same old, at her grandfather's diner. Then the door chimed.

~*~

Jake steered toward the flickering neon orange sign that declared Earl's Kitchen. He parked in between a huge, old sedan and a bevy of trucks. Engine off, he pulled out the key. Studied it, solitary in his palm. So, this was what starting over felt like. Eyes closed, Jake prayed that this time he'd do it right. No compromise. No settling. No running away. No one to know who he was or compare his sermons to his father's mega-ministry. He stepped out into the noonday air to meet his congregation. The door jangled.

Heads swiveled to view his arrival.

Senses greeted with the siren song of roasting coffee and frying bacon. Silverware scraped plates as the masses devoured breakfast. He palmed his midsection with the notion of real food and scanned the jam-packed dining room. Kitchen in back, cook busy flipping flapjacks. A bleached-blonde waitress in orange walking shorts and crisp white blouse shot soda into glasses from the huge dispenser. Above, a propped whiteboard with handwritten daily specials and artfully drawn trout declared "Papaw's Catch of the Day!"

The booths, barstools, and tables were filled with all manner of folks dressed in megastore five-dollar button shirts and rock-bottom bargain jeans. The only seat in the house was a lone bar stool between two men—a heavy-set, sun burnished construction type, and a thin, elderly man with a spray of white hair and smudged glasses.

"You must be Pastor Gibb," a resonant country twang from the half-circle booth halted his progress.

*Parishioners before yourself,* his father's voice reminded through the hunger. *Here goes.* Jake changed course, parked his pastor's smile, shook hands with the man, and nodded to his pregnant wife, doing his best to remember the rattling of names. Scott Thompson. Emma. Kids. He nodded to their stair-stepped, blonde-headed children ranging in age from a bored-looking high school girl to kindergarten twins. "Nice to meet you. Thanks for the welcome."

Their toddler stopped fiddling with fish crackers from his highchair perch and reached toward Jake's belt.

"Here, Dewey." The mother, Emma, filled the tyke's hand with an orange bite and looked up with a smile. "You stumbled into the local meetin' place. Everybody's here, most days. My Scottie's one of your newest deacons." She gave her husband's lanky arm a pat.

Scott scanned the packed room, then his full table with a slight shoulder jog. "We could pull up another chair—"

"Dad!" The girl shot a mortified look at her father, then to Jake, finally ducking her attention low, over a mobile.

"Oops!" A splash of white as one of the twins' milk toppled.

Emma sopped the reaching splash with a fistful of napkins. "He don't want to sit with us, Scottie. Let the man eat a meal in peace."

"Another time, maybe." Jake gave in to the urge to ruffle the highchair toddler's curly hair.

The kid actually giggled, the rest of the family following suit, save for the red-faced texting teen.

Just then, the blonde waitress hurried up to greet him. A flash of recognition told him it was the same girl from the parking lot, but no freckles, too bleached hair. Her sister, maybe? Her nametag read, Eden, pinned over a lace hankie at her shoulder as she squeezed his hand in welcome.

"I'm Eden Dale. You can call me Edie." Hand to hip, she smile-chewed, and snapped tiny bubbles with her gum. "Now, where shall we sit ya?" Everything about her spoke confidence in volumes.

He read nothing but trouble coming at a million miles an hour. "I think maybe I'll just order to go." *Should have gone to the drive through, then straight to the church. What the heck am I doing here?*

"If you're done greeting our new celebrity...order up!" Another voice called from the back. The tone and timber of voice was identical to Eden's, minus the Ozark-ian twang.

He followed the sound, doing a double take at the woman's face. Not just a sister, but twins.

"Coming, Lilah," Edie snapped, then plastered her grin back in place. "That's my sister. She's a bit on the serious side, but don't mind her. She needs all the prayers she can get." Aside, she whispered a bit too loud, "She's gettin' a divorce."

Jake nodded. Getting, as in, still married. That slippery slope of the almost divorced was familiar territory. Limbo that could be over in a snap, or last long torturous months. He'd counseled so many to avoid that trap of falling for the still involved. A stolen glance at the glowering figure at the grill, and he caught the message loud and clear.

Lilah Dale was off limits. Her freckle dusted nose scrunched in annoyance. The same fresh-faced woman who'd startled him awake, not an hour before. The one he'd been thinking about ever since.

Brows lifting with recognition, she stared him down, as if the small town had plastered a scarlet letter on her chest.

Jake's expression remained placid as he nodded a greeting, refusing to look away. If he could send her his thoughts, she'd know she wasn't alone.

Her frown deepened until a buzzing timer drew her attention elsewhere.

Eden, "call me Edie," seated him at the counter between the burly construction guy with the faded anchor tattoo and the eighty-something man in khakis and a golf shirt.

Pausing, Eden removed the elderly man's reading glasses, wiped them clean, and deposited them back into place. She kissed his cheek, and then rubbed the gloss lip print away as well. "There you go, Papaw."

"The better to see you with!" He winked. "Thank ya, Rebecca. Best daughter a daddy can have."

Her sunny-bright smile faltered a moment. She inhaled it back into place and turned with an easy drawl. "Mr. Steadman, you keep our Pastor Gibb company, now."

Jake watched in fascination as she collected herself and gathered up the back order platters in her arms. She efficiently negotiated the floor, clattered heaping pancakes in front of Scottie and Emma's brood, the kids barely waiting for her to set the plates down before digging in.

"Oh, yes. That's right. Eden..." the old man stammered with foggy confusion way beyond smeared glasses, Jake realized. Edie's papaw turned to face him, as he cleared his throat with a rattle. "Pastors get younger every season. Couldn't be me getting any older, could it, Tom?"

"No, sir, Mr. Dale. That'd mean I'm gettin' older, too." Tom, the heavy-set man, rumbled a laugh, sipped his coffee, and gestured for another cup.

Eavesdroppers from nearby tables snickered.

Tom continued. "Where d'ya hail from, Pastor Gibb?"

Before Jake could answer, Eden returned with a mug and sloshed fresh, steaming coffee into all three.

"He's from out west." Her neat eyebrows danced up and down as she turned to the soda machine to fill a glass with ice and juice and hustled off.

"That's fine. That's right fine. Spring's the best time of year out here. Fishin' and basketball..." The old man turned back to his plate, fork in hand, and then blinked at the scraped clean dish and crust of toast. Replacing fork for mug, his hand trembled as he sipped coffee. "Think Quentin and Scottie can take us ta' state this year, Tom?"

A silence floated around them and all heads swiveled to the front booth.

Scottie paused and spoke up, loud but kind. "That was back in '88, Mr. Dale."

The other diners resumed their breakfasts, though quieter now.

"Last time Mammoth made it to the finals." Tom's disappointment was obvious in his frown.

"Scottie's got the jump shot, but Quentin's the

three-point leader." The gentleman blinked over his coffee, giving Jake a wink. "My Rebecca's taken quite a liking to Quentin Marshall. Don't tell her mamma, though. The boy's Catholic."

"Uh, no, of course not." Jake eyed Tom with a knowing look.

Signs of the man's dementia were unmistakable.

He buried his attention in the faded menu. The thing didn't look updated anytime this century. Instead, Jake perused the hand-drawn Monday breakfast and lunch specials, written in curving script by an obviously careful hand. The idea of a chipotle grilled trout sandwich set his stomach rumbling and his mind tripping back to his days fishing with his dad off the California coast.

Maybe this place wouldn't be so bad after all.

Tom twisted a bit on the barstool. "I'm the contractor the church hired to see to the repairs. Last pastor left things in an awful mess—he brought in all kinds of animals, strays, you know. You'll probably see cats under the porch, a dog'll show up from time to time wanting supper. He never could say no to anything. Didn't care much for his politics."

Jake drank in the gossip with placid expression and washed worry down with a steaming sip.

Across the room, Edie bumped her way through the buzzing crowd, chatting and gossiping with two thirty-something women, sending a glance over her shoulder his direction. She turned back with a giggle.

"So, Pastor. You bring your wife along with ya?" Tom asked with an appraising stare.

"No." Jake sipped coffee and swallowed a hot ball of regret. "Truth is—"

The interrupting kitchen door flung open and out

popped Edie's doppelganger. Light and quick on her feet, she gathered a cup and shoved it in the dispenser to fill with ice, then water.

"Hello, again." She slid it his way. "Sorry about that."

"Thanks, uh—"

"Lilah. Lilah Simpson." Her chin jutted forward, pale green eyes stared at him through slits, as if daring him to say something about her different last name.

"Jacob Gibb." He offered a hand over the counter divider.

She shook it, a tiny smirk reaching her generous mouth. "Nice to meet you. Officially." Lilah's sun-streaked hair fought against restraint in a curly ponytail, tendrils escaping around her ears and face. She looked fresh, natural, and annoyed. "What can I get you, Jacob Gibb?" A smile tinged her mouth, adding sparkle to her gaze with her refusal to say Pastor. "Since you've forgone fast food for our humble diner."

"Not much on breakfast...how about that chalkboard lunch special, if you're serving it this time of day."

That made her blink.

He pushed the coffee cup aside. "And a lemonade. Please."

She nodded as she piled empty dishes high, and hustled to the back. She worked in the open space, confident in her element as she moved, grilled, chopped, and plated his sandwich. A few minutes later, she returned with his meal and filled them each a glass.

Lilah leaned to the cutout window at her back and hollered, "Raymond! I'm on break."

An affirmation mumbled through as a hand shot up to the spinning rack and grabbed the next dangling ticket.

"That's the first and only special I'll sell today." Lilah grinned. "I could start orders before any hit the wheel. Don't know why I bother."

"It's hard to step out of your comfort zone." Jake sipped the tart-sweet lemonade. He took a bite. Flaky, hints of heat, fresh and succulent with garden fresh salsa.

"Good?" By her tone, she knew the answer already.

Jake nodded, took another bite, and turned to the contractor. "I was just talking to Tom here about renovations over at the church."

"That's right." Tom clapped him heavy on the shoulder. "One thing's been causing me trouble, though. It's that blasted stained glass window. Last estimate showed it'd be more than our annual budget to fix. There's a crack, top to bottom, through several of the panes. Might have to replace it with glass block, or just plain glass. We'll see what you want to do."

The man Jake assumed to be Earl Dale straightened tall in his seat for the first time, eyes bright and focused. "You can't replace the lost sheep. You can't..."

"I know, Mr. Dale. I know." Tom averted his eyes, pushed off the stool. "I'll see you up there, then, Pastor. Nice to meet you." Tom hitched up his belt and headed out, the crowd mumbling goodbyes as he ambled toward the door.

Jake added succulent tomato and red onion to a bite of trout. "Excellent. Papaw's catch of the day?"

"Caught this morning at the landing." Her smile

seemed harmless enough, though her ocean-green eyes flashed a warning over the implied truth.

"That's good he still gets out there. Fishing." Dipping his gaze, he did his best to offer a word of encouragement, if not understanding. "Keeps him with you."

"Hmm." Her expression went frosty as the awkward silence.

Sounds of dishes clattering into the sink brought her to sigh. "Looks like my break's over."

"Yeah. Guess I'd better check out my new church." He downed a mouthful of lemonade. "This ought to be fun."

"You'll be fine," Lilah reassured. "People around here want to like you. They'll give you a chance as long as you don't rock the boat."

"Got any suggestions for a new guy in town?"

"It's like the specials." She thumbed to her board. "I offer them, don't expect to sell any. Mammoth's not a place that likes change. I wouldn't expect much in that department."

Edie appeared with more orders, and Lilah excused herself, kissing her papaw's cheek before she went. "Want more coffee?"

"Thanks, Rebecca. I'd love some." He smiled as she poured from the glass carafe. "Nothing like a fresh cup o' joe."

"I'm Lilah. Remember, Papaw?" she reminded patiently with a reassuring squeeze to his hands.

He nodded. "D-did the fish bite this morning?"

"Got a few good strikes. Saw ole' Moby Dick jumping this morning."

He smiled wide, revealing gold-rimmed dental work as he turned to Jake. "Moby Dick's the only one that ever got away from Lilah, there. Best fisher-woman on the river."

"Is that right?" Jake relaxed. "I guess you're the man to ask about good spots on Cherokee Spring?"

"Grew up on its banks. Best fishin's still out near Taylor's Ranch. Our cabin, Lilah knows where. Carved that lot out with my bare hands. Best view on the river." He went on, words heavy with memory.

Lilah backed away, and he saw regret flash in her sea-blue eyes. The cabin must be just another muddied memory, he guessed. Still, she mouthed a silent "thank you" as her grandfather talked about the fish hatchery, the falls, and the split at the fork.

Jake returned to his meal, interjecting where needed, until the old man's enthusiasm drifted off like a fallen leaf downstream.

Around him, customers ate, talked, paid, and disappeared into their lives. What did people do here?

Jake savored the final bite of the fish, the crunch of the toasted fresh-baked roll—a little taste of home from a thousand miles away. He left a generous tip as a thank you, bid Mr. Dale goodbye, and slipped out the door, sparing a last glance to Lilah as she cooked for the populace with subtle efficiency, then to her sister, Edie, with equal and opposite flamboyance. Two sides of a coin, each of them were keeping Earl's Kitchen running in their own way.

Jake promised himself he'd come back, along with the regular crowd. If for nothing else than to see Lilah smile again.

# 3

Three o'clock.

Lilah glanced at the front door. The bell announced the entrance of Kimmy Johnson, the postal carrier. Dressed in her official blue shorts and shirt, towing the mail cart, she said her heys and ambled to the counter. Kimmy fished through the jam-packed handcart and dragged out a stack of rubber-banded envelopes secured to a priority mail package, then ordered up a Coke to go.

Edie traded the cup for Kimmy's dollar and thumbed through the mail, casting a frown at the oversized red and white envelope. "What's this? McDougal, Finch, and Hawthorne?"

The Lawyer.

"That's mine!" Lilah pushed her way around the bar and took the thick package.

"Grabby!" Edie spat. Then her brows rose in understanding. "Those your divorce papers?"

"Could you be louder, *Eden*? I don't think everyone heard you." Lilah purposely over enunciated her sister's name, watched her twin's hackles rise, and then focused on the sealed envelope with the California return address.

"That's your freedom in there, sister." Raymond peered over her shoulder, giving her a quick squeeze. "Just in time."

"For what?"

"Did you see the new pastor?" Raymond's eyebrows rose.

Lilah's cheeks rushed with heat.

"They're sayin' he's a widower. Maybe you could—"

"Shame on you, Ray!" She snapped a towel at his leg. "And of course I've seen him. He lives at the parsonage, right across the street from us."

"So, you bake him some cookies. Offer to show him around town—"

"Uh-uh. You might not buy into it, but until the courts say otherwise, Nana's right. I'm still married."

"Just want to see you happy again, Lilah." Raymond pushed the back door open. "I got you covered. Go on and take a break."

Lilah strode out the back door, package crinkling in hand. He was right.

Any flesh-and-blood woman would double take at the pastor's square jaw, capable-looking hands, or that jolt of heat that came with a handsome man's attention. But guilt oiled any romantic notions.

She sat hard on the weed-studded concrete and tossed the packet to the side. She'd vowed to God that she'd love Ryan Simpson until death do they part, even if it was in a seedy Vegas chapel. Now, their promise was as broken as the rear stoop cement. Her thoughts went muddy as she plucked a stubborn dandelion seed head and considered the white fluff.

Pastor Jake was all moved in now. In the one week since he'd arrived, she'd barely seen him except for a quick wave. Maybe Ray was right. She should bake him some brownies or a plate of chocolate chip cookies. It'd be the neighborly thing to do, but it was wrong. Deep down, she knew it. Her penance for choosing the wrong man, following the wrong road, was waiting in this idle purgatory. Not married, not single.

At her steady breath, the cottony puff exploded, its frothy white seeds flew on the breeze, over the gravel drive, down the long slope of grass. Like little white flags of surrender, the seeds angled down to a woody spot by the river's edge, the churning pool just beyond the waterfall, toward the old mill where she'd spent the morning.

Papaw's landing. She had a vision of his capable hands over hers, his quiet, resonant voice, and his smile of approval when she at last understood how to angle the rod to cast, and the satisfied, subtle plunk of bait in the water.

Though the restaurant still claimed his fresh catch of the day, Papaw's secret fishing hole remained clear and plentiful, while his mind had glutted up with weeds and overgrowth. He hadn't so much as baited a hook since the dementia took the desire from him, leaving only a well of empty stories.

Swallowing tears, Lilah rolled her attention up to the bright blue, late-April sky, the same color as Jake Gibb's eyes. That brought to mind his sturdy shoulders, and a tan that screamed Southern California. She tossed the empty stem aside. No sense looking for love when she was still paying off her last debt. She'd bet on love once and lost everything, a gamble she'd never make again. Lilah slid her thumb under the tape, popped open the metal tabs, and reviewed the lawyer's letter. One week to give up rights to everything. All she had to do was sign. Freedom's bitter cost turned her stomach.

Gravel crunched, jangled a dim alarm of someone

coming, but she didn't look up until the shadow blocked the sun, darkening the "whereas," "heretofore," and other legalese in the papers.

From her seat, she shaded the glare, spying the gray face of the stranger. Ratty pants, t-shirt, green army jacket. Homeless, she guessed, not a common sight in Mammoth but in California, she'd seen them in spades.

"Can I help you?" She'd been wrong about Jake when she'd spied him in that parking lot, but this man had the look of hunger on his face.

"If it's not too much trouble..." He cleared his throat and held out a bright yellow sheet of paper. "Just wanted to know if I could post this in your window, ma'am."

Lilah reached up for the handbill he offered and read out loud, "Reunion Carnival."

Bright lights, the spin-whoosh of the rides, the raucous calliope music, laughter, all in a whirlwind of lost youth and promises.

"Is it almost Memorial Day already?"

"Three weeks. We're settin' up early this year." He shifted weight, backed deeper into the shadow from the building cast across the alley. "If you wouldn't mind, I'd appreciate you hanging up the notice for your customers."

"Mm-hm." Numbers of carnival employees filling tables warred with the improbability of Nana allowing it. "You look hungry, sir. Can I get you something from the kitchen?"

"Oh." A work-worn hand scratched his thin midsection. He shook his head. "I don't want to trouble you none..."

"No trouble. Wait here." Lilah stood, brushed the

dust off her shorts, and stepped into the kitchen. She dropped her package and flyer on the desk and hurried to slide a fresh-plated burger and fries into a to-go box.

"Hey!" Edie frowned, her brow raised into a loop of annoyance. "That's my order!"

"Raymond." Lilah's tone made him pause mid-dish wash. "Make another number three for her royal highness, there."

"Funny."

Raymond dropped two fresh patties on the sizzling grill.

Lilah headed outside but the steps were empty. The alley was vacant, but a long trailing shadow showed which way he headed. "Wait up!" She trotted down the weed-studded gravel road, passing dumpsters and brick-backed buildings.

The man secured a handbill to the light pole, covering a faded Mammoth High School car wash announcement.

"You forgot your burger."

"I didn't forget." He slicked a hand over thinning gray hair. "I don't need charity, ma'am. I get three squares a day for doin' my job at the carnival."

Though he protested otherwise, she doubted the stranger had a decent meal in weeks, plus the diner could always use more business. "It's a free sample." She shoved the white box in his hands. "Maybe you'll bring some of your friends by the diner. Everyone's welcome."

"Much obliged." Grasping the container, he slanted a smile. "But, I wouldn't count on it. We keep mostly to our'n."

"We'll see about that."

Back inside, she slid behind the desk and thwacked the lawyer's thick package on one side, the carnival announcement opposite.

From the floor, Eden's slow southern drawl offered pie with coffee to the ladies book club. Ray's grill sizzled to match his humming, the chug-slosh of the dishwasher his back beat.

Lilah wondered how to get that handbill in the front window without her grandmother raising a holy fit.

# 4

Jake's apartment was only slightly improved from his dorm room back in the day. Not where he expected to be at age thirty. He plucked picture hangers from the hardware store hooks. The storefront faced Main Street, and Scott Emerson was marching four children into the squat library building. He needed to pay quickly and go, then say hello—another plus for small town life. Jake stuffed the change into a jar on the counter for the high school basketball team.

"Thanks, Pastor. Kids appreciate it."

Jake sauntered after the Emersons for his next greeting. He could learn to like it here.

Across the town square, by the Cherokee statue, a very pregnant Emma pointed in the face of a down-on-his luck type. By her finger in the man's startled face and his back-peddling, she was reading him the riot act. She marched into the library.

The ragged, white-haired man knelt amid a shattered fifth of whiskey.

"Hey, pal," Jake said. He squatted and began to help. "Saw the whole thing. Sorry Mammoth gave you less than a warm welcome."

"I'm used to it." The homeless-looking man rolled his stooped shoulders. "Can't say I blame her, after all. Young'uns are priceless beyond measure."

"True." Jake glanced to the library where more trekked in for weekly story time.

The drifter swept the last of the glass splinters into a flyer.

"I'm Jake Gibb. Pastor at the church."

"Folks call me Guthrie." Eyes downcast, he tossed the mess into the sack. With a bitter laugh, the man stood to his full height. "Getting harder to kneel down every year that passes."

"Depends on who—or what—you're kneeling to."

"Amen, Preacher." Guthrie shot a wistful look at the dissipating puddle.

Jake clapped him on the shoulder. "Have a better day, friend, and God bless."

# 5

Lunch rush was over and Lilah's mind spun to the lawyer's packet she'd stowed in the desk days ago. She had a deadline to keep, today, or the latest deal was off. Freedom meant more than pride, didn't it? Time to just get it over with. Lilah hunted the desktop for a pen, sifted paper stacks for the packet. Menu ideas, a shopping list, the flyer from the drifter that was still not posted in the front window.

No package.

Lilah rifled through the desk drawers. She opened and slammed each shut. She stomped from the tiny office. The clock edged its way past four o'clock as her rubber soles squeaked through the kitchen and the now empty diner.

Eden stood, back to her, counting out tips from the register jar into three neat stacks.

"Where is it?" Lilah palmed the counter in between them.

"Where's what?" Eden jogged her right hip under her hand.

"Don't play me. Hand it over." Lips clamped down choice words she'd much rather say. "I've got to sign and have it postmarked today or the deal's off."

"Don't worry, hon. You're not signing that garbage." Eden gave her shoulder a pat and turned back to sifting bills like a Vegas dealer. "I returned it to your attorney, along with some notes. Then, we'll see."

"You did what?" Lilah gave her sister a firm shoulder shove.

"I took a glance at that cockamamie offer while you were daydreaming. Made some notes, a counter offer."

Lilah removed her apron, tossed it in the laundry heap. "You had no right to look through my things."

"You need legal representation or that son of a monkey's gonna walk all over you. I thought—"

"Well, don't. Don't think. Don't go through my mail, and don't get into my business." Lilah stormed toward the kitchen. "I got myself into this mess and I'll get myself out. I don't need help from you or anybody." She grabbed her purse from her cubby and dug through looking for the attorney's number. Maybe she could stop the mail, or call, or—

"If I thought you'd a' listened to me, I would have discussed it with you first. But I know you better than you know yourself."

"You don't know me at all." Lilah found a business card amid gum wrappers, makeup dust, and sticky change. She flipped it, scanned the gold-filigreed logo of the hair salon on Melrose. *Yet another place I'll never go again.* She crumpled it and tossed it in the can.

"Well, guess what, sis." Eden blinked back tears. "You don't know me so well, either." She hot-stepped it out the front door, the bell ringing frantically in her wake.

Great. Lilah's hands shook as she grasped the purse in a surrogate wringing of Eden's neck. She tossed the bag aside and watched her sister's melodramatic display out the front window.

Raymond ambled over to Lilah's side, head cocked in curiosity, though he said nothing.

Eden marched to the corner mailbox and slid the door open until she could peer inside.

"Tell me, Ray." Lilah watched her sister try, fail, and try again to wiggle her arm into the dark blue bin. "How did this switch to Eden being the wronged one?"

"That's family guilt for you." Raymond covered his chuckle with a cough. "You might hear Eden out, though. She might even be able to help."

Lilah blasted a laugh.

Eden help with something other than her own minutia?

"Highly unlikely." Lilah walked outside.

Afternoon sun cast long shadows, outlines of the buildings across Main Street. Birds sang. No cars. No sign of anyone milling about. Up on the hill, the school buzzer sounded, releasing classes for the day.

Eden crouched by the lock, jiggled it with her manicured hands.

"Edie..."

"What?" Eden's voice seethed through gritted teeth. She yanked on the door, again, unsuccessful.

"You really put it in there, didn't you?"

"Yep." She pulled the front lid down again and frowned. "Along with a couple of letters to Afghanistan. Seemed like a good idea to play lawyer for you. At least, it did at the time."

Lilah's hands went limp at her sides. Fresh anger balled in her belly. "Why on earth would that have seemed like a good idea?"

"Well, you said you weren't signing away your rights to some two-timing, two-bit loser who still has a house in Santa Monica, a car, and a full bank account. I looked him up on the internet. He's living off of your reputation and taking all the credit."

"But what in the–" Lilah counted to ten, eyes squeezed shut, waiting for the curse to leave her lips. She opened her eyes.

Eden deposited herself on a wooden bench, nestled next to a weary looking planter by the pharmacy door.

"What on earth makes you think you can play lawyer?"

Eden took her twin sister by the hands. "I watched everyone in town hoof it to college or get married and pregnant, and not always in that order. Fine. You left town, married the wrong guy, and I let you do it. All the while, just me, Nana, and Papaw, running things. Watching him fill and refill the salt shakers. Hearing him tell the same stories over again...he's so much worse now..." Eyes to heaven, she gathered wits and turned to face Lilah. "This time, it's my turn to do something. I'm getting my law degree over the internet. And there ain't no way I'm letting you get divorced by yourself."

"You're in law school. Online?"

"Can't wait tables forever." Eden squeezed her hands. "Got my bachelor's from State that'a'way. Signed up for the bar."

"You graduated? From college?"

"Not that Nana cares." Eden jogged her brows in a little victory dance. "Just trust me, honey. That man put you through enough grief. It's time for you to give him some in return."

For a minute, they were eight years old with matching skinned knees and falling down socks, waiting for the principal to give them a talking to. She jogged her sister's elbow and hazarded a smile. "So.

Afghanistan, huh? I thought you left your heart in Iraq."

Eden's eyes filled.

"I'm sorry." Lilah wished she'd kept her big mouth shut.

"No, you're right. It's like an addiction." She lifted, dropped her shoulders. "I've got two soldiers writing me back this time. How's a girl s'posed to pick just one?" Her sister—identical underneath the makeup and hair bleach—dished about the two soldiers, a world away. She'd written every day for six months, sending pictures, letters, and care packages to each.

How anyone could juggle not one, but two budding long-distance relationships was more than Lilah could comprehend.

"So, I hurried the mail together to get your package out before you could tell me not to—and I'm now pretty sure I put Tony's letter in Eli's envelope." Eden sniffled a sorrowful laugh.

"And one doesn't know about the other?"

"Nope," Eden said. "And once something's been mailed, you can't break into the box. It's a federal offense."

"So speaks the budding lawyer." Lilah pressed in a bubble of laughter.

Together, they collapsed in a fit of girlish giggles.

"Somewhere, someone overseas is about to be very disappointed."

"Yeah." Eden wiped her eyes and sighed, a halfhearted laugh bubbled up again. "Someone in California, too."

Lilah squeezed her sister's hand. All amusement vanished like the breeze, an icicle of worry skewered in its place.

# 6

Thursday. The weeks blurred by in a spring haze. Lilah's hand rake clomped into the cold earth, dark mud seeped through the gloves. A shiver ran the length of her spine that had little to do with the slow-creeping early morning light, and everything to do with the letter Eden had so cavalierly shipped off to California. Her well-meaning, well-intending sister had a heart of gold and a head full of rocks.

With each thud, the claw alternately dug up rich, red clay or upturned broken stones. Danged rocky Ozark soil.

Up the road a figure was jogging toward her. A jogger? In Mammoth? He approached from River View Drive. Good form, easy stride, arms pumping.

She considered going inside and grabbing her own running shoes. She turned her attention back to a corner of stubborn rock, slammed it with the rake's handle. The stone fractured, but the claw popped off the hand tool. "Of all the stupid–" She tossed the useless tool aside, followed by the first, second, and third rocky lumps. "Idiotic... Imbecilic..." She teetered and landed in a whoosh of breath.

"Usually people don't arrive at that opinion of me until they've known me at least a month." Pastor Jake's voice rained down. He walked toward her in worn running shoes, black jogging shorts, a gray Cal State t-shirt, and a music player strapped to a well-formed bicep. Indeed, the new pastor of Mammoth, Arkansas's Cherokee Spring Memorial Church, could be jogging the Santa Monica strand rather than through a humid Ozark neighborhood.

"I'm a little busy." Lilah spoke to the ground. "Something you need?"

"Nope. Just out for a run."

"Unusual pastime for a preacher, isn't it?"

"I could quote you several lines of scripture saying otherwise, but somehow..." He picked up the handle and claw head, worked one back into the other, and handed it back. "I think you're just ribbing me."

"You got me." She put the rake to good use, hiding the soul-surging grin. Not just a handsome, single man right next door, but a pastor, too? That was just God being ironic. Had to be. Still in his shadow, she wiped loose bangs, rake in hand. "Can I do something for you?"

"I was just wondering." He scratched his chin, smiling. "What is it you're so angry about?"

He stood, checked his pulse, fingertips to throat, staring at his watch while her mind reeled. So that was it. Her personal business, everyone's coffee talk, Eden's prayer chain must've finally linked to the new pastor.

"What makes you think I'm angry?"

"That's a deep hole for tomatoes. Looks like you're burying a body."

"You got me." Lilah stood. "I'm just turning negative energy into something more productive. Trying to, anyway." She peeled off her gloves, brushed off her muddy knees, and set a foot to the gray-planked front steps, leaving the six-pack of plants unplanted.

Jake obviously had no intention of leaving.

"Uh, you want a cup of coffee or something?"

"That's mighty neighborly of you."

She pointed toward the downward slope of lawn and the river below. "Deck's got a great view. I'll join you in a minute."

Inside, Lilah would never get used to the bright red painted walls, the white slip-covered couch barely visible under throw pillows in a rainbow of chartreuse, ginger, and electric blue. Equally colorful framed photographs of red barns and other scenes were clumped together on the trunk serving as a coffee table, and atop the enormous antique steamer that contained dog-eared romance novels. Eden had become quite the photographer.

It didn't dawn on her until this moment that there wasn't a single person in any picture. Lilah frowned at a shot of mist over the river. A blue heron fished by a downed tree. Pretty. Eden should sell these to tourists at the register in a postcard rack. She straightened the shot of Big Bird, the heron, balanced on one leg. Satisfied with the now level picture, Lilah opened Nana's old double-door pie safe, which Eden now used as a china cabinet. The rooster clock above the kitchen back door chirped six a.m. Startled, she juggled two ceramic mugs to the counter.

"You're up early." Eden spoke through her yawn as Lilah filled cups.

"Couldn't sleep."

"Me, either. Wanna go yard sale-ing today?" She unpinned her curls, shoving the ties into her robe pocket as each platinum spiral curl stuck out in a new direction. "Emma's having one. Should be some fun bric-a-brac and whatnots. I'm gonna try to convince her to sell me her sewing machine. She needs a new one, with all the home goods she's been making. What is it about getting pregnant that makes a woman want to sew?"

"Wrong person to ask." Lilah gave a quick prayer for strength to deal with Eden as she talked about praying for Emma's baby, just discovered to be breech. "Course, Emma's a pro in the delivery room. Five babies. Can you imagine? Mmm. Coffee." Eden's pink slippers shushed across the kitchen floor. "Thanks."

Lilah gave it to Eden and went for another mug.

"You got company?"

"Just, um, well–" She thumbed toward the porch where Jake sat, waiting. "Yeah."

"The preacher!" Eden hooted a laugh. "Well, well, look at little Miss Divorcée."

"Not divorced yet, remember?" Lilah spat. "Might have been if you hadn't decided to help me."

"That hurts." She stared at her coffee, took the cream and stirred it. "My guess, we wouldn't have had this problem with the last'n."

"Nice, Eden." Lilah shook her head at her sister's offhand slur. "Real nice."

"What?" Eden blinked.

Lilah trayed two steaming mugs, pitcher of milk, and negotiated her way through the screen door. Maybe she'd lived in California too long.

Twin dragonflies zipped along the grassy slope by the deck, sailing along through shafts of sunlight to light on the river. Papaw and Nana's home up on the hill cast a long shadow over Eden's backyard. A light winked on in Nana's kitchen.

Below, river music played over rocks, its rhythm a steady blend of rushing water and bird calls. The warm humidity promised a pretty first of May.

Jake smiled, took the offered mug, and inhaled French roast. He drank deep, a rumble of pleasure in his throat. "So, wanna talk? Or shall we just watch the river go by?"

Lilah sipped as she sat beside him, gaze trained on the river's dance over the rocks. "Down a bit for this time of year." She hoped he'd get the message. No amount of chitchat would excuse the prayer chain for their spread of gossip. Or what he knew about her by now.

"Tell me about Mammoth." He leaned forward, cup in hands.

"How much time've you got?" She took a long drink, and considered his hopeful gaze. Might as well tell it like it is. "Seriously? It's fading. Shops are closed, most people leave, a few stay. It's a place people drive past, you know? On their way to somewhere else."

"Well, not everyone." He glanced to his church across the street. The rooftop, missing a few shingles, could just be seen. "I'm here. And you. You came back."

"You've heard my story by now, I'm sure."

"Actually, no." He leaned back in the metal rocker. "Is it a comedy? Or a cautionary tale?"

That made her laugh. Her elbow jostled and coffee splashed her thigh. She blotted it with the cloth he handed her. "Thanks. Sure the prayer chain hasn't left you a list of my latest debacles?"

He frowned into the dark brew. "They mean well—"

"It's just a way to use God to gossip," she said, blowing the heat from her drink.

"It can be." Jake nodded, his clear gaze reflecting the hurt that dogged her soul.

They sat in silence while a kingfisher dive-bombed the water and sailed up to its nest, a thrashing trout in its beak.

Jake launched into a story about a similar issue at the church he'd just left.

She drained her coffee, glanced at the house, longing for another.

He smoothed it over with his pastor's story, drawing her in, leading her down a path where she could consider the prayer chain's well-meaning intentions. After a pause, he added. "Try not to be so hard on them."

"Is that why you stopped by?" She set the mug on the metal table. "To mend my proverbial fences?"

"Actually, I did have a reason. I was thinking about Mammoth's single population."

"Singles?" Her stomach dropped. "You looking to meet some?"

"Funny." He leaned back, the springy chair creaked in response. "I was just thinking there's not much to do, for teens or single...newly single adults. Might be nice to offer something at the church, a movie night, or games. Something."

She collected her mug to have something to hold. He hadn't been asking about her, just brainstorming, so why was her stomach jumping?

"Might be nice. Keep kids out of trouble. Anyway, you should talk to Eden. I've only been back a couple of months. And I'm not in that 'newly single' category yet." She scrubbed her bare ring finger, a wide gulf between her and the future.

Below, the heron swooped down to land behind the reeds.

Jake watched the bird stilt its way through the

fishing grounds. "You know, you don't have to persecute yourself forever."

"Just a few more weeks." She snorted a laugh. "Hopefully."

His mouth drew into a lazy smile. "So, friends?"

She considered, a heaviness washing behind her eyes. At last, she nodded. Friends it would have to be. "I don't know why you've decided to make me your focus group, Pastor Jake."

"Let's just say I'm a sucker for hard luck cases."

She laughed. If only he knew the whole truth.

"I think we're being watched." He sipped his coffee, tipping his head toward Eden's kitchen window.

She caught sight of white lace curtains flicking back into place.

"Not getting the wrong idea, I hope."

Nana would be standing at the back door, white hair pinned, brows raised, housecoat zipped to the neck, a disapproving scowl on her pinched lips.

"No. Of course not." Lilah angled a glance back, considering the cozy scene they must have made. "Not Eden, anyway."

But Nana was another story altogether.

# 7

Jake held the white sign in place, allowing the cement to fix around its base as he thought on that morning's coffee with Lilah. Sweat dampened his brow and he wished he could shake thoughts of the troubled, beautiful Lilah Dale. No, wait. Simpson. Her last name was Simpson. Better remember that for now. Whatever, her in-process divorce was the source of small town scandal that rivaled the ousting of the last pastor, based on the prayer request messages that flashed daily on his machine.

*Pray for Lilah, for healing of her marriage.*

*Please pray for Lilah, that God forgive her for leaving her husband, even if he was a two-timing loser.*

*And please, pray for Lilah, that she get her name back. It's all she really wants. After all, that man took everything from her.*

He'd kept his distance, but that merely sharpened his hunger to know more about her. Lilah challenged him, first delivering on a promised excellent meal, then sparkling morning conversation. But nothing had startled him more than his instant focus on her. His burning need to find out what made her tick and why she put up with the whispers that circled every time she entered a room. They had so much more in common than she knew.

He could wait until she was free, but would she want to date a small town pastor with small time aspirations? Distant, melancholy, intent on keeping him at arm's distance, but not pushing him away. So why did that make him want to break down her barriers? He'd never felt like that about his ex-wife. Margaret simply was perfect pastor's wife material. Nothing he did ever surprised her, not even when he confronted her about her emotional affair with his more upwardly mobile best friend. She'd just serenely suggested they seek counseling. Never once considering the fact he'd end their marriage. But wasn't that what she'd done? Murdered their chances of happily ever after? At the memory of discovering her trail of texts, all that came after, his hands wrapped tight around the wooden stake.

"Time," Dad had said. Time and space would heal that wound.

"We'll see." Jake spoke to the sign. Rubbed the painted office hours. His shortened name, itself a lie.

Was it possible for anyone in the modern era to start over? He doubted it, gave the sign a solid jiggle, and judged it safe to not topple.

Lilah was more likely too wrapped up to care, and that was better for both of them.

Placing the balancing level on top, he pushed and righted the thing, adjusting until the bubble rested in between the black lines.

"Looking good, Pastor Gibb!" Tom's voice called down from the rooftop.

"My sign? Or the roof?"

His contractor hustled down the ladder with ease. Tom thumbed toward the roof. "Unfortunately for the parish, I was talking 'bout your sign."

Jake straightened. "I think it looks all right—"

"No. Not that." Tom clapped a work-worn hand

on Jake's shoulder. "It's the roof. It needs re-shingling before storms come through. Tornado did a number last year, and that joker—your predecessor—never did have a mind to fix it up right."

"How much?" Jake thought of the coffers, already low from declining membership.

"Enough." Tom wiped a bandana across his forehead. "We'll work it out. Fundraisin'll improve after this year's Revival."

"Revival." Jake hooked thumbs to belt loops. He'd read up on previous years' turnouts.

"I wanted to talk to you about that..." Tom scratched behind his ear and gave him a wary look, as if unsure of what Jake stood for. "Not really my place to ask, Pastor, but I gotta do it."

"Go ahead." Jake fought to keep his smile even and waited.

Tom cleared his throat, turned toward the river. "Mammoth's been through some ups and downs with our little church here."

Jake nodded, mind scrambling.

"I'm speaking out for the deacons, mind you." Tom drew a well-worn handkerchief out of his back pocket and rubbed his nose. "We just don't want to cast our lots in the wrong basket, if you're just passing through."

"I'll stay as long as you'll have me, friend," Jake said. "No pressing engagements elsewhere."

"Not exactly a jumping off point for a career."

True. This man, a small town contractor, hit the nail on the head. Jake studied the post, gave it a pat. "I'm just looking to start my life somewhere that matters. The center of the map seemed a good place to do it."

Satisfied, Tom nodded. "We sure need it this year, with the Reunion Carnival back in full swing for the first time in a decade. You've seen the trucks. The RVs pulling in? We'll be battling the devil at our door, I promise you." Tom strode to his work truck. "See you at the deacon's meeting tonight, then."

Tom Steadman, the only contractor within two hundred miles, buzzed on his merry way down the hill. Toward Earl's Kitchen, Jake gathered. Maybe Lilah was there, slinging burgers, or maybe she'd dreamed up another succulent fish sandwich. The thought of her homemade potato chips set his mouth to watering. Or was it the thought of her slightly crooked grin? The way she cocked her head, looked into his eyes, and really listened to him. Movement across the street caught his attention.

An older woman in pink walking shorts rounded the corner of the chapel, wire-framed glasses and a grin on her crinkle-lined, slender face.

He'd seen Naomi Dale, but had yet to become acquainted with her.

"Well, hey there, Pastor Gibb."

"Hello."

"You've met the rest of my family." She beamed, waited a beat. "I'm Naomi Dale. Earl's wife, Edie and Lilah's grandma."

"Right." He clasped her outstretched hand, along with a cloud of plaster dust. His hands were grimy, and he wiped them on his jeans. "Sorry. Working today."

"Hard work's good for the soul." She handed him the container. "Brought you a bite of lunch. Eden figured you'd be wantin' something about now."

"Be sure and thank her for me." He opened the

container to a fully loaded cheeseburger and kettle-cooked chips, surprised at the sudden longing for Lilah's fresh fish sandwich. He closed the box and looked up at the woman who measured him so openly. "Incidentally, how is Lilah adjusting to coming back home?"

"She's still suffering from a case of bad marriage. Until that divorce finalizes." Mrs. Dale's pale blue, rock hard eyes studied him like a bug to swat. Or step on.

"Those things take time." He offered a sympathetic smile. "Even when they're fixing a wrong thing."

"Mm. Time, and a toll." Nana nodded, sharp. "On all of us."

"Thank you for thinking of me, ma'am." He crunched the fried potato chip, hoping for a change of subject.

"They say you've got some plans for this ol' place." She waved toward the faded white structure.

"We've gotta keep moving forward, don't we?"

Her thin-set lips showed Naomi Dale obviously didn't agree. "I was married in this church. Baptized here, same as Earl and the girls. Been to countless funerals here, too." She turned on her heel, heading to the little rose garden and plucked a few curled brown, fading leaves. "It'd be a shame to change much when this here's the glue that holds Mammoth together."

"I'll try and remember that."

With a curt nod, she headed home, up the hill.

Lilah had been right. Folks in town didn't want change, her grandmother most of all.

*Lord, tell me what to do.* He stared at the white, ivy-covered steeple against the bright, spring sky, heart full of ideas and longing. *I didn't come here to do what they wanted, but to give them what they need.*

*Is that why you came, Jake? Really?*

Thoughts speared back to the day he left, the way his father squeezed his shoulder, told him they'd take him back in a heartbeat, get him on target for a larger, growing church, should he change his mind. If all else failed, his dad would fix things for him. Again. The knowledge was oil in his gut as a greedy vine of wonder grew in his thoughts. Would he want to go back?

His gaze took in the trees, their new, bright green leaves rustled in a slight spring breeze against a vivid, cloudless sky. The roses announced blooms would soon return with tight buds and purple leaves. From the dry and the dead, new leaf buds transformed the thorn-covered stalks into something beautiful. In the back meeting area, a large plot of grass sat, poised and ready to be covered by Revival tents and chairs.

Revival. What were they reviving exactly? Would the existing parish sing, pray, and congratulate themselves on their piety while true revelry went on as always over at the fairgrounds? Carnival folk hawked rides, ring tosses, and feats of strength, and in turn hosted an array of clandestine activities in the tents and trailers.

Both Tom and Naomi said the church and town needed a change of spirit and funding. He'd been fishing for ideas with Lilah on how to involve the younger set. Maybe this was a good time to see how the next generation of his congregation could set things in motion.

An idea seeded in his gut. Jake checked his sign. It looked firm, but he knew from construction that it would continue to set for days, if not weeks. Just because it looked strong on the outside didn't mean it was finished. And neither was this little church. He trotted up the trio of steps, inside the unadorned sanctuary. At first sight? It looked naked. But now? Maybe that was just as it should be. Plastered white walls, save for handmade quilts—each a work of art in its own right, centered with a verse from scripture—made by the women of the Quilting Guild, of which he'd read Naomi Dale was in charge.

In the back, light streamed through the cracked stained glass.

The image startled him in its clarity and unique style. Jesus as a shepherd, a lamb cradled in his arms, stood before the rest of the sheep on a distant Ozark hill. In between the thoughtful shepherd and his flock, the river flowed around black rocks; a lake bloomed out from the spring, the message of the parable clear in the stylized face. The artisan set the scene at the heart of Mammoth, at Cherokee Springs Park.

"I asked for it, didn't I, Father?" Jake stood in wonder, bathed in the warm, vibrant rainbow of color streaming through that window. "Just go easy on me until I get my footing."

A floor-to-ceiling crack in the panes that split the hillside flock in two. The breeze sailed through. That'd have to be fixed, for sure, somehow.

Someday.

If he stayed.

*Decide.*

With the boxed lunch out on his desk, he rattled ice in the cup and sipped. Jake dragged out a phone book, note pad, and pen and set to work.

# 8

By the time the deacons arrived for their weekly meeting, Jake had more questions for them than answers. How did anyone get anything done here in this trough of a valley? Businesses didn't answer their phones, and the ones that did weren't interested. As far as he could tell, Tom's assessment that he was the only contractor within two hundred miles wasn't far from the truth.

Another car parked. Out the window, a trio of "Hey" and "How do" in that Ozarkian twang had him smiling. The slow speech matched the snail's pace lifestyle he wasn't sure he'd ever get used to. He stepped out of the office and into the main meeting room.

Metal folding chairs were set up across the tile floor. Someone dusted off the podium. A table had cookies and brownie bars, next to a perking industrial coffee dispenser, and Emma Thompson arranged paper cups and napkins. Pregnant belly tenting the dress she wore, she nodded to her tall, lanky husband. "That'll set you up, Scottie. Evenin', Pastor Jake."

They said how d'ya dos and nibbled her homemade cookies. He lasered attention on her sweet, twanging tone. Most certainly, she'd left one or more of those anonymous prayer requests about Lilah.

"This'n can't get here soon enough." She rubbed a protective circle over her broad belly. "I got hands to help, with my eldest daughter, but she's got high school midterms and college scholarships to apply for. She don't need to end up mothering four kids before she's thirty. No offense, Scottie."

"None taken, doll." He kissed the top of her head and smiled. "Go rescue Charla before the little ones tear her project to shreds." Love shining in his gaze, Scott watched his wife leave then turned to Jake as the door closed. "We got married right out of high school. Never had much. She worked as a grocery checker until I got my teaching degree."

"You've got a beautiful family."

"The Lord just gave us a hefty blessing in that area."

That brought a handful of laughs from around the room.

Scott clapped Jake on the shoulder. "Go meet the others. This here ministry's mine and Emma's."

Jake caught the slightest tinge of concern in Scott's eyes. The look vanished as quickly as it arrived, but no one else seemed to take note. He was quite sure no one noticed Scott at all, aside from a back slap and a ribbing on yet another Emerson family impending arrival.

The rest of the men arrived. More chairs were hauled in from the storage shed. It seemed every deacon, elder, and male parishioner had come to the weekly meeting to check out the new pastor.

Jake's hand repeatedly pumped in greeting. He memorized names, faces, and listened to veiled concerns.

The men cycled around one subject. The carnival. Each had their own thoughts of how to stop, confront, or tell folks to avoid it.

Jake did his best to listen, but he couldn't stop thinking about the previous exchange at Scott's expense, that still haunted the man's eyes. Regret, maybe? Not for his wife, or his children; his love for them shone. Something else, buried deeper and laying heavy. He'd catch up with him later and get him to talk when they didn't have an audience.

Jake went to the podium. He led them in a quick but powerful prayer, and then gazed around the room after the "Amen!"

He gave a silent plea for strength to get through what was sure to be a difficult meeting. "Thanks, everyone, for turning out tonight and for the warm welcome."

They applauded and settled into a respectful silence as he explained the announcement from Tom about the new roof and the budgetary concerns for the renovations.

Mumbling went through the crowd, and Tom stood to explain the costs and materials, but no one seemed focused on his report. There were nervous stares and the folding and unfolding of the meeting's agenda pamphlets. Everyone, it seemed, was concentrating on the next discussion point.

"Thanks, Tom." Jake resumed his place. "I guess you know we're here to talk about plans for the month. The Revival—"

The doors opened with a flourish and all heads turned. Naomi led Earl Dale into the room with shuffling steps. "Forgive me, everyone. Earl here's having a good night. I thought maybe he'd enjoy listening to your meeting. If you don't mind, Pastor Gibb." Her gaze was a cold stare daring him to say no.

"Earl's always welcome, Mrs. Dale." Jake strode

across and took him by the elbow. Someone vacated chair, and Jake directed him to sit. "I'll get him home after, unless of course, you'd rather stay?"

Naomi's brows shot up.

A slight gasp went through at what was obviously an unwritten rule: Men Only.

"We'll help him get back over," Tom spoke up. "Never you mind yourself, ma'am."

Naomi departed.

Earl settled. "Thanks, boys. That woman hovers about me like a mother hummingbird."

"Always has, Earl." A portly man in a red checked shirt clapped his shoulder.

"Always will, I reckon." Earl chuckled. He sipped coffee that someone brought. "Mmm. That's a good cup o' joe. What're we talkin' bout tonight?"

"Revival Meeting," they answered in a chorus.

Jake exhaled, shuffled papers. "I was about to discuss plans for location."

"We can get two hundred souls in tents in the back," the owl-eyed fellow offered. "If we go with that rental company from Thayer again."

Mumbles of approval rattled through, along with budget and traffic concerns.

Jake drummed his thumbs on the table. He didn't hear one question that stemmed from the real purpose for having a revival. He held up a hand, but no one seemed to notice.

"Knock off the racket!" Earl spoke up and the room fell silent. "Our pastor's got something to say." He frowned then turned to Jake. "Go ahead, son."

"Thanks, Mr. Dale." Jake held his hands out. "Now, it's all well and good to talk rental companies, tents, and traffic control. But I've got an idea that you should take under consideration."

They sat in rapt attention.

"The Reunion Carnival's scheduled for the same weekend as the Revival. I'm sure that's not a coincidence."

"Been that way long as I can remember," Scott spoke up.

"Longer than that," Earl acknowledged.

"We've got to combat the elements that those travelin' folk bring to the valley." Tom wagged a finger.

"And how are we going to do that, exactly?" Jake's voice quelled the rabble.

The crowd sat in silence.

"How, indeed?" He continued, "Unless we host His Revival where folks happen by. Maybe they'll come in from the Reunion."

Their instant disapproval soaked him in a wave.

"Drunken revelry" and "Heathens!" followed by "Trouble-makers, all of 'em!"

"That may be...but what good is it, re-saving ourselves every Sunday? We need to throw out life rafts to those in need. And where better, than across the fairgrounds from the carnival?"

More disapproval. Owl-eyes stood to leave, crumpling his pamphlet for effect.

Earl Dale struggled to his feet and walked up to the front in unsure steps.

The crowd hushed.

Jake grasped the elderly man's elbow, then stepped back to let Earl have his say.

"When I was a boy, I hunted those woods every day rather than go to school. That old school house is still out there, you know. It's a monument, I guess, or some crazy thing."

"Yes." Tom spoke up, impatient. "My company renovated it last year. They have weddings out there, family picnics."

"I know Naomi thinks otherwise..." Earl grinned. "But I was saved out there on that plot of land, in that very school house, at the first of Cherokee Spring's revivals. Back when I was just a boy..."

Jake stared toward the back at a trio of stained glass windows. Glowing with the bright farm lights from the Dale property, he saw scenes of pastures, rolling hills, baskets of fish, and crowds on a hillside. A simpler time, maybe the one that Earl saw in his mind's eye as he stared off.

Someone cleared his throat, breaking the silence.

"All in favor of moving the Revival location to the park, above the carnival grounds?" Jake offered, and then added. "If we can make arrangements with the city?"

"Aye!" Earl shouted, and laughed until a coughing spell overtook him.

"Ayes" salted the crowd, along with slowly raised right hands.

Tom begrudgingly raised his own, his scowl showing his true heart.

"Nays?"

Silence. No one dared speak opposition.

"We'll see to permits and discuss further plans next week." Jake adjourned the meeting, leaving the crowd to mumble at his back. He darted through milling men, their previously hopeful and expectant faces now full of doubt, concern, and worry. No doubt, he'd be getting a call tomorrow from the church elders, demanding explanation.

Fallout from this decision would be legendary. There'd be plenty of time to hear complaints after church on Sunday, for the weeks leading up to the event, and to his email, newly posted on the sign out front. He hot-footed it after Earl Dale, and placed a hand to steady his gait, to see he made it safely back home.

He'd avoided discussing the ousting of his predecessor, the prayer chain, and his own history, but the Lord worked in his own way. In Jake's experience, it was never the way anyone planned.

# 9

By six AM the diner's kitchen hummed with prep for Saturday's morning special. Lilah dumped the colander of washed potatoes on the cutting board already littered with onions, rosemary, and bright red, gold, and orange peppers, her knife rat-a-tatting against wood.

Raymond swept up the remnants that fell to the linoleum. "You know they're gonna complain, right?"

"I know." She tossed a red potato up, caught it, and added it to the veggie victims. She cleared the surface into a large steel bowl and handed the knife to Ray. "Like that. Only lots more."

Knife tip down, he mimicked her movements, and then smiled. "Hey, that's kind of fun!"

Lilah turned back to the bowl, drizzled olive oil, dashed sea salt, and tossed the mixture. She added a generous heap of Parmesan cheese, poured the seasoned contents into a parchment-lined baking sheet and set the industrial oven to broil. "There. Shake it around in ten, with a handful more parm. Add the next batch."

She washed her hands, and knowing Raymond would do her bidding, wiped off last night's advertised corned beef dinner special—unsold and untouched. With a quick scrawl, Lilah penned the morning's special: corned beef hash, poached eggs, and home fries. Maybe she'd actually get someone to eat it.

The bell rang, and Jake came in, shaggy hair damp from a shower. "Too early?"

"Why, hey, Pastor!" Eden hopped around the counter to give him a friendly hug and pat on the cheek. "I just flipped the sign."

"I was heading to the market, but I saw you were open."

"You sit anywhere you like. I'll bring you some coffee." Eden went to the coffeemaker near Lilah. "It's like God knew we needed a new, single man in Mammoth. He could use a haircut. You're good with scissors, ain't ya?" Voice low, Eden elbowed Lilah.

Jake settled at the bar.

Eden went to him and poured a generous splash of coffee into a fresh mug. "Here you go, Pastor."

"Thanks." He did his thing with the creamer and slow stirred, his gaze fixed on Lilah as she lifted the board. "Need a hand?"

"No, I got it." She smiled and propped the day's specials above the drink machine.

Bright blue, red, and white lights swirled—a paramedics vehicle—pulling his attention away from her sign. The siren burred once and then went silent.

"Someone call for an ambulance?"

"Nah." Lilah poured a cup of coffee and leaned on the counter. "That's just Jeremy and Luke. The B shift, come by to drool over my sister."

The bell jingled again, and Eden welcomed the paramedic team.

After nodding a friendly hello, Jake absorbed himself in the menu.

Conversation settled into a comfortable hum.

Raymond announced his chopping task done.

Scents of fresh brewed coffee wafted around the

roasting potatoes and peppers.

"Smells like heaven." Jake observed the Specials board. "What'd you do to spice that up?"

"How d'ya mean?" Lilah dialed the radio and landed on a ministry station tuning in to Pastor Bill Gibson's rich, welcoming tones of forgiveness and hope. With a smirk to Jake, she decided on country.

"Leave it!" Eden shouted out.

Lilah grabbed a bag of napkins and assembly-line jammed them into a waiting row of silver dispensers. She pointed to the board. "I've learned that's where you put your best stuff. Not that they'd know this."

"So, all those peppers and potatoes?"

"They're in there." She raised her eyebrows, daring.

"I'll have the special. Please." He slid the menu back into the rack. "I don't think I'll ever read this again."

"What an honor." She kept her tone light. "It'll be up in five." She went to the cooler, dragged out ingredients, and commenced to shred, mince, prepare, and set it sizzling on the griddle. The salty aroma mingled with the vinegar-steam and roasting veggies. His comment unnerved her. Cooking her special for the handsome pastor shouldn't get under her skin. She had no right to anticipate anything.

It was only a few days since the overnight package should have arrived back at the lawyer. She shouldn't be expecting anything save for trouble arriving once all parties were informed of her revised demands. Gooseflesh broke while she spooned frothy white poached eggs from simmering water. Not the time to think of that now. She glanced at the wall clock. Saturday at six-thirty, she had time for a quick bite and one for Eden, too. She made two plates and slid in beside Jake at the otherwise deserted bar.

Raymond poured glasses of freshly squeezed orange juice for each then disappeared into the back.

"Hope you don't mind. I needed something before the rush comes in." She shot a glance at Eden.

Her twin set a hand to Luke's shoulder and gave it a squeeze. The paramedic lit up like the neon "Open" sign in the window. Poor Luke gazed at Eden as if she were the only woman in the world.

Irritation balled in her gut. "Eden!" Lilah called.

"What?" Eden came over, frowning.

"Don't be short with me." Lilah pointed at the artfully plated hash. "You need to try the special."

"Why?" Eden's look darkened. She bookended Jake at the bar, speared a poached egg, and took a dainty bite.

Lilah watched the two of them as they ate; the expressions on their faces as they each experienced the subtle explosion of flavors. Jake was just in from a morning run and in need of sustenance, while Eden was starving on a completely different level. From what Lilah could tell, her sister barely ate anything, intent on keeping herself the same size since high school. Lilah's own frenetic energy had always been enough to keep her metabolism steady. Something her twin insisted was a constant battle.

"Wow." Jake mopped up the last drops of yolk with his sourdough toast.

"Yeah." Eden's brows rose. "Wow, indeed."

"Now, you can recommend it." Lilah dragged the plate back away from Eden's searching fork, and took a bite herself.

Eden set off to chat up an elderly couple and

expound on the morning special.

"My work here is done." Lilah pushed off the stool. "Big plans today, Jake?"

"Working on the church this morning, then I thought maybe later—"

"Two specials, Ray!" Eden swung the order on the rack. Frothing drinks into ice-filled cups, Eden caught Lilah's attention. "I get it. Why it's important to you."

"Thanks." Lilah carried Jake's plate to the sink. She waited for that flush of accomplishment, pride, and joy but her heart was hollowed out. None of them knew how much she'd sacrificed to return to Mammoth.

Not even Eden.

Nana and Papaw wandered in at seven.

Eden wrapped her arms around them both and pecked her grandfather on the cheek.

Nana held on an extra minute, as if Eden was her life raft.

Lilah tossed more empty dishes into the sink, a bit harder than necessary. She loaded glasses into the trays. Seeing Nana and Eden hug like that shouldn't bother her. She dragged the orders off the rack and set to work. Two specials. So far. She was sure to sell out by lunch. She showed Ray how she wanted it plated, then set the white platters to the window. "Order up!" she called and blinked at Jake still at his barstool.

Her Papaw sat on Jake's left, his time-worn fingers worried the sugar packets.

Nana stilled him with a steady hand.

Lilah poured them each a coffee and said her good mornings. No hugs. A hand squeeze for Papaw. A measured stare at Nana. She nodded, turned back to Jake. "You need something else?"

"Just—" He cleared his throat at her approach. "I was hoping maybe you'd show me where to catch a fish later. If you're not too busy."

"Lilah's the best fisherwoman on the river." Papaw's smile touched his clear, green eyes. "Knows just where to cast. And when. That's the trick."

"I hope she'll show me. I can cook up a mean trout."

"You want to cook trout. For me?"

"Maybe." Jake grinned. "Maybe I could teach you something about grilling fish."

"Pastor Jake..." Nana interrupted the repartee. "You should know something about our sweet, wayward Lilah here."

Lilah's heart speared with her grandmother's tone. "Really. It's OK—"

"No," Nana interrupted, tone sweetened with southern drawl, but her meaning sharp as her stare. "I don't believe it is."

Suddenly Lilah was ten, sitting in the corner, her backside stinging as Eden cried a river in the living room. Sweet little Eden, who never did anything wrong. Lilah would remain mute, not saying a word to defend herself, eyes wide, hard focused on the future and her someday escape. Frozen, she stared down at the counter, praying for this to end. Fast.

"Lilah's still married in God's eyes." Nana's ice blue eyes flashed with intensity. "She can't go hanging around with single men."

"People get divorced every day." Jake splayed his hands around his coffee cup, then reached for the glass of ice water. "It's part of life."

"Not part of our Lord's plan, surely." Nana turned her disdain from the new pastor to her wayward granddaughter. "He should know the truth of it. He's your pastor, after all. You followed someone we barely knew out to California 'bout five years ago." Nana's words sliced deep. "Thankfully, she's come back to us. But, what's done is done."

"Apparently, that means our romantic interlude over fish guts is off," Lilah spat before she could bite the sarcastic comment back. Her stomach dropped, but she hid it with a wavering laugh. "Sorry, Jake."

"I suppose you think that's funny?" Nana shook her head, turned to face her new pastor. To give him a lesson in what was moral, no doubt.

Back to them, Lilah grabbed a cloth, and set to drying coffee cups.

"She's still married in God's eyes," Nana challenged with her piercing gaze.

"I think God knows I've not been married for quite some time." Lilah shot the barb back at her grandmother. "Not in the Biblical sense."

Jake choked on his ice water, coughing into another napkin.

"Lilah Dale!" Nana snapped.

"Order up!" Eden called cheerily as she clipped tickets to the teetering wheel, blatantly ignoring all the tension from Nana and Lilah's tight exchange.

"Excuse me, everyone." Lilah angled past her sister. "This bit of damaged goods has work to do."

# 10

That afternoon, Lilah dragged her feet in the cooling rush of water, her fishing pole in its Y-branch rest at the river's muddy edge. The constant roar from the river's head did its work to douse the fire of her anger.

Some folks said the pool beneath went down ninety feet, others said only twenty. No one agreed how deep, and no one cared enough to do a study on the matter. Most thought the fish didn't stay after the hatchery dumped them off every Friday.

Lilah knew otherwise, and that's why she came here to fish. She cast her line toward a fallen tangle of tree roots from a stump. That shady spot, this time of day, was a perfect hiding place. Her gift was knowing more than anyone ever needed to about the best hiding places.

Lilah tilted her head back to the pre-dinner sun. Its warmth through the cotton clouds wrapped her in a golden glow. Just her private chapel here at the water's edge. With ear buds in place, she watched the line and flipped to the playlist carefully designed to mourn her failed marriage.

A singer crooned of letting go, and someone had to go. That someone was her, though it hadn't been love that she had abandoned back in California. It was icy-cold indifference. Her soon-to-be-ex-husband's bitter, unexplainable resentment of everything she did or said.

It didn't take counseling to see the mistakes she'd made with Ryan Simpson. One thing she had stood her ground on: getting married in Vegas, on their way to California, as if that bit of subtle propriety would matter to her grandmother. She'd hoped it would have meant something to Papaw.

Ryan delivered on one or two of his dangled promises in the beginning, then left the brunt of his dreams weighing on her shoulders. He'd worked her, made a name off of her recipes in public, while he'd broken her spirit in private.

It shamed her to the core, how many nights she'd stared into the darkness and prayed to return to the edge of those falls. Walk that thin bridge by the old electrical plant and grain mill. To gather up one of those big, heavy millstones and just let the cool of the spring wash over her while she took the plunge. To find out how deep the water really went.

Freeing her ear, music was replaced with the pounding chaos of water. Hand to head, a gasp at her lips, she turned.

Jake Gibb stood smiling, fishing rod in hand, his gear slung over his left shoulder.

Lilah powered down her player. "Hey."

"Hey, yourself." He sat at her side and opened his tackle box, gathered a golden barbed hook from its plastic case. "Beautiful spot you've got here."

She checked her reel, to have something to do with her hands. "How'd you find me?"

"Just prayed for a friendly face." He shrugged, baited a hook with a wiggling minnow from his bucket. "Guess you'll have to do." Jake angled his line with a practiced hand. The bait plopped into the root ball's shadow, just next to hers—a perfect cast.

"Nice."

"Soda?" He offered a soda from the cooler and cracked one open for himself, his grin acknowledging her compliment.

They didn't talk.

His silence spoke volumes to her soul.

Lilah observed his profile.

Strong chin, his hair curled long about his collar, neat but unkempt. He'd rolled shirtsleeves up to three-quarter length. Scabbed knuckles showed he'd been working, faded blue jeans were worn over tattered brown work boots. This wasn't a man who stayed behind his pulpit or in a stuffy office. He got to know every one of his parishioners. Wouldn't he be disappointed the next morning, if he expected to see her in the crowd?

That thought brought a morose, yet satisfied smirk to her lips.

"What?" he finally spoke.

"Just an idle thought." She crushed the can and stuck it in her tackle box. "This'll be your first Sunday at church. You ready for them?"

"Not the first time I've faced an angry mob."

"Angry? About what?"

"Your grandmother didn't tell you?" He arched an eyebrow and laughed.

"We don't talk much—or, didn't that translate back at the diner?"

"I made some decisions about the Revival. Voiced them at the meeting last night. Didn't go over so well with some folks."

"Some folks. Meaning my grandmother."

"Her. Others. But this place is desperate for

change. They just don't know it, yet."

"Like my specials?"

"Sure." He adjusted his grip on the pole. "It's a lot like fishing, actually. Toss an idea out there for folks to circle around. Decide whether or not they're interested. Some'll bite. Others'll swim right on past, ignoring it, or come back. Strike." He shrugged. "Or not."

"The curse of free will?"

"Or the blessing. It depends on your point of view." His mouth upturned a grin. "He'll get through to them." Jake played out his line, settled his rod back, and waited. "All I've gotta do is show up."

"You honestly believe that, don't you?"

"I believe...that river fishing's night and day to fishing off shore." He tilted his head to where line met water. "Cast, and wait. No seaweed, no pull of the tide. Just...wait."

"Off shore? I meant to do that, but—just never got around to it."

"I used to go with my dad. But, his work took off—kept him busy every weekend." He exhaled and picked up his rod, slow, keeping the line slack where it met the rippling water. "Last time, I was about twelve. I caught a barracuda trolling in a sailboat, off Malibu."

"Lots of bones." Lilah's thoughts drifted to the best way to serve up fresh barracuda, grilled in olive oil, salt, with chopped tomatoes, red onion, garlic. She licked her lips and grinned. "Good eating, though..."

Jake's line tugged, silencing any reply. The rod tip bowed down to the water. He gave a cautious, achingly slow spin to his reel. Within moments, the fish swallowed the bait. He gave the line a confident jerk, setting the hook. They stood, side by side, as he played out line, then drew back in with a swirl of the reel. "Good size, you think?" Grin splitting wide, he nodded to the rod's tip, practically touching the surface of the water in a tight arc.

"Maybe a one pounder." Lilah grabbed the net and, barefoot, squished into the ankle deep water. "River trout know how to fight."

At last, through the lens of the surface, they saw it swimming.

Lilah laughed, turned a quick I-told-you-so grin, and looped the net under the foot-long rainbow trout.

Trading pole for net, Jake scooped up the trout. It flashed in the sunlight, scales reflected a brilliant rainbow, wide gills gasping, hook looped clean through its lip. "Beautiful..." He breathed hard, smiling like a little boy.

"Good enough to keep?"

"Nah. Let's let him get bigger." He freed the creature and set it back into the water. With a flick of fins it disappeared faster than it had arrived. "Get you next year!"

"Sign of a confident fisherman." She returned to her pole, fingering her reel in a slow twist.

"Not confident." He shrugged and re-baited his pole with a struggling minnow from the bucket. "Just not in that big a hurry to fill up our stringer."

"Ah." The smile bloomed within, though she did her best not to show it. "Sure your parish won't mind if you sit here with a fallen woman?"

"What fallen woman?" He winked. "There's no one here but us. We're friends, remember?"

"Friends." She elbowed his ribs. "It's kind of nice. Here you know my deep, dark past and want to hang with me, anyway."

He said nothing, but she sensed him pull back, as

if a veil fell over his thoughts, a shadow cast over the perfect afternoon. Why had she opened her mouth?

"So. About that dinner?" he offered, and behind his hooded gaze, she saw something she almost missed. Hope.

"Sure, why not."

He sat taller, but her shoulders sank with the hornet's nest of trouble she was about to cause. Nana embarrassed her at the diner, so her reply would be missing Saturday night's family meal. Relaxing to the idea, Lilah reeled in, recast. "If we're gonna have anything to eat, no more tossing back."

They turned back to their own lines, their own thoughts, as the sunlight played on the rush of water.

# 11

The Saturday evening rush settled, Eden washed up, ready to go. "You good to close, Ray?" Eden finished applying lipstick in the small hand mirror. She pressed her lips into a full, glossy pout.

"Yes, Edie." He sprayed water over a tray of white ceramic dishes.

"Thought Lilah'd be back to help. Bein' Saturday night, after all."

"No big deal." He trayed the plates and then shoved them into the industrial washer. "I'll set this to run and be out behind you in ten minutes. Half hour, tops."

"Thanks." Eden tossed him the set of gold keys. "Pharmacy'll be closing soon. Nana's expecting me any minute. You know how Papaw gets if we're late." Her gaze dimmed.

"Live by schedule..." The laughter vanished from Raymond's eyes. "Right. You get on, now."

Eden picked up the pie box and hightailed it across the street to the drugstore. The checkers board game was folded and pieces stacked. She held the door for stodgy, old Martha Anderson, a prescription bag clutched in her hand.

"Evening, Mrs. A."

"Oh, hey there, Eden." Martha's doughy face folded into a smile, she pushed at gray curls that sproinged from what looked like a healthy shellacking of hair spray. "How's your Papaw?"

"Same. I'm on my way up there. I'll tell them you said hello."

Martha's throat rattled as she cleared it, her circus tent flowered shirt rustled with the cough that followed.

The pharmacist's bald head tilted to the sound, but no one else browsed the low aisles of thinly stocked first aid kits, stomach remedies, and hair dye. Mrs. Anderson lowered her voice anyway. "You just tell them not to worry if we're not in church. I'll be visiting my sister over in Jonesboro on Sundays for a spell."

"It's not like you and Mr. Anderson to miss a Sunday service."

Hiking up her walking shorts, she shoved her pill bag into her satchel. "Donald was at the meeting last night. He's not convinced that new pastor's gonna serve Mammoth well. Not at all."

"That right?"

"Ideas. Plans. Schemes. Why folks can't just let well enough alone is beyond me. It's enough that the riffraff are showing up again." She flopped a hand toward the broad swath of grass that served as the fairgrounds. "I thought a nice, widowed pastor would be just the thing—maybe even catch the eye of one of our young, single ladies. Like yourself."

"Hmm." Eden cast a fleeting thought toward the strapping, tall pastor. Nice enough to look at, but not at all exciting, or adventurous.

"Anyway. Mr. A and I aren't the only ones thinking of not attending. That's all I'm sayin'. Goodnight, Eden."

Mrs. A puttered up the hill in the fading light of day. Was it true? Were folks that fickle? They'd had a taste of getting their way ousting the previous pastor for his eccentricities, and now they were gunning for a sensitive guy who lost his wife? What would this idiotic town think of next?

Eden strolled into the store to the back wall and the squares of gold PO boxes. She keyed hers open and smiled at the airmail envelopes. The address for the foreign offices were so long, so complicated, it was no small wonder she'd gotten a base wrong here, a barracks number wrong there. Too soon for her soldiers to notice, though, of course. Didn't it take a few weeks to get mail overseas? It's why she insisted on writing letters longhand, not email, not instant messaging. There wasn't any romance in electronic communication. It was all about seeing their handwriting styles, to see what kind of men these really were. And why, out of all the men she'd sent letters to, she'd chosen these two, Eli and Anthony, to correspond with.

Eli. He was strong, confident, brazen, and brash. Tony, on the other hand, made subtle, sweet attempts at romance. So unsure, so charming. She'd been unable to choose between them, and in the end had decided not to decide. She'd continued her love letter relationship with both. Her gut speared and fell to her shoes, imagining Anthony reading her response to Eli. Her only hope was finding some way to explain before—

"Evening, Edie." The pharmacist interrupted, his nose-perched glasses gleaming in the incandescent light

"Hey, there, Mr. Hackleberry." She folded the unopened letters into her purse, juggled the pie box, and turned. "D'ya have anything for Papaw and Nana?

I'm headed up that way."

He turned to the alphabetized rack of plastic baggies, grabbed several from the D loop, and handed them over. "Just have your grandma drop by Monday and pay the tab."

"Thanks."

"Lots of mail for you, there."

Eden laughed. "For now."

"Not trouble on the front lines, I hope." He shot a worried look. She'd heard the stories time and again of his trips overseas, his time in Vietnam, again in the first Gulf war.

"No." She sniffed a smile. "More on a personal level. See you tomorrow?"

"I'll be there." Mr. Hackleberry ran a hand over fringe of white hair. "I figure our new pastor needs all the support he can get."

She headed out for a swift walk home. Her thoughts sifted back towards the two soldiers who'd been romancing her from Afghanistan.

Each one touched places in her heart that hadn't been awakened in years. What a mess she'd made. Too selfish to let go of either, even though her soul sparked with guilt. Now, with the great letter swap, she had a tiger by the tail. She was pushing thirty, unmarried, and likely to remain that way as she'd just spoiled the best chance at love she would get. Eden walked to the carport and blew at her bangs. She unearthed Anthony's letter. She couldn't open it. Not yet.

She opened Eli's envelope instead. His coarse script looked hurried, just a few lines, and most of it crass innuendo. What had she seen in him? Was it the fact he bragged about his future as a lawyer? He wanted her to meet him in Branson this Memorial Day weekend while he was on leave. Right. In a huff, she crumpled Eli's letter.

She flipped to the next thin envelope and sighed.

Anthony's opening read like a poem, to his delicate Ozark rosebud.

Who writes like that anymore? She read on, absorbing every word as if it were living water. Then, on the next line, his fine, block letter spelled out her doom.

"Of all the..." She wanted to laugh, cry, scream, and kick something. Instead, she sank to the large stone that edged the garden and read his careful script again.

Anthony was coming out to spend her birthday with her, over Memorial Day weekend. He'd be arriving in Mammoth the weekend of the Reunion Carnival. And the Revival. If she'd have him, that is. He'd booked a room for himself at the Mammoth Inn on Route 67, the easier to visit her. No mention of wanting to do anything more than ride a Ferris wheel by her side, maybe hear her shriek in joy on a roller coaster.

"Eden!" Nana's voice ricocheted from the porch.

"Coming, Nana." She waved. "Just gonna change first! Got a pie for you."

Nana slammed the screened-in porch door.

So far, the only one who knew about her little fiasco was Lilah. Maybe it would stay that way. Maybe she'd just hide in the closet where she waited out tornadoes.

The sun arced closer to the rocky hills, backlit the canopy of new green leaves. Soon, it'd be summer, the Memorial Day weekend, and that meant—oh, she didn't even want to think about what that would mean. This year's Reunion was coming in with a hand-basket of trouble, and she was the one hauling the handle.

# 12

Lilah chopped red onions in Eden's tiny kitchen until her eyes streamed with tears. The well-used plastic cylinder sat in the sink, full of water, ice, floating lemons, and cleaned trout fillets from her fishing expedition with Jake. She sealed in the smile. No matter what Nana said or thought, Jake was intent on becoming her friend.

"What're you so happy about?" Eden's voice preceded the back door close.

"Who said I am?"

Eden set the pie box on the counter. "Hmm." she shrugged her purse onto the stool, and sat. "You fish the river out?"

"Yeah." Lilah smiled at the tub of white fillets chilling at her elbow. "Papaw's spot still works."

"'Course it does." Eden twirled a pen with manicured fingers. "Nothing changes here. Or have you forgotten?"

"Some things change." The smile wove its way to her lips. Whether Jake's concern was with her soul in the hereafter or her life in the present, Lilah didn't really care. For some reason, Jake wanted to spend time with her, and that was worth everything when the rest of her world was falling apart.

"What?" Eden studied her like a butterfly on a pin. "Something you're not telling me. Isn't there?"

Lilah flipped the focus back to her twin. "Did you

ever think, the older we get, the less alike we seem?"

That brought a blast of laughter. "Don't change the subject. What're you hiding?"

"Nothing." Lilah slid the knife into a stream of faucet water, rinsed, dried, and returned it to the knife block. "I'm an open book, remember?"

Eden's crunched eyebrows showed she wasn't convinced. "When're you taking that up?"

"I'm not."

"It's Saturday."

"Yeah, and I said I'm not."

"Did you tell Nana?"

Lilah gave a quick shake of the head.

Eden's jaw hung open. "If you don't come and aren't the one to tell her—" her voice shook. "Oh, wait. I get it. You're leaving this on me again, aren't you?"

"No. It's Saturday night, and I'm having a friend over." Lilah clattered the knife into the sink. "I'm a grown woman, Edie. I don't have to do anything."

"But...Papaw..."

"Will be fine. Just give him another pill." Lilah hated the bitter tone, but in truth, this morose Saturday ritual since she'd come back was more than she could stomach. She picked up the loaf of fresh French bread, sliced it open and slathered garlic butter on two slices. "I'm not going. Like I said, I made plans." She read Eden's thoughts just by looking at her: *What am I gonna tell Nana?*

Lilah tossed the tray into the waiting oven, cranking heat to broil. They'd sit across the table in the same seats they'd parked their rears in as children. He'd go over the same conversation that they'd had when she was five, ten, fifteen years old.

"Well, isn't that the limit." Eden's voice rose in a

gale of fury. "You made plans. Just like always, Lilah gets to lay down the law. Make her way. Get on out of town and on with her life. Have a date while she's still married. That's just perfect."

"That's not my fault and you—"

"Not another word." Eden's nostrils flared with distaste. "Ten, fifteen, twenty." Eden finished counting out loud, temper controlled—in that, at least, they were identical. "There." Eden challenged, her brows high. "I'm taking a bath. You go wherever your plans are taking you, or up to Nana's by the time I get out. But, I refuse to leave you in this house where they can see you and I have to listen to her complain about it. D'ya hear?" Her sister stormed down the hall. The raised floor rattled under her wake. Eden went to their shared bathroom. The door slammed, and even the panes in the windows shook. The plumbing rattled and the pipes clattered, the shower started.

Lilah mulled over their argument. She should have known better than to try to change things. Things didn't work that way here, and it was time Jake knew about it before he got himself in more trouble than he bargained for.

Beaten, she dialed the church number from memory, but Jake didn't pick up. A frown to the clock showed he still had half an hour to arrive for dinner. She smelled something burning and rushed to open the oven door. Lilah slid the tray out and shut off the broiler. She wrapped the crispy, semi-blackened bread in foil, set it on the counter, and went across the street to the pastor's cottage.

The May night embraced the oak trees in blue-gray twilight. The cooling breeze sent a shiver over her bare shoulders and she adjusted her peasant top. She knocked, then waited. Impossible not to peek through those back porch windows framed by cheery lamps glowing inside.

The radio played a this-century tune. Shouldn't he be listening to Christian music or ministry tapes? What kind of a pastor listened to songs about not being born to follow?

She knocked a little louder and heard steps to the back door.

"I thought you invited me to your place?" He buckled the belt on his just-pressed chinos, a confused loop between his brows. She browsed his attire, inhaling the scent of soap. He stood barefoot, a towel draped over his neck as he scrubbed at his damp hair with a corner.

"Yeah." Lilah fought a battle to look away and lost. "About that..."

The phone rang.

"Can you wait just a sec? I'm still technically on the clock." He turned and darted a glance to where she leaned against to his doorframe. "Hey, Mrs. Dale."

Lilah's stomach dropped.

No! She tried to get his attention, batting at the air.

"Dinner plans?" He shot a quizzical gaze at Lilah's frantic waving off. "Uh, no. No plans. Sure. I'd love to join you all. See you in a half hour, then."

"Thanks." Lilah exhaled. "That's why I came over, to tell you. I sort of owe Eden. We do this family get-together thing every Saturday."

Jake joined her on the stoop. "Why didn't you say so?" His face softened with understanding. "It's not like we were going on a date or anything. Friends. Remember?"

"I thought I'd mix it up a bit. Do something

different, you know?" She shifted, backpedaling across the patio. "It didn't go over so well with Eden. Probably would have gone over like a card game at the Baptist church..."

His gaze went stormy before his eyes closed. Opened again, he seemed to have regained lost composure. "Go on up." He drew her to stand. "I'll see you up there in a half hour. All things considered, let's not mention our fishing trip today, OK?"

"You want me to lie?" Lilah's jaw hung. "Some pastor you're turning out to be. Isn't misleading by omission still lying?"

"This isn't misleading. Just something she doesn't need to know. We're friends and I don't want it misconstrued." His hands covered her shoulders. "Let's just not talk about it. Not after—"

"Not after today, you mean. After Nana specifically told you just how much trouble I am?" Lilah flopped her palms up, heading across the street. "Fine. Whatever."

"Lilah!" His preacher voice stopped her. Resonant, commanding.

Perhaps he'd apologize. Say there was more to her than just another divorcee looking for love. She turned back to face him. "Hmm?"

"Please, try..." He waited a long beat, swallowed, and sighed. "Try and call me Pastor Gibb? Just in front of her?"

The comment cut deep. Now it was her turn to count to ten. Fifteen. Twenty. She gritted her teeth together until enamel ground. "See you at dinner. Pastor."

"That's not what I meant and you know it." He stepped forward, tried to take her arm, but she jerked out of reach. His voice gentled. "Lilah, you've got some heavy stuff going on, and so do I."

"Don't tell me your sob stories, and I won't tell you mine." She stood toe to toe with the half-dressed pastor, fought to calm the hurricane brewing in her gut.

He dragged the threadbare towel off and tossed it over one of the resin porch chairs, landing it instead on a broad-leafed fern.

"You need to make up your mind about me, Pastor Gibb." Lilah met his gaze.

"I know." He stepped a bit closer. Longish hair drifted around his neck in a shaggy mane, desperately in need of a trim. She wondered if it was true that with reddish hair came a fiery temper. How long had he mourned his wife?

She'd never be able to ask. "I'd better go." Her neck heated. "Sorry my past is so disappointing to you."

He blew a long breath. "I've been in town less than a month, and I've managed to alienate the elders, the deacons, your grandmother, and now you. And you haven't even heard me preach yet."

"Not alienated." She resisted a tiny smirk. "I'm only slightly annoyed."

"Give me your hand." He offered her his broad palm outstretched, and waited.

His touch thrilled in a wave of ripples from core to spirit, like pebbles tossed into the Cherokee Spring. "I don't—"

"Shh." The warmth of his touch flooded her skin as he pressed an achingly sweet kiss to her knuckles, staring up at her through those charcoal lashes. Her hand still to his mouth, he spoke low, throaty. "I'd like to start over, if you don't mind."

Lilah's heart did a flip and twist before splashing back into the depths of her exasperation. "This doesn't change anything. I'm still not divorced yet." She tugged her hand away.

He let her go, remorse tinged his hooded gaze. "I know."

She left him standing, half-dressed for their friendly dinner that wouldn't happen, and the full knowledge that if left unchecked, her emotions for the preacher would spiral to a depth she dare not go.

~*~

"C'mon in Pastor Jake, it's open!"

At Eden's invitation, Jake entered the barn-style house and stepped into another world.

Rough-hewn plank floors ran the length of the Dale's riverfront home. Along the back wall, floor to ceiling windows framed a breathtaking view of the river. Beyond the long slope of hill and past the subtle bend of the river toward the spring, spotlights flooded the scene into a High Def picture of the lower falls, the river rushing past the opposite bank.

"Excellent view. Looks like a painting." He handed Eden his light jacket and a fistful of tight-budded roses wrapped in a soaked paper towel.

"Smell that perfume!" Eden buried her nose in the opening buds, delighting at their scent. "Go on in. I'll just go put these in some water. Uh, they're Nana's favorite."

"There's a few early buds behind the chapel." He admired the view, curtains wide, windows open, amplifying the crickets' evening song. Beyond the river's bend, a train's mournful cry pierced the night, announcing its presence with a growing roar and pinpoint of light. Across the river, it journeyed around in a flurry of wheels, gears, and engine. Then, all was silent again but for the growing night sounds. Jake realized he wasn't alone in the room.

"Darn that Percy!" Earl Dale grumbled. "He knows better than to blow that horn. It'll wake the twins."

"Easy, Paw. Here's your medicine." Naomi Dale hurried in, watched him swallow, and then took his glass. Satisfied, Naomi strode toward Jake, looking sharp in linen pants and a teal jacket. "Welcome, Pastor Gibb." She wrapped both hands around his. "Thanks for coming on such short notice. You know Eden, and Lilah—of course."

He smiled at Eden and glanced at Lilah. "Hello."

She picked up a magazine, but didn't look up at his greeting. Instead, she crossed her legs, revealing purple painted toenails and suntanned ankles.

He turned to her grandfather, seated in a well-worn green velvet chair, glasses perched on his nose. "Lovely view, Mr. Dale."

"Thought so when we built it," Earl said, and turned to view Eden setting the table. "Can you believe my daughter, Rebecca, is this year's homecoming queen?"

"No, I—uh—"

"He means my mother." Lilah closed the magazine, tossed it to the table. "Mama was beautiful, wasn't she, Papaw?"

"Eden looks more like her than you do." Earl turned back to Jake, thumbing a disappointed wave to his granddaughter. "California."

"Right." Lilah stood, and slipped her arm through Jake's. "Papaw calls me California. It's how he tells the two of us apart."

Jake eyed the built-in library shelves behind the living room chairs. He ambled over. There were a few well-worn paperback novels and nonfiction books he recognized, but the shelves mostly displayed pictures. One in particular drew him and he stepped closer, the picture of Mammoth's homecoming queen displayed for all to see. The young woman in a pale blue prom-style dress wore a sash over her shoulder and held an armful of white roses. Her face—the spitting image of Eden and Lilah. She looked off into the distance, a wistful and wanting look to match the slight smile on her glossy lips, as if she knew something the world didn't.

"That's her." Lilah came up behind him. "Rebecca Rose Dale." Her gaze stayed glued to the photograph even after he set it down again.

"A beauty." Earl Dale searched his pockets, came up with an empty pipe. "Smart. Sassy. Too big for her britches, Naomi. She needs to be at the Revival, not at that danged carnival. And you can tell her I said so. I mean it."

"I'll tell her, Paw." Naomi stepped to Earl's side, relieved him of the pipe and replaced it with a handkerchief. "Let's get you some dinner and off to bed."

He turned a confused glance to the white cloth and then his wife. With a distracted nod, he followed her to the table.

"He needs dinner right after the pills." Naomi spoke in a low tone. "You young'uns go on out to the patio—he's agitated tonight. I'll get him to bed early."

She shooed them out the sliding glass door.

The screened-in porch held a trio of enormous ferns, a white porch swing and a table with four matching harvest gold chairs. Jake walked to the swing, sat, and accepted the lemonade Eden offered.

"Sorry about that." She sighed and settled in one of the yellow swivel chairs. "Papaw's getting worse."

Lilah smoothed her skirt and sat alongside him, but close enough to clasp her sister's hand.

"How long's he been this way?" Jake pushed back on the swing, feet firmly on the floor as he took mental notes.

"Five years, give or take." Eden exhaled.

"Has he been diagnosed?" *With dementia* he almost spoke the words, but stopped at the look on Eden's face.

"It started out slow." Eden's soft drawl gathered strength as she shared. "You know, brushing his teeth ten times a day. Forgetting where he parked the car. Or left his fishing gear. Then, lately..."

Lilah finished. "Lately it's more like he's flip-flopping through time. Thinks Mama's still alive one minute, we're babies the next. Then he's back, for real, but only in flashes."

"I hate it." Eden's shoulders shuddered. "He was the neatest man ever. A story for every occasion. Our rock. Now—"

"He's just there," Lilah shrugged. "And Nana's mad at everyone. Or maybe it's just me."

"Your mom." Jake looked from one sister to the other. Seeing them so close together—aside from shape of face and smile—he wondered how anyone ever confused them one for the other. "How old was she when she died?"

Eden and Lilah shot a silent laser beam of communication to each other.

Lilah turned back to the river in silence.

"Eighteen," Eden answered, pouring lemonade. "You know the curve in the road, on the way up from Hardy? With all those big, yellow arrows? The night we were born...there was a rainstorm..."

He nodded, recalling the bumps in the road that nearly rattled his poor truck to death.

"Story goes, Mama was in a car on the way to the hospital to have us," Lilah continued where Eden had trailed off. "She lost control—maybe wet road, or maybe another car. Anyway, she didn't make it. We did."

Eden kept her gaze trained on the river.

"Nana got those signs posted and the bumps to rattle you awake. Kids still call it dead man's curve. She never did get the carnival to stop coming through."

"Did her best to stop folks from going, though," Lilah added.

He leaned forward, elbows resting on his knees. "Why focus on that?"

"It's the time of year. School's out. Kids get in trouble there." Lilah shook her head. "Not that there's anything else for a kid in this town to do besides get into trouble."

"So, Nana and Papaw raised us here on the river. The end." Eden jangled ice, sipped lemonade.

"And your dad? He died, too?"

The women made brief eye contact but allowed the question to remain unanswered.

"We can go in now," Eden said.

"Ready to finish making dinner?" Lilah hopped

up to go into the kitchen.

He followed, a glance to Eden, still paging through a *Southern Living*. "You coming?"

"Nah. Lilah's the chef. I'm just gonna watch the river go by."

Inside, Jake leaned against the counter and observed the master at work. Tawny curls escaped their restraint and framed her face with wayward strands. A dishrag apron tied at her waist, Lilah rolled out parchment paper, lined a soldier course of their trout filets over a baking sheet, sprinkled sea salt liberally. A maestro's hands, she drizzled golden olive oil, a squeeze of lemon, diced cubes of tomato and onion and set it to broiling. In no time, heavenly scents of caramelizing onions wafted through the house.

Cornmeal and an empty bowl of batter were on the counter. A basket of fried, round biscuits waited, draining on a cloth. "Those hush puppies?"

"It's a prerequisite for having fish in this house. Eden's one specialty. Plus, I scorched the garlic bread." Lilah plucked a fried ball, blew it cool, and then popped it in her mouth with a crunch. She held the basket out to him, gave it a tempting shake. "Careful, you can't have just one."

"I'll risk it." Jake allowed himself an eyes-closed moment to savor the combination of flavors. Salty-sweet, a subtle hint of onion. He plucked another from the basket. All the while, he couldn't shake the description of their mother's tragic end. What must it be like for Naomi, for the girls, to live right across from that stretch of road. *Lord, how do I help, here?* "Is it very difficult for you?"

"Difficult." Lilah chased her hush puppy with a long swallow of lemonade. "Is it difficult for you?

Having lost your wife?"

"Uh—"

"How long has it been since she died?"

Skewered, his heart spiked with the unspoken truth, a sinking notion it was now a lie. "I-I don't—"

"No." She stopped him with a word. "I'm sorry. That was cruel of me." Hand whisking fast in the pan, she spoke again. "I'm sure you understand. It just is. It's my life. My normal."

"What's normal?" Naomi shuttled into the kitchen and pecked Lilah on the cheek.

Lilah stood blinking as her grandmother moved to sink, rinsed remnants of the earlier fish fry. "Thanks for making dinner. Sorry, hon. You know your Papaw won't eat the fish unless I fry it." Naomi turned to Jake, apology welling in her clear blue eyes. "Earl had a great day yesterday, even today up until sunset—or I wouldn't have offered you up."

"I'm glad you did." He assured her with an earnest smile. "I'm sure looking forward to seeing the whole Dale clan at church tomorrow."

"Oh, Pastor Gibb!" That brought a bitter blast of laughter as she left the room for more dishes. "If you can get Lilah back to church, the angels'll sing the Hallelujah Chorus. I'll take the lead."

Lilah stiffened, but said nothing as she stirred a creamy-looking sauce in a pan, balancing it over another pan of boiling water in her makeshift double boiler.

"You don't go to church anymore?" Jake stepped to her side, voice low.

"I'm undecided."

"That's rich." Eden clattered in with a tray of empty glasses. "Lilah's not been inside a church since she got married in that Las Vegas chapel."

Lila's stirring hand screeching to a halt. "Of all the—"

"It's true." Eden's look all but dared her to say otherwise.

"Just because something's true, doesn't mean you have to shout it to God and everyone. Especially your little gossip partners."

"Prayer chain!"

"If the shoe fits!" Lilah sniffed and fast whisked her congealing sauce. "Now I've gone and done it."

"Is it broken?" Eden stepped forward, stared down at the separating sauce.

"I can fix it. Maybe." She scowled. "Get the lemon juice. Another egg."

Side by side, the sisters worked the congealing hollandaise. Eden added in more egg yolk, a drizzle of lemon at Lilah's command, unflinching at her sister's drill sergeant tone. To them, there was no one else in the room, as if one mind moved four hands.

He hazarded a glance to Naomi, watching with equal awe, and then she drew him out to the dining room. They sat at the table and waited while the girls worked in the kitchen.

"Are they always like that?"

"Always have been." Naomi tilted her head toward Lilah, a look of pride on her face. "Lilah's the leader. Eden wants to be. She was a bit lost out here without her sister. But, Eden's also why Lilah came home."

Another train passed going in the opposite direction.

Naomi twirled a napkin ring. "We raised them for Rebecca. Did the best we could."

"And their father?"

"There's no father." Naomi shrugged her slight shoulders, though her ice blue eyes went hard. "Never was."

"Biology would say otherwise..."

"None that we knew." Her tone was dismissive.

A cheer interrupted. A victory dance was taking place in the kitchen.

"You are healed!" Lilah pronounced over the sauce in a televangelist voice.

Riotous laughter erupted, followed by immediate silence, and two identical sets of eyes peeked at them from around the corner. With laughter and hugs, any disagreement between the sisters was gone.

Jake caught the slight, sad curl of Naomi Dale's smile, and wondered what she wasn't telling him.

# 13

Sunday morning, Lilah skipped rocks on the river in the chapel of her own making. She walked the shoreline, hunkered down at the lapping water's edge, and selected a river-smoothed wafer of white quartz. Its surface warmed in her grip as she shook it into the sweet spot between her fingers and let it fly. One. Two. Three. Four skips! A scattering of rings bloomed as the river accepted her gift.

Cherokee Spring falls deafened in an endless watery curtain. But wasn't that the point of being here? This eternal thunder, the mist and scattering of rainbows—this she could understand. Better than the raging words of a brimstone preacher. Perhaps God Himself roared and raged at all of her misdeeds, or perhaps He was just smoothing her like a rough chunk of quartz.

Somewhere, people worried about what style of shoes would be inappropriate at church or wondered if the new pastor would notice the patch on their son's best Sunday britches. Somewhere, people had things to worry about other than getting divorced or whether or not your husband would come after you with murder in his eyes, or if he'd just sign the blasted documents that would set you free.

A blue heron drifted out of the oak trees, broad wings floating it to the ideal place to fish. It dipped toes and long stilts into the water, made a few careful steps with a ducking head, its slender neck cocked, as if daring her to throw another stone.

The soft skid of running shoes sounded before she saw him.

Jake was jogging, sweat beading on his muscular arms darkening the neck and folds of his faded gray t-shirt.

"You're gonna be late for church, Pastor." She chucked another stone.

The heron floated up, away.

"Whoops. Sorry, big bird."

It landed farther down the river.

"Just wanted to ask you to come. As a favor."

"To you? Or to God?" She chucked another. Six skips this time, and the small stone nearly reached the other side. "Some say that nature is the best church of all. Look here, for example. It's almost impossible not to worship Him when you're standing at the base of these falls—amidst His creation. Nana told you I don't go to church? I say, I come to it every day."

"Just this once, Lilah. Please."

Hearing her name on his lips sent her stomach to butterflies on the breeze.

He prepared to skip a rock of his own. It sank with a heavy *sploosh*. "Out of practice." He picked up another stone, held onto it. "I could use a friendly face when I say my piece today."

"You don't need me there, Pastor Gibb. Eden always smiles at speakers, especially the cute, widower ones. She says it makes them more comfortable." Lilah skipped another. Five hops, nearly bank to bank. "'Course, the last one never smiled back. She knew he was gay long before anyone else."

"Actually," He cleared his throat and continued, "I

do need you there. People've got a wrong idea in their head about me. I'm gonna set them straight today. Please come."

"Wrong idea about what?"

"Just come." Not waiting for an answer, he plodded toward the little church.

The heron perched himself on a rock in a batch of reeds. Poised, serene, and waiting for the perfect strike, he plunged, drew out a good-sized, wriggling trout and swallowed it whole.

No reason not to see what Jake planned on preaching. He'd looked so worried. So sad. Why he decided to latch onto her for friendship and support, she'd never understand.

The river swept by, gurgling, chuckling as if mocking her. If it knew the reason, the waters weren't telling.

~*~

The church filled from the vestibule door. The stained glass window cast disjointed, multi-hued morning light over the pews. Thick ruby carpet still held its new-chemical tang, mixing with equally pungent fresh white paint, even though the women's auxiliary had aired out the sanctuary the entire day before and lined the altar with vases of the sweet-smelling roses Jake had ordered clipped from the chapel garden the day before.

While the choir sang about building a cabin on the river, he watched Naomi Dale flinch, and turn to him with an acidic glare.

No, he hadn't noticed the dedication at the entrance to the Rebecca Dale Memorial Rose Garden until that very morning.

The doors opened and another family stumbled inside, found their seat. No sign of Lilah.

He drummed his fingers on the doorframe and considered their chance meeting that morning. Starving for his alone time with the Lord at his side, jogging always cleared his head. Sometimes, he even came up with a last minute sermon idea or answer to a long, drawn-out problem, like when he'd awoken in a cold sweat with no idea what to preach this morning.

Every note sent to him by his parishioners, though with the kindest of intentions, rang empty and God-less. Not that they weren't written with the Lord in mind, but none rang with the truth the Lord placed on his heart.

Last night, Jake returned home alone, as expected, but lonelier than he'd been since his first night in the hotel after leaving Margaret.

No messages. Jake lay awake late into the night, trying not to care that his father hadn't called to offer some encouragement. He and Dad were locked in another stalemate, for his stubbornness, for not working out a bad marriage with a woman who didn't love him and maybe never had. With his father's stubborn streak, there was no chance their deadlock would end soon.

He fell asleep with no sermon ideas. Not until this very morning and the sight of Lilah at the river's edge, tanned legs curled underneath her, her curling blonde ponytail golden in the dawn, skipping stones across the water.

Lilah was alone and yet not lonely. She had a spine in the face of adversity, remained steadfast, an open book, while everyone around her tutted tongues over her sins while shielding their own.

He looked around his church. Wood pews that could hold about two hundred souls. Did place make a difference? Wasn't God everywhere? They'd skipped stones. Thrown them into the...

The sermon knocked him back, as it always did when the pieces clicked into place. The threads of His message became clear. Jake thought of the exact passage he'd have them turn to in their Bibles.

The hymn drew to an end, and Jake walked out past the altar. His palms slickened around the podium while the parishioners raised their voices in the Amen. He spied familiar faces, some he hadn't yet met. The deacons scattered themselves around the sanctuary, though God's house was far from full.

By the time he finished today's message, he knew next Sunday would be far different—they'd fill the place, if for no other reason than to run him out of town. When this group found out Jake was not a widower, but a divorcè—he was sure they'd find fault.

Rita smiled from her seat, hair teased into a gunmetal gray helmet. She shot a slight wave from behind her program.

The room silenced. All gazes turned to him as he read the day's passage from the book of Matthew—the intervention at the stoning.

Eden grinned her support, as predicted by her sister, sandwiched by her grandparents. With a loud creak, the back door opened.

Heads swiveled to view Lilah Dale striding in, her head high, eyes daring, she scrunched in on the other side of her Papaw, carefully avoiding the quizzical gazes from Naomi and Eden.

A rise of joy in his soul, he heard the murmurs

even as he finished the verses.

She settled in and raised a daring eyebrow to him while dragging a Bible from the pew rack, fluttering pages.

"Good morning, Mammoth." He un-pocketed and palmed a flat river stone to the podium's surface, and as he'd hoped, drew questioning looks.

"Why did ancient cultures partake in such a brutal punishment of those who broke God's law? Did the Lord bless this Old Testament practice?"

He looked everyone in the eye as he spoke, praying all the while for direction. He explained about stoning as punishment in ancient Judea, and how the Romans added it to their own methods of dealing with thieves, traitors, and liars. "Our Lord ended it, there on that day, when he asked the blameless to step forward. Not one among them could. A stone tossed in a pond, or a river, does nothing but make waves. Not one of us on this earth is without sin, without a past."

Gazes darted to Lilah, sitting stock-still.

*Here goes.*

"And that includes me." His words evoked gasps and whispers from the audience.

Tom Steadman shifted in his seat, while his wife fanned herself with the day's announcement.

"There's a misconception about me that must be cleared up."

Whispers surged.

"I am not a widower. My ex-wife is very much alive and still in southern California." Murmurs and discontent rose in a wave as he held up hands for silence. "Now before you go gossiping, here's what you need to know in accordance of our church leadership. We divorced for reasons that don't concern anyone here, but as the Lord reminds—divorce shouldn't burden anyone with an eternal shroud of shame." But it did. And they will judge you, just as they did in California; just as they judged Lilah, now.

His heart died a little at their stone-faced expressions. Still, he went on, "I want you to ask yourselves something before you go writing Hot Springs and asking for my replacement." He stared back at each eye that remained trained on him. Many looked down, closed in prayer, or looked away. He allowed the silence to drag. "Who says divorce is a greater sin than lying or omission? Who would cast the first stone my way?" He clenched the rock in his fist and raised it, an offering. "It's right there. And I'm guilty."

That brought a nervous chortle.

"There was a time I'd have thrown it myself," Jake went on, giving the rock a toss-catch. "So, I have another question for you..." Palms slick, he fought the urge to wipe them on his pants. He cocked the stone toward the stained glass window like a Cardinal's pitcher and paused for effect.

"No!" someone shouted.

More gasps, he turned to show them the palmed chunk of Ozark chert. "What if Jesus Himself closed His hand over yours? What if He stopped you from flinging that stone just in the nick of time? Before you had to ask for His forgiveness?"

Some of the teens blinked.

Scott and Emma's teenage daughter looked near tears.

He sighed, continuing through his message, though his heart sank faster than that un-skipped stone at the river. They'd never allow him to stay now, so he segued into his plans. "God doesn't want us standing around congratulating ourselves for being pure or forgiven. He wants to be there, to stand in front of the one being stoned." *Please*, he prayed, and glanced around the room again.

An almost imperceptible chuckle filtered through the crowd.

*Good. Still have them.* "People are coming to Mammoth in a few short weeks. They want the joy of the roller coaster, the excitement of the tilt-a-whirls and shooting galleries. I say we give everyone the chance to experience eternal joy. Let's move the Revival to the park, near the carnival. We can open those tents to everyone, just up the hill—catch the curious, like in the days when Earl Dale was a young man."

All eyes turned to the white-haired man nestled beside his wife and granddaughters.

Nods and thoughtful tilts of the head indicated he'd caught their attention.

Naomi Dale's cheeks flashed a hot flush of red.

Some of these fish had swum right past, pretended not to notice, but most were circling now. Soon, they'd bite, especially the younger crowd. Raymond, the dishwasher from Earl's Kitchen, gave a fist pump as he nodded, mop of black hair falling into his eyes. There were more reasons for relocating the Revival to within stumbling distance of the Carnival Reunion than any of them realized.

"We're here to be the light. So, let's go down there and shine. I filled out the paperwork with the city parks, and we're just waiting for an answer."

"So give it to him, Mayor!" Someone he didn't recognize elbowed the late fifties woman in the dark blue pantsuit, front pew, center.

She surveyed the others, let out a laugh, and nodded. "Is that what you all want?"

Subtle mumbling at first, then murmurs.

"If that's what y'all want, that's fine with the city council members?" Three nodded. The mayor stood up, giving her a head over the crowd, her voice strong and sure. "Mammoth's fiftieth reunion will take place at the Cherokee Spring City Park."

Applause peppered the crowd, the atmosphere lightened. Their expressions were open, receptive to his idea. Including Lilah's, lips pursed in silent wonder.

Others sat, still as statues, as he called them back to silence, offered the benediction.

But Naomi Dale's challenging blue eyes chilled his blood like twin icicles.

He'd wrangled a fair share of the crowd to his line of thinking, but not all.

Not yet. And maybe, not ever.

# 14

Eden swept the floor on Monday afternoon, before the dinner rush began. The lunch crowd had cleared out, except Luke Traynor, who apparently decided this was a good spot to wait for someone to need emergency services.

Kimmy was late with the mail today. The soda cup left a water ring on the counter and Eden wiped it away. If only all messes could be cleaned that easy.

"What's spinning around in that brain of yours, Eden Dale?" Luke asked.

Same dopey look, buzzed blond hair, but for that stubble of gold on his face, he could be seventeen, prom night, in that ill-fitting tuxedo.

"I'm wondering why you park that infernal thing right in front of my window every blasted afternoon."

"I didn't know you minded."

"You've gotta park it somewhere, I s'pose." She swept up a pile near his feet. "But why here? Why not in front of the furniture place, or over across from the hardware store?"

Luke's gaze bored into hers, his deep, resonant drawl thrummed as he spoke. "I park it there because I need to keep it close. And, because I like to come in here and talk with you for some reason, though you hardly ever look me in the eye anymore."

He spoke the truth, like a stone to the heart. Just like Pastor Gibb's sermon. His boyish adoration, the puppy-dog look she'd gotten so used to over the years, now transformed into something different. Something she didn't like nearly as well.

Blunt, focused, and sharp, he continued, "You're so worried about those letters you write, about getting your mail, that you can't even see what's right in front of your face."

"What do you know about it?" She gave another halfhearted sweep.

"Plenty." Still seated, he lifted the small notepad out of her pocket.

"Give that back!" She snatched for it, but he held it aloft, scanning the half-starts of letters to both Anthony and Eli.

"You're playing a dangerous game with those guys, Edie." He circled an arm around her.

"I'm not playing anything."

"So, the almost-homecoming queen still needs her court." Luke tossed the pad to the table, retained his hold on her waist. "This isn't high school. Those are real men, fighting over in some God-forsaken place, looking forward to a letter from a pretty girl. Hoping to meet her someday, maybe."

"I—"

"Not everyone who joins the military's exactly stable, Eden." Luke's warning jarred her.

"Who's gonna be around to protect you when you get yourself in a heap of trouble?" He let her go and pushed back his chair.

Luke towered a head taller and a lot stronger as he captured her shoulders with broad hands. Why hadn't she noticed how handsome he looked in his paramedic's uniform? "Luke, listen..."

"Don't speak, Eden." His look matched his dead-serious tone. "The carnival opens next week, and I know the Dales don't usually go—but consider coming to watch the fireworks with me next Friday night."

"That's my birthday, y'know."

"Well, who better to spend it with than me?" His mouth set in a confident grin. "Don't say yes, and don't say no. Just think about it. I'm not gonna ask again. And that's a promise." Luke left the restaurant, a gust of wind blowing in at his back, pressing the door open.

She had a full view of his leaving and a sour taste of wanting more.

# 15

Lilah hadn't seen Jake after church.

Now that the gossip mongers had someone else to pray for, Eden's group dropped her like a bad habit.

She should've high tailed it to the river house. Spent the day fishing the falls, sitting on the dock in the sun, stayed until after the sun set. But carefree days were over, and she'd be danged if she let Jake off that easy. His manipulation of her predicament, while almost understandable, was unconscionable in every regard. And an unspoken truth was by definition a lie. She'd looked it up.

Cleaned up, changed, and bursting with righteous indignation, Lilah marched across the street with every intention of laying it into him.

But the door opened before she even had a chance to knock.

Jake stood, tall, lean, and worried by the look in his eyes. "You came."

"Hmm." Anger simmered as she darkened his doorway with crossed arms.

"Please tell me you're OK." Jake folded her into a friendly hug. "Are we OK?"

His relief rattled her to the core. She was prepped and ready for ten rounds, and he'd already thrown in the towel. "How do you define OK?"

"I'm so sorry. About everything. I should have told you where I was going with the sermon, but it just kind of...came out." His gaze so hopeful and so very vulnerable—how could she crush him? Her fury shut off as she noticed the little notepad. He'd filled every line.

"What's that?"

"My list of things to do." He looked even more pitiable. "The elders are behind moving the Revival, as are the quilting guild and the ladies auxiliary, but I have to get it set up on my own."

"The whole thing?"

At his nod, she understood the truth. They'd set him up, all right. To fail and fail big. No way she'd let that happen.

~*~

Hours later, Lilah cradled the phone. "That's it for folding chairs, tents, and tables."

"And for our budget." Jake tossed the ledger on his desk. "Somehow, every company in two hundred miles raised their prices since yesterday."

"Well, that's what the collections are for, isn't it?" Lilah stood, stretched to loosen muscles sore from sitting.

"No, actually it's not." He ambled to the window. "Feel like getting your feet wet?" He thumbed to the river.

"You want to go fishing?"

"No." He pointed. "I want to try that."

A trio of bright red canoes drifted toward the bend.

"Now, wait a second." Lilah shook her head. "Locals don't canoe. It's—it's what people from out of town do. They go to Many Falls, rent canoes, drink beer, carouse, and call out to us locals to beg for a bathroom to throw up in, or worse."

"Maybe in the height of summer, but there's hardly anyone out there." He tilted a cheeky grin her way. "You scared?"

"I'm not falling for that." She wagged a finger. "I'm not scared. Just practical. We've got a money crunch, and you might forget, but we're not allowed to date. Thanks to my birdbrained sister, I'm still married—and you. I don't even know what you are anymore."

"Divorced." He sighed.

She splayed hands, the victor, but feeling none too great about it. "Would you settle for a jog around the park? We can check out the site again, see if we missed anything."

"Better."

She raced home, changed, and found him waiting by her mailbox ten minutes later. No need to ask why he didn't come in. The ever-present house looming from the hill was reason enough. Naomi Dale sat out on her porch reading a paperback, or pretending to. Lilah knew her grandmother was a silent sentry, always watching.

"Hey, Nana!" Lilah called, smiled bright, and tossed a wave. She elbowed Jake. "Wave to my grandmother, Pastor Jake."

"You're never going to forgive me for that, are you?" Jake laughed, bumping shoulders with her.

"Nope."

"You two, be careful, now," Nana called, her warning a bit stronger than it needed to be.

If not for the mail lady chugging up the road, Lilah might have delivered a barbed retort. "She doesn't care what I do." Lilah stepped it up from a stroll to a jog. "Never has, never will."

Jake fell into an easy, matching pace at her side. "Why'd you say that?"

"Eden's hers. I'm Papaw's." She shrugged. "It's the way it's always been."

"His and hers. A pair of bathroom towels, huh?"

"Like an old sixties movie." Lilah had gotten used to it, but the dividing up of love caused more than a few heartaches.

They jogged past the carefully manicured front lawns, then down beyond the chain-link fenced houses.

Posters advertised the Reunion Carnival on street posts and the sides of old buildings. None of the carnies had yet ventured into the diner.

They ran under the freeway bridge, taking careful steps on the broken, root-rutted sidewalk. Just beyond, they passed over the gravel, graded entrance to the Cherokee Spring State Park.

Tulips reached for the heavens; broad-leafed green bushes hugged each side of the freshly painted redwood sign. Rita had done her best to keep the park tidy, neat, and ready for an expected bushel of visitors.

This was the only time of year that Mammoth saw more people stop than drive by. Those folks would probably get hungry—the smart ones would seek out a real meal close by, rather than deep fried food and funnel cakes. Had they prepared for enough extra stock at the diner? Probably not. *Have to remedy that when I get back,* she thought, calculating the order in her head.

Jake ran like he could go all day, keeping a pace that she had to work to match.

Something was bothering him other than his announcement at church. Cabin fever? A case of jangling nerves? Nothing cured that like a jog around one of the prettiest parks on earth.

They passed the squat, brick building of the park center, opting to jog on the dirt path edging the rushing water. Ducks flew off toward the lake as they tromped over the freshly stained redwood bridge. She matched his strides, grateful for the shade from broad-trunked oaks, leaves shimmering in the sunlight. The constant babble of water, pounding of feet, and steady breathing worked its magic. Muscles loose, thoughts free as the breeze on her skin.

Jake ran up and paused before the bronze plaque that explained the river head aquifer. The cross-section picture depicted water rising from a fissure in the earth, the natural river forced up through a crack to this stone-lined pool—the scientific explanation for the aquifer's presence, not nearly as elegant as the Native American legend on the next sign.

Jake swiped a hand across his perspiring brow. "A constant water temperature of fifty-eight degrees," he read aloud with the wonder of a kid in school. "No matter what season?"

"That's what they say." She wiped her own face with the corner of her t-shirt. "Cold is cold."

He scanned the myth of the native chief. "Funny where 'why' stories come from, isn't it?"

She shrugged, scanned the story. "A chief comes to bury his son, who died searching for water during a drought. The water comes out of the newly dug grave, never to go dry again. I always thought the myth kind of ironic."

"I'd go more with tragic than ironic." He stared

back at the lake. "Seems this place was born in tragedy."

"Kind of like Eden and me." She kept her stare level, sure of what he was thinking.

He opened, and then closed his mouth. So he knew when to keep silent.

In the distance, a team of workers called orders and answered back to each other. The rides and freak shows would be in full swing by the end of the week.

"Hear that? Let's go check it out." She turned and pushed on down the path, not waiting.

Lilah ran beyond playground swing sets, monkey bars, and scattered outbuildings, and into the dapple-lit forest. She went cross country star again, dodging limbs and rocky outcroppings. The pastor wanted to see the park, the spring, so she'd show him. *Mamma ran away, pregnant too young. Took her reasons to her grave.* Skidding on loose gravel, Lilah slid down the hill on her rump, scratches pierced thigh to knee.

"Lilah!"

Chewing back choice words, she stood, dusted off, and twisted to view the back of her leg. With a hiss, she touched raw skin. Bright dots of blood and two long scratches. Beautiful.

"Where's the fire?" Hand outstretched, Jake pulled her to stand. "You OK?"

"Yeah." She judged her weight on the leg. "Nothing damaged. Except maybe my pride."

"What was that about?" He placed a steadying hand on her arm. "You turned into a gazelle all of a sudden."

"Just—felt good to run off track. I'm just not the sixteen-year-old cross country star anymore, you know?"

"Who is?" He released her.

"It's just this time of year. This place." Lilah plucked a leaf from her shorts, the pain of her injury an ache to match her heart. The approaching anniversary of her mother's death and her birthday, as always, tied in a big messy bow. "Bad memories for all of us..."

"Bound to be hard on all of you." He pulled her to stop. "Do you want to talk about this?"

"Not really, no."

"So, we'll look at the field, then head to Earl's Kitchen. Dinner. On me?"

"On my day off?"

"Sure."

"Only if we go Dutch. My papers aren't back yet."

He nodded. "Any word on that happening soon?"

"Just a waiting game."

"Dutch." Jake stuffed hands in pockets as they refound the trail to town. "Let's stay on the path this time."

They walked the rest of the way, side by side, to the field reserved for the Cherokee Spring congregation's annual Revival.

She couldn't tell which was worse—her own or her mother's bad choices.

# 16

"Thanks for dinner." Jake smiled.

Lilah mirrored his slow blooming happiness, as she hesitated in the door frame. She glanced at the two teens in the corner booth. "You sure you're OK to close?"

"Fine. Go on now and stay out of trouble, you two." Eden corralled her twin in a hug

Lilah followed Jake out the door, up the hill, with only Riverview Drive to separate them.

Eden was alone with her miserable throbbing feet, two more customers, and a night full of worry. Returning to the office, she slipped off a silver sequined tennis shoe. "Why'd I ever think these were a good idea?"

"Because you can't resist the bling." Ray laughed, snapped behind her knee with the towel. "Who cares if they feel like boards strapped to your feet, right?"

"Funny." She perched on the counter and rubbed out the ache at the ball of her foot. "And true. I wanna go home."

"So tell Andy and Charla to leave." Raymond dragged his bandanna off, turned to the mirror by the back door and swept a hand through his dark hair. "But you won't, will you?"

"Nah. They can finish their sodas." Eden switched feet and rubbed the other one. "Turn up the radio for them, will you? Where else do these two kids have to go?"

Raymond obliged.

The singer begged a boy to see that he belonged with her. The words set Eden's own heart to tugging.

"Where'd you go when you were that age?" Raymond squirted soda in two glasses and passed one to Eden.

"Charla's what, now? A year younger than you?"

He nodded. "Seventeen."

Her mind drifted back to senior year. She'd been on the cheerleading squad, up for homecoming queen. Lilah's big cross-country race. The talk of three counties, even a nod from the local paper—small town twin sisters with big aspirations.

When forced to choose between staying to win the crown or watching Lilah in the cross-country tournament, there'd been no contest. Eden conceded in order to cheer for her sister, and Charla's perfect mother, Emma, wore the crown. That was fine with Eden. She had different ideas of what happily ever after looked like. At the time, it looked like Marty.

"Spill, Eden." Raymond sat, arms resting on the chair back. "That far-off look tells me you got a great story."

Eden's memories bloomed so big they wouldn't stay inside. "Marty graduated the year before." She described the boy who'd cheered next to her on the bleachers and then stole her heart. "He'd never paid me much mind, though we'd practically grown up together. You know the type. Not tall, but cut in the best of ways. Muscles out to here." She gestured, laughed. "Oh, it felt so good to be held in those arms. So warm. So safe. As if nothing in the world would ever touch me."

"Oh, this is getting good." Ray tilted his head back in a laugh. "So what happened to Mr. Perfect Marty? Where is he now?"

"He only had a few days' leave, in town to see his family before heading–well," Eden slow blinked, "before heading to war."

"Always you with the soldiers."

"Hmm." Eden's eyes darted closed in memory. "He was the first. The one. I knew it the first time he kissed me. We wrote. So many letters we had to number them when mailing. No email or cellphones back then, you know. Or texting." She muffled a laugh at the horrified wonder on Raymond's face. "Life just poured out of both of us, and longing for the future. Marty signed up for another tour of duty. He wanted to buy us a house on the GI Bill, give me a proper wedding. I had big dreams and went on and on about them. Never thought how hard he worked, how much he sacrificed to try and give me what I wanted."

Raymond stayed stock-still, hands curled around the backrest, eyes wide and waiting. Both pretended not to hear his cellphone buzzing in his pocket. He waved a circle. "Go on."

"Marty came back six months later." She chewed her lip. "We buried him in the Mammoth cemetery, next to his grandparents. His mama never was the same. They moved away, said it was too painful to stay. She did give me this, though..."

Eden dragged the long chain from around her neck, fished out the band of gold, the bright and shining trio of diamonds. "He'd told me he had something special made just for me."

Raymond's gaze washed with emotion as he clasped her hand. "Girl, that's not the story I expected from you."

"Yeah." She forced a wooden smile, pressing back tears. "T-telling, I know."

"So that's why you write to those boys in Afghanistan?"

"No." She dropped the chain back into her shirt. "Marty has nothing to do with that."

"You can't tell me you're not thinking of him every time you put pen to paper." Raymond dazzled a confiding grin. "Are you writing to them? Or are you writing to Marty?"

The song switched to the lonesome croon of another country singer.

"Time to close." Eden put her shoe back on, hopped off the counter, and leaned around the corner. "Charla! You let Andy walk you straight home, and I mean it. No long-cuts through the park!"

"Yes, Miss Dale." Charla grinned, her fingers knit through Andy's as they stepped into the night.

"Kids." Eden checked her reflection in the pie case window, swiped frosty-pink lipstick across, and smacked her lips. "You go on, Ray. I'll close up."

"You sure?"

"Don't you have a date or something?"

"Band practice." Raymond tossed his apron into the laundry bin. He kissed her on the cheek, brotherly, sweet, and flipped the closed sign. "G'night, Eden."

She turned to clear the table. The band of gold whispered against the chain at her neck as she stacked dishes to wash. She paused at the song on the radio, a man singing how his dear friend walked with Jesus, sayin', "Don't worry about me..."

"Really?" She cast a watery glare at the ceiling. The dam broke. Tears spilled. For Marty, for what they'd missed, for the shattered dreams and box of letters under her bed, tied with a ruby string. Eden quaked with a fresh rush of grief. She clutched the counter.

Somehow, she got through the song. She finished her chores as the West Plains station went to commercial. Restaurant dark and locked, she set towards home beneath the stars. In the distance, a storm cloud lit with electricity. Eden hummed as she made the trek uphill, from one amber streetlight to the next, singing near-forgotten words. How many nights had she and Marty trained their eyes up to those constellations, drawn the pictures and picked their stars that they could each see—drawing comfort in knowing that the same stars shone on them both.

But now she was alone.

# 17

With the house scented with flavors of butter, baking, and warm fruit, Lilah plunged her hands into soapy water. She was still scrubbing when the door slammed. One thump, two, her twin sister shucked shoes and padded down the hall toward the bathroom. Water pipes rattled.

"Must've been a long day." Lilah hefted cobbler to counter, steam rising. Maybe she should take it over to the church now, a pick-me-up for the volunteers transporting supplies to the Revival tents. The volunteers were her friends now. She should let the cobbler cool, along with whatever intentions she wasn't admitting. "Did you see any cars over at the church?"

"No." Water splashed. "Go look yourself, if you're so curious."

Darting a look through the front window showed no action, but the handful of envelopes peeking out of Eden's purse caught her attention. Still sealed. Usually those letters came and Edie would rip into them, devour each word, and then reread the good parts aloud, following Lilah around with them until she wanted to scream. What was with Edie's sudden emotional jag? There was only one thing possible. Yet Eden hadn't spoken of it in ages. Marty. Heart jogging, she knew Eden needed cobbler and company more than Jake did.

"You gonna be in there long?" Lilah rapped a knuckle to the door.

"Go away."

"It's a one bathroom house, Eden." She leaned on the wood door. "You can't stay in there forever."

"Try me."

"I've got fresh triple berry cobbler, cold milk, and a shoulder." Lilah pressed her forehead on the wood frame. "Come out when you're ready."

Thirty minutes later, Lilah flipped magazine pages in her usual place on the couch.

Eden wandered in, plate of cobbler in hand, white terry cloth robe wrapped around her body, hair in a towel-turban. Washed clean of makeup, she mirrored Lilah's skin tone, shape of face, and blonde lashes.

"You want to talk about it?" Lilah asked.

"Nope." Eden swallowed, speared another bite. "I thought this was for the church?"

"There's another in the oven." Lilah dragged her plate from the trunk-turned coffee table. "Don't think they'll notice."

"Pastor Jake won't, so long as you're the one who brings it." Eden gave her spoon a thoughtful lick. "He's getting sweet on you."

"Aw, come on." Lilah's cheeks heated. "Don't care what the movies say. Not every guy-girl friendship has to be that way."

"You're gonna sit there and tell me there's nothing going on between you and the divorced preacher?" Eden arched a perfectly-plucked eyebrow. "Really?"

Lilah replayed their moments together. The way he'd helped her back onto the path. The broad surface of his hands, the line of his jaw when he laughed, his eagerness despite the folks of this town endlessly set in their ways.

"You got it bad, girl." Eden spoke through her mouthful. "So bad, and you don't even realize it. All over your face."

Lilah turned her glance to the window, the sentinel house on the hill. Nana's kitchen light was on, that ruby glass shaded lamp guiding weary feet through darkness for a glass of water or a midnight snack, the same as when they were children. "Nana disapproves."

"What else is new?"

Lilah couldn't have agreed more, but changed the subject. "What do you suppose life was like for them? Before—before Mama..."

"Before she ran away?" Eden settled her empty plate on top of Lilah's and curled her bare feet underneath. "Or before she was born?"

"Either."

"I like to think she was happy. But I don't think Nana ever gave happiness the time of day. Too busy worrying about where she was going, about what comes next, to think about where she was."

"Now, with Papaw..." Lilah blew a sigh.

"Yeah."

Their thoughts circled around the image of their grandfather when they were kids. Whittling carved bears or fish they'd play with for hours. Telling stories of his ranch horse, Broomtail, how they herded up lost cows and chased off rustlers from the Taylor range.

Stories of when Nana was but a girl of nineteen, when their entire future was before them. She, the lady's maid, and he, a cowboy. In a time when the country was a dustbowl, they'd found love and risked everything to marry.

The next winter, when the house burned to the ground along with every precious belonging, the ranch folk and neighbors gifted them a friendship quilt made from gunnysacks and bits of bright colored, worn dresses. Each square signed with embroidered hands of those doing their Christian duty, wrapped them in subtle kindness. The same quilt Nana used to wrap them in during the storms, back before her heart had hardened to stone, before she'd wrapped the quilt in paper—the offering of comfort and caring, now hidden in the back of her closet. Along with that quilt, she'd hidden away a part of herself, her dreams, and secreted away a portion of her soul, never to be discussed again.

Lilah's eyes went damp at the thought of Nana as she'd been when they were little, when knees were scraped and bruised from tumbling down a hill. The Nana who dried her tears as she watched Eden and Papaw meander down the hill on a clandestine fishing trip, thinking Lilah wouldn't know or notice. The Nana who'd taught her how to cook, how to sew, how to turn nothing into something, and knew her, inside and out. The Nana who'd look her in the eye.

Eden squeezed her hand, drawing her back into the here and now. "Your timer's buzzing."

Lilah blinked. The air hung with scents of baking fruit and crust. "Cobbler's ready." She pushed up off the sofa as Eden gathered scraped-clean plates.

"Remember when Papaw dragged us out of the blackberry patch? I never knew two girls who were more stuck!" Eden jumped up to follow her into the kitchen.

"We ruined our new shirts." Lilah lowered the plates in the sink with a clatter. "Then Nana made me wear mine anyway, with that big 'ole purple stain."

"No. She didn't make you do that." Eden furrowed her forehead. "Remember?"

She'd ruined hers by slinging ripe, dripping blackberries across the front. She'd sobbed while Nana tried to lift out the stain, but declared the garment destroyed. Lilah wore it anyway, in spite of Nana's best efforts to sneak it into the ragbag.

What other memories from her childhood were skewed like that?

Up on the hill, the ruby glow from the kitchen blazed.

# 18

Cherokee Spring fairgrounds bloomed with the red and yellow striped tents. Clouds on the horizon sparked with lightning.

Guthrie checked a rope on his own structure, then stepped over the counter that would be his home for the next few weeks. The Glass Shack sat just east of the ring toss and south of the Tower of Strength. He unpacked his equipment—the mask, the long clear glass cylinders—and unrolled his pliers and tongs from the green felt bag. One tool slot remained empty. He checked his blowtorch. Tanks full. Guthrie had inherited the booth, and the knowledge of his craft when he was a young man, the day his mentor was caught with one ace too many in a card game with the carnival master.

"Cheat at life, face your death." Randall had spat the eulogy as Guthrie had shoveled a final pile of dirt on the unmarked grave in the Ozark backwoods.

They'd given him the Glass Shack as consolation, near thirty years ago, since no questions were asked. From that day on, Guthrie knew he had to give up the sauce, at least on driving days. He couldn't make figurines if his hands shook, or spin molten glass while doused in an alcoholic haze. This was the only place left to call home. He was out of options. This was his purgatory. He barely remembered what came before, as if it were some dream from which he'd never roused.

"You all right there, Guthrie?" Maya Randall, the carnival master's daughter, walked over. She was sixteen with curves where she used to be stick straight. "Just making sure everything made it safe."

He averted his attention. "Yes'm." He twisted to glance at the exhibit pieces, flicked the spark to his blowtorch, adjusted the narrow blue flame, and lowered his visor. "I'm all unpacked."

Across the field, near the forest's edge, other tents popped up their tops. White canvas ghosts, they floated under the moonlight, near the skeleton of the old schoolhouse. "Look at them, up there."

"That'd be the Revival folk setting up." He swallowed a shard. "Wrong side of the highway."

"You ever been to one?" Maya leaned her elbows to the edge, the fire red of her hair dangled across one shoulder.

"Not for quite some time." The blue flame whooshed, heat and light. He tightened until it almost burned invisible. "Pastor's getting ready to save some souls."

"Pa'll snag a few down here, too, I reckon." She tilted a wicked grin as she reviewed the figures in the haphazard display, a mini carnival in its own right. She pointed to the clown. "You gonna finally give that to me this year?"

Guthrie shook his head. "Nope."

Her lips pressed into a full pout. An idea brightened those agate-colored eyes. She reminded him of a tiger, ready to pounce as she leaned halfway over the counter. "Make me something?"

"Already started." He dragged the amber stick of glass over, warmed it, set his hands in motion. Guthrie made the same form that he made for her time and again, bunching the tiger's shoulders, jaws open, tail swirled around its lithe body. He used the fine tongs to twist the cooling glass just so.

Maya scrunched her lips. "Why do you always make me tigers?"

"It's what your eyes tell me." Satisfied, he set about cooling the figure, using a heavy cloth to draw the heat out.

The girl in the alley had eyes that showed him something altogether different. His mind replayed the scene he'd witnessed a few days ago, and he started his next project for the menagerie. The heron. The trout. With competent, quick fingers, the animals took shape from tubes of glass.

Lips pursed in an O of surprise, Maya ignored the tiger and watched him work. Childlike, she clapped.

The sloshing bottle pressed in his breast pocket as the glass sparked under his hands. He cleared his throat as he wove in bright blue for the bird's wing. A slight line of yellow melted under the blaze of his torch. He tweaked it with the finest pliers, forming its beak, the crest at its head.

"I want that one." Maya blinked brandy-colored eyes.

"Always want what you can't have, don't you?" Guthrie gave a swift shake of his head. "You take care of the tiger now, Maya." He cooled the heron, quick-like to keep it from breaking, and secreted it away between heavy cloths.

"I never will get how you do that." She frowned, turning the cat over.

"Tried to show you once, remember?" He smiled, teeth hidden behind his lips. "You didn't give it a chance."

"Patience isn't my strong suit." She flipped her ponytail, a laugh on her lips. "I ended up with a blob."

"Paperweight," he corrected. "Everything deserves a chance—even if it needs to be re-melted. Formed into something new."

"If you say so. I call it trash." She set off toward her pa's trailer without so much as a glance back.

Looking back up the hill, Guthrie's heart throbbed. The last of the Revival tents bloomed out. Someone sang, a guitar hummed through loudspeakers. A voice lilted, laughed.

Inside, curtains drawn, lights burning, Maya's father—Carnival Master Randall—plotted and planned the next moves for his carnival of fools.

# 19

Lilah scrawled an unrecognizable signature on the electronic form while the delivery driver muscled out a large paper supply box, topped with the slim envelope that would decide where she went from here.

At the box truck's departure, Emma and two of her besties giggled and compared him to the actor from that latest dystopian movie. "He could save my life, any day." Emma fanned herself.

The Thursday lunchtime crowd fell to a hush.

Eden paused, pad in hand, her pencil poised mid-order. Her eyebrows jogged, but she didn't budge.

Lilah took the thick packet to the back room and sat at the little desk. The letter opener ripped with a zip. Inside, the hand-scrawled note from the attorney in Los Angeles had her blinking. She read it again, just to make sure that she got it right, and glanced up as her sister centered herself at the dining room window.

"Order up!" Eden called. She spun a receipt on the wheel, and then hurried through the tables with water pitcher, refilling glasses with a *sploosh*. Wasn't she even curious?

Lilah smiled as she read the note a third time. The attorneys had reviewed her requests, made the changes. The final comment made her snort a laugh.

"What? What does it say?" Raymond stood, though a pained look in his face begged her to share all.

"Eden?"

"What?" Eden appeared as if she'd been hiding behind the wall.

"As my attorney, can you make sure it's OK to sign?" Lilah pushed the papers at her sister, who quite stoically perched reading glasses on her nose, and quick scanned the wheretofores and hereafters.

"For real?" Raymond paused mid-apron tying. "You mean she actually helped you?"

"She did one better than that." Lilah jogged Eden's elbow. "Looks like I can keep my car after all."

"And your name. He doesn't get to ride your coattails any longer." Eden raised her chin, handed over a pen with a ceremonial flourish. "Sign away, Miss Dale."

Lilah scrawled where Eden pointed, at each sticker-marked sign arrow. Finished, copies made, and final documents secured in a return envelope, she wrapped her sister in a firm squeeze. "Well done, sister." She hoofed it to the door before her lungs exploded. She needed air. Fast. Stepping into the warmth of late afternoon, Lilah upturned her face to the sun.

The truth of it spun out faster than line on a hooked trout. Eden had helped. She'd forced that Los Angeles attorney into reworking most of the figures at his law firm of That's Mine, This is Yours. Even though throwing in the towel would have been easier, this was the best thing by a long shot.

She'd fallen for a pocket full of lies and received a sack full of trouble while he'd profited from her and reaped all the rewards. Now, her sister, chock full of surprises, had freed her. And Ryan? He'd be footing the legal bill for both sides. Even Eden would get a tiny commission.

And this is the price of freedom?

No contest in the state of California. Everything was a fifty-fifty split, whether dollars, debt, or despair, and Eden made sure the man who'd kicked her to the curb would hurt where it counted and not take any more than his legal due.

Why did it simultaneously feel wrong and right to celebrate this ending? She floated across the street to the corner market and buzzed through, choosing fresh meat, ripe produce, and a few fixings for dessert. On her way out, she slipped inside the pharmacy, said her how d'ya dos, and checked for any new prescriptions.

"Your Nana just came by about an hour ago." The pharmacist grinned over the glass partition. "Saw that truck stop at your place. Drop off anything important?"

"Yep." Lilah forced her shoulders back. "My papers are final. That, and a carton full of paper towels. Can't decide which is more important today."

"Both clean up quite a mess, I reckon."

Lilah paused, heart light as she browsed bright tubes of lipstick. "More true than you know." She claimed the lipstick shade she'd shied from since moving back, and purchased it along with a pack of chewing gum and tin of mints. Money wouldn't be so tight now, and neither would her determination to stay away from the handsome pastor across the street.

~*~

Jake paused by the mailbox at the edge of her driveway. He scanned her carport and her dusty red convertible, tires low from disuse. He gave the back of his neck a thoughtful-looking rub.

Lilah walked up the road, hefting up her groceries. She smiled in anticipation of his question. Why did she have a car in the driveway if she never took it anywhere? She'd never registered it in the state of Arkansas, as if doing so would admit failure: that she was staying once and for all. Just another hillbilly failure—Ryan Simpson's favorite accusation.

Jake's finger traced a dust track across the hood.

"Hey," she called. "You made a clean spot."

"Funny." He stepped to her side with hands out. "Looks as if it hasn't moved in an age."

"Hasn't." She shrugged. Even if she could keep it, the sporty ragtop fit in Arkansas about as well as…well, about as well as she did. She pushed the thought aside. "After all, I can walk everywhere I need to go. I promised I wouldn't move it until I was free. How about we take it for a spin?"

"It's done, then? Your divorce?"

She nodded. "Signed today."

He met her gaze, eyes hooded simultaneously with a pastor's concern and a man's unveiled interest. "Want to put the top down?" Jake shot her a wicked-looking grin. "Drive it out to the carnival?"

"Like a date?"

He plucked the bag from her, his intentions to carry them inside obvious. "Sure."

They walked inside.

"Aren't you worried about someone seeing you there?"

"At first." His gaze turned heavy as he unpacked the contents and watched her put each item in its place. "Then, I had an idea maybe by going we could remind folks that it's OK to have fun. In moderation, that is."

Milk, juice, apples, and bread properly stowed, she turned back to him. "Moderation?"

"Mmm." He discovered a tube of lipstick among the breath mints and magazines at the bottom of the bag and rolled it to her.

"In moderation." Lilah raised her brows and swiped her lips without looking—loving the heated spark in Jake's gaze. "Well? What do you think?"

"Jury's still out." He drew her to him, thumbs hooked in her belt loops. His head angled down until she stood in his shadow. He trapped her in his warm, heavy-lidded gaze. "May I?"

"I'm a free woman now." She nodded, waiting.

His eyes closed; his lashes nested together, expression soft, restrained, yearning. He met her lips, a caress more than a kiss. Sweet and shaking, their dance subtle yet undisguised.

Utterly lost, her arms drifted around his neck, her hands intertwined in his hair, in the kiss. Heat flooded up, rocketing through her entire being and into him, as if their souls met and melded somewhere in the heavens.

"Come with me." He pushed her from him, his gaze pleading. "I was thinking we could take your car."

He looked so hopeful, so anxious for her to say yes, she couldn't resist the tease. "I don't know...Driving around in a car that dusty? People might talk."

# 20

He steered the convertible into the carnival's paved lot. Though sensible, after the hour he'd spent on the wash and wax, she laughed when he paid an extra dollar so as not to park it in the dirt. After a brush to her wind-mussed ponytail, she flipped the visor mirror, taking his hand as he opened the car door.

Fingers laced, they walked to the ticket booth. Even after helping wash the car, the tips of his fingers remained ink stained. Did he handwrite his sermons? She really knew little about him.

"Evening!" the buck-toothed lady behind the window called.

Lilah offered a twenty. His answering frown told her everything. This was a date, and he was paying.

Jake accordioned the bands of script tickets, and they followed the line through the gap in the chain link fence.

She skated a foot on the dry grass, momentarily second-guessing the soft yellow sundress she'd selected. The cool breeze danced the hemline just above her knees. Her white sneakers, already smeared with a line of dust, would be dirt-brown before the night was over.

"Ready?"

They crossed under the brightly lit sign into the opening night of the Reunion Carnival.

She hadn't been in years.

The locals—especially the members of the Cherokee Spring Memorial Church—claimed they would never walk through the gates into such a heathen display of drunken debauchery. Some of the parishioners who'd screamed the loudest on Sunday were actually here, with kids and wives in tow.

Jake sauntered down the midway, passing the petting zoo and fortuneteller booths, the tattooed man and freak show. He nodded their way through the massing crowd, tossing waves, how d'ya do's, and smiles to the shocked faces of his flock.

*He's enjoying this!*

"See you at Revival tomorrow?" he asked Eddie, a burly man standing in line with three or four of his friends. Neon bulbs over the kiosk spelled out "Beer Garden."

"Uh, yes, Pastor. I'll be there." He shook Jake's outstretched hand, his right wrist wrapped with a bright orange band for entry to Beer Garden.

"Have a good time!" Jake clapped him on the shoulder and ushered Lilah ahead.

She tilted a glance up.

Mammoth's new pastor.

Her friend. Her date.

Jake positively glowed under the red, yellow, and blue swirl of lights. His smile easy; his manner deliberate but somehow uncalculated.

Teenagers tossed rings for prizes and measured their strength with huge wooden mallets.

Jake stood in line behind them, waiting his turn. He wanted to try everything.

She almost choked on her funnel cake when Jake led her over to have their palms read. Mouth full of sweet pastry, she wondered if the woman in the purple shawl and dark green eye shadow had any idea she'd just told a pastor about his past lives.

"Why am I always Elvis or Napoleon?" He frowned at his hand. "Just once, I wish someone would say I was a sheep herder in south Angola, lived a modest life, and had seventeen children who took up the family biz after I passed to the great beyond."

Lilah laughed powdered sugar onto his shirt. "Sorry." She swiped it away with a brush to his chest and felt hard muscle and warmth beneath.

He clasped her hand, held it there.

Melodies jangled in the background along with the whirls of color, the merry screams from the roller coaster. She finished brushing away sugar dust. "You're a mess."

"In more ways than one." He accepted the last bite of funnel cake in exchange for a light kiss. He glanced around to see who was watching even as her ears set to burning.

A handful of carnival attendees caught the sight of Pastor Jake kissing Lilah Dale. She could hear it now, even as that dark-haired banker lady sharp-elbowed her husband; that new checkout girl from Ultimart, the one with the ropy braids and ocean gray eyes, sucked on an ice cream cone, watched a moment, then cast her gaze down and went the other way.

"That ought to get them talking," Jake murmured.

"Why are you doing this? What's your message, Pastor Gibb?"

"I want you to win that panda bear." Jake slanted a smile. "Doesn't every girl want the big panda?"

She glanced at the display of stuffed animals dancing in the soft breeze. "Is it that the girl wants the enormous bear, or that the boy wants to win her one? Like some bizarre male rite of passage?"

They wandered past feats of strength to the softball throw. Seven chances to knock over the trio of stacked milk bottles, a sallow-faced carnie with a cocky grin challenged passersby. Seven to win the oversized bear.

Lilah picked up a ball, gauged its weight against her palm. Tossed it up and caught it with confidence. "Tell you what. I win? You carry the bear."

He waved her forward. "This I've gotta see."

Seven bull's-eyes later, he accepted the treasured bear. The man behind the counter replaced the red-ribbon-tied animal with another.

"So, what?" Jake adjusted the creature under his arm. "You ran cross country and played softball?"

"Four years in high school. Could have been state champs if, well. If." Lilah jogged up her brows. "That made me thirsty. Want anything?"

They wandered toward the food court again and sipped sodas while listening to a band play a tune. The singer donned the same dark glasses as the one he impersonated and did his best to match high notes.

"What now, Pastor?" She turned back to Jake, cringing at the pitch. The panda perched on the chair next to him. "I'm pretty sure you've shamed most of your parishioners into facing their inner sinner."

His straw stuttered, soda meeting ice. "That's what you think we're doing here?"

"Isn't it?"

Their fun evaporated into the humidity.

They left the court in silence. Every attempt she made to rouse the former mood fell flat. Why had she spoken so sharply? Questioned his motives?

"Do you want to leave?" She waited in line next to him, while the Viking ship swung screaming riders back and forth in the background.

"Do you?" His dark eyes were unreadable; his tone, measured.

The ship came to a rest and the carnie called up the next boatload.

Jake tilted a glance to her and then looked away, his focus trained on the passing crowd as they sat, side by side, lowered the safety bar, and nestled the big bear between them.

The teenagers around them raised their hands and hollered as the ship swung higher and higher.

Jake gripped the bar, didn't touch her, and didn't move to hook hands with her again. Off the ride, his manner was easy with everyone he greeted—everyone but her. He greeted Scott, Emma, with their cotton-candy-eating kids. The family shook their heads, laughing as they headed for the fun house, as if all shared some inside joke.

Lilah's stomach sank from either too many sweets or her own sour mood. No amount of amusement rides or cotton candy could revive the jovial bond between them. They walked on, separated by more than the bustling crowds.

"Here." She relieved him of the oversized prize and clutched the panda bear before her like a shield. Feet dusty, her stomach churning, she kept worry to herself. "I guess we should—"

"Wait. One last thing." He dragged her away from the food court. "Follow me." Jake paused in front of the glassmaker's stand: The Glass Shack. On the other side of the counter, the glass man sat on a stool with a blowtorch in one hand and a glass rod in the other, his protective headgear obscuring his face. A crowd of gawky pre-teen girls waited while he worked.

Lilah leaned in to watch the form of the bird take shape.

The glass bender wove and spun the quick-melting glass rod through the blue flame. With pliers, he pinched, pulled the neck, added details to the wings. Quick cooling the figure in oven-mitt-like pads, he flipped up his mask to focus on the small crowd. One of the tweens paid, took the figurine of a swan, and went down the hill.

"Well, hey there, Pastor." The glassmaker shoved up his hood, studied Lilah. "Didn't expect to see you here."

The sick feeling kicked up to near panic. The man making lovely, delicate glass figurines was the guy she'd mistaken for homeless weeks before. Their gazes met, and Lilah forced a weak smile. She shifted her panda shield up.

Jake stepped forward, stuck a hand in his pocket. "Evening, Mr. Guthrie."

"You know each other?" she asked.

"Sure. We go way back." Jake shook the carnival worker's hand.

Lilah frowned through the same exchange Jake made with everyone all evening.

Except this time, the man paused, unrolled the paper between gnarled thumbs. The glassmaker tilted his head. "What's this?" He cackled as he read. "Passing out scripture?"

"Figured a subtle reminder couldn't hurt. You're welcome to join us at the Revival."

The man laughed. "Don't'cha go waitin' on a sinner like me."

"Invitation remains." Jake freed the panda and shoulder-bumped Lilah. "Hey. How about you make something for my girl?"

Her gaze remained glued to the roll of paper the glass man pocketed. This is what Jake had been doing here all night? She wished she could vanish into the dust and float away on the breeze.

Lilah upturned her gaze into the face of the man from the alley and smiled.

The glassworker nodded as he fired up his tools, voice muffled behind his lowered mask. "I've got just the thing for you."

The solid glass tube stretched, loosening in the flame; fire-heated, he swirled and elongated the strands into a mass of melting crystal. His tools set to work. A pull here, a twirl of red-hot glass, and a subtle form of a bird formed. A heron, with a curved neck, long beak, and wings outstretched, watchful and waiting.

Panda under his arm, Jake placed a rolled up, inch-wide piece of paper in her hand.

She shifted weight, wanting to bolt in any direction, yet she remained, waiting, as the man she'd so misjudged finished the tiny work of art. She unrolled the note, read its contents. "Be joyful, as unto the Lord!"

How many of these little notes reminding of God's love did Jake have in his pocket? How many hands, hearts, received Jake's subtle messages as she wandered beside him, oblivious, her mind tripping elsewhere? Spirit slain, she realized she wasn't worthy of this man. How could she be friends with someone who kept so much out of sight? Let alone date him. Everything needed to change. Now. Before it was too late.

"Here you go, ma'am." The glass artist's low voice rumbled. He edged the heron toward her. Its neck arced, a trout held in its open beak.

"Lovely," she whispered. Picking up the bird, she turned it in the light, catching the strands of green and blue woven among the clear glass. "Looks like it's gonna take flight any second."

Jake reached to his billfold. "How much?"

"That'n's a gift." He looked down at her, then back to Jake. "For the message." The artisan didn't look anyone in the eye.

She blinked at the little figurine and turned back to the display. "How do you do that? Decide what to make."

"It was waitin' in the glass."

"Allow me." Lilah picked up Jake's note, took the glass bender's stained hands across the counter, and did her best to capture his sinking gaze. "Thank you." Her elbows dug into the worn, gray carpet, scorch marks like tiny constellations burned into the counter.

He released her grasp, though he did keep hold of the paper, muttering a goodbye.

"Come on." She tugged Jake's sleeve and pulled him toward the carnival exit. She sneaked a glance back as the glassmaker reread Jake's paper.

The faces of all that they'd seen, both citizens of Mammoth and points beyond. From shame to amusement, each had their own reaction at the sight of the pastor strolling through. But, not one among them had that look of honest wonder, as did the craftsman in their wake.

~*~

On the midway, Eden strolled alongside Luke eating sticky feathers of cotton candy. The last time she'd gone to the carnival, the skinny jeans fit her a tad better. Her loose-fitting peasant blouse masked the harder to restrain parts at her hips.

Luke seemed pleased when he'd arrived in his truck to pick her up. A tad too pleased, she reckoned. How he'd ever talked her into this she'd never know. Mulling this over, she spied Lilah and the pastor, her sister moping along in last year's yellow sundress.

Pastor Jake had her on one arm, an enormous black and white panda slung under the other. So, he'd won her a prize.

Eden flicked a glance at Luke. Well, maybe if there was a game with a basketball hoop. "Hey, Lilah!" she called.

Jake and Luke shook hands, exchanged pleasantries, then the pastor shuttled her sister on to the exit.

"See you at home," Lilah waved, a sparkling figurine cradled in her hand.

Eden's attention focused on the tiny figure. Instantly, she wanted one. Before she could ask Lilah where she'd gotten it, they were gone, disappeared through the crowd.

The band kicked up above the merry-go-round's incessant calliope music, and she steered her date in that direction. Luke had a pocket full of tickets; ready to buy her whatever she liked, and this, the perfect night to test her theory. Luke, the always faithful friend who appeared to save the day whenever she so much as said, "Boo." Too easy. But, a nice enough distraction before the dam broke.

She ticked down the hours until her soldier fiasco would begin. Plane landing in Little Rock at just after midnight, he'd be at his hotel by three. Maybe he'd stop by for breakfast at the diner? Her heart stutter-stepped with the possibility.

Luke slipped his large hand through her arm and guided her around a muddy patch. He stooped, picked up a spilled soda cup, and tossed it into a trash can. "Two points."

"Hmm. Let's go listen to the band." Boredom settled its blanket over her mood. She smacked her dry lips, then glossed them from her tube without looking. "All this dust makes you thirsty, doesn't it?"

Luke took off to fetch sodas while she watched the singer.

Clapping, she swayed to the rhythm and sang along, thinking about her own soul sister. Lilah, so easily soothed. So open. Nothing hidden in any regard. Maybe that would be a better way to live than all this clandestine nonsense.

Luke's blond head popped up across the crowd, then he disappeared from view again. He knew she wrote to the service men, but hadn't a clue her soldiers were coming home. So, why was disappointing him tying a knot in her belly? She brushed the thought away.

A few little kids spun and bumped, giggling into each other.

The lead singer sang to her, feeding off her energy, making Eden his audience of one, for the moment.

Luke shoved a drink in her hands and stared down the singer with a scowl.

The singer caught the eye of a beauty more his own age.

Eden turned the force of her displeasure on Luke, crammed the last of the pink fluffy sugar into her mouth, and downed it with a fizzy sip. "Thanks."

He dragged out a resin chair and sat a bit too hard. It wobbled underneath him.

She applied another layer of lip gloss, then popped in a fresh stick of gum.

"You wanna go?" Luke dragged a hand through his curly blond hair.

"Why?" She darted a glance at her watch. "It's only nine."

He wrapped palms around his bony knees. "I'm just gonna ask this once."

"OK, Mr. Serious." A slug of soda didn't soothe the tightness in her throat at Luke's charged-up attitude. He looked angry. Not the Luke she was used to.

"Are you here with me tonight, Eden Dale?" He stared at his shoes, and then raised his glittering eyes to meet hers. "Or just the idea of me?"

"Don't do this, Luke." She challenged the man she'd always considered her back-pocket ringer if all other attempts at love went south. By his look, that wouldn't be the case much longer. "Can't we just stay the way we've always been?"

"I know all about your letters. Your soldiers. But they aren't here."

Not yet. Her thoughts raced to the two army men. They both wanted her. Both headed here over Memorial Day, her birthday weekend, each without an inkling of the other.

Luke's boot stomped a puff of dust. "I'm a flesh and blood man, and I'm right here."

"Maybe that's the problem." She scooted her chair

back, wishing they could just listen to the music and enjoy themselves that things could go back to the way they were.

"I'm done waiting for you to figure this out." He dragged her to stand. Hands clamped on her shoulders, he stared into her eyes as if he could peer into her soul. "I'm the one you call when you're scared. I know what makes you laugh. When you need something, I'm there every time. Not them. But I'm not gonna wait forever."

"Luke, I just can't—"

"I get it. You can for everybody else, but not for me." He nodded, hand scrubbing his scalp. "I'm not a drinking man, Eden. But, heaven help me—you might just drive me to it." He backed away, the white plastic chair toppling. She reached for his forearm, but Luke's outstretched palms stopped her advance. "Don't count on my being there when you wake up from dreamland." He crossed over to the line waiting to get into the beer garden and showed his ID. He paused to scan the crowd, then waved and strode over to a group of EMTs sipping from pilsner glasses. He accepted a drink and settled. Back to her, he drained his glass until it was empty like her heart.

# 21

Lilah followed Jake's long steps up the grassy hill toward the park, opposite from where they'd parked. "I thought we were leaving."

"Gotta check the tents. Make sure things are ready for tomorrow."

She followed him at a jog.

In the shadows, Raymond strummed a guitar from a rocky perch.

"Hey, guys." Jake smiled. "How was band practice?"

Raymond slid the guitar he was holding around to his back. "I finished learning those songs you brought, with Ted's help, here." Ray gestured and Ted offered a wave. "He knew a couple of them. Progressive, man." Ray cleared his throat. "You think the church's ready for a real worship service?"

"We need it." Jake's voice dropped to the serious, pastor tone. His gaze darted to the hill, then back to Lilah. "Coming?"

"You go on, Jake. I'll be there in a minute." She shooed him on, turned to Ray. "Having fun?"

"Hey, Lilah. Thought you were Eden for a second." He introduced his new bass guitarist.

"What're you all planning?" Lilah asked.

"Revival. It's gonna rock." He and Ted's high five sounded with a smack.

"Maybe you should take breakfast rush off

tomorrow—if you'll be up late practicing."

Raymond's cellphone washed blue as his ring tone mimicked a guitar. His face illuminated with the text message, then went dark again. "You sure?"

"Absolutely."

Jake disappeared into the Revival tent's shadow.

"I've gotta go help. You two stay out of trouble."

"No worries." Raymond turned back to Ted. "Just think where we could take this, a worship band!"

Creativity in action—two friends sitting together under the stars, thinking up worship songs. Lilah couldn't stop thinking about them as she trudged after Jake. Young men, poised to take over the world, but with a purpose. She'd never had a purpose—just floated where the breeze had blown her. To California, as far west as one could get without getting feet wet.

Just as her mother tried and failed to do an age ago. Rebecca Dale never even made it beyond the city limits. Maybe she was the blessed one. No pieces left to pick up. No sins to repent. Forever young in everyone's mind, especially her father's.

Lilah drifted to the white peaks on the hilltop. Twin tents backed by the schoolhouse overlooked the carnival; folding chairs awaited the crowds, the stage was set for the Revival.

"Think Ray and his band can really do this?" she wondered aloud, her focus trained on the drum kit gleaming in the moonlight, the microphones, the amplifiers hooked in and ready to go.

"They're good." Jake surveyed the room. "I heard them yesterday and his voice blew me away."

"Yeah, I've heard him sing in the kitchen. But…"

"You really don't get it yet." Jake pulled her up on the stage. "Do you?"

"Not sure what you mean."

"I've been doing some research on this place." He checked the distances, walking the stage between a set of natural looking branches in containers flanking the podium.

The ladies' guild had made simple arrangements of young oaks and lilies. Not enough money in the budget for a huge floral display, just what they could grow and gather.

"Mammoth." He quirked a smile, dropped to dangle his feet off the edge of the stage. "Even the name and the town that grew up here are at odds with each other."

"Ironic."

Jake patted a spot. She sat, cupped her hands in his while he spoke. "We're bringing hope where there's none. We're waking up souls who've slept for too long. This is a revival of sorts, in its purest form. Just us, here, now..." His thumb traced the lines of her palm. "...as friends, or something more?"

Lilah swallowed, his voice sounded so earnest. "More."

Hallowed, this place on the hilltop, the sounds of the tilt-a-whirl whooshing, and clanging bells and bright lights below. She inhaled his scent, something inherently Jake, being near him warmed her heart, her spirit, as never before. Silence stretched, as she fought to fill the void, as a good pastor's sort-of girlfriend should.

"If you need to practice, I'll listen." She watched more than listened, gaze trained on his mouth, his lips, as he preached to her audience of one. Almost more important than what he said was the way spoke. The determination. The passion. The depth of his dedication. The well of his belief.

*So, is this what it means to fall in love with a preacher?* Her heart fluttered with the question. A surge of guilt worked up as they sat in the newly ordained space. She had no right to feel this way for him, not in church. Not anywhere. An icicle pierced her heart. "What if no one comes, Jake?"

He said nothing, grabbed her hand, and joined her in staring at rows of empty folding chairs. A wave of sadness simmered through her soul. She'd finally found someone who understood when words would only make matters worse.

# 22

Lilah paced the diner before it opened, swiping tables. It was the right thing to do. Raymond would be up late for three nights in a row. Until yesterday, she hadn't fully admitted it. This wasn't his life, after all. This was a weigh station—a stopping off point. Ray had hopes and dreams, and she...she had this.

Leaning back, she poured a steaming mug and added a white waterfall of cream. Her spoon created a muddy whirlpool. *Happy birthday to me,* she blew it cool, sipped.

Birthdays were rarely celebrated in the Dale house. One anniversary marked another. Her mother's death...so young, so tragic. But, every time someone mentioned mothers, Nana came to mind. Not the ghost of Rebecca—her birth mother, pregnant at eighteen, who chose something other than the straight and narrow path and died because of it. Because of them.

Lilah slammed a hand against the light switch and the main room illuminated, declaring the "Open" sign. She set to filling dispensers with equal numbers of white, yellow, and blue packets as she waited for the morning rush to begin.

What made a mother, after all? It was so much more than biology, it had to be. Mothers could wither with a stare and spear your soul back to the right path or comfort your aches with a lingering embrace. Someone with whom you could share anything and not be judged, in fact, be loved in spite of it.

She curled her hand around her mug, doctored her second pour, and then sipped the bitter brew.

Since Lilah had returned home, she and Nana could barely be in the same room. They'd been at odds so long, they might go on this way for years before either one of them mentioned their stalemate.

The door chimed, and Nana ushered Papaw to his regular seat. "Morning, Lilah. Ray didn't open today?"

"Told him to sleep in," Lilah said. "His band's playing tonight."

"At the carnival?" Nana's nostrils flared distaste.

"Nope. The Revival."

Nana's gaze shot heavenward. For a moment, it wasn't clear whether she was holding up Papaw or vice versa.

Papaw fiddled with his glasses case, eyeglasses still perched on his nose. "Morning, Rebecca!" he waved, his blue eyes bright.

"It's me, Lilah, Papaw." She covered his hand with hers, squeezed. "I'll get your coffee."

"Fry up that bacon. We've got the hatchery crew meeting at ten."

"Hatchery crew?" Lilah lifted a questioning brow at Nana. "That's a new one."

"Earl. Think. The hatchery hasn't met here in over thirty years." Nana shook out her white curls. "Been a long morning already, and it's not even seven." She sighed. "You sure you can handle him and the breakfast rush?"

Lilah patted her shoulder. "I can manage. Eden'll be down in an hour." She walked Nana to the door, hesitated a moment, then wrapped arms around her grandmother's slender, brittle frame. Squeeze too hard and the little woman might just break in two. "I love you, Nana."

"Where'd that come from?" Nana's quizzical look blended with something akin to nervousness. "You're not going away again, are you?"

"No."

"Good." Nana's brow relaxed with her curt nod. "See you by ten. Busy night tonight. Better hit the pharmacy for some earplugs if Ray's band's playing."

Would her grandmother ever be comfortable with her again? Leaving town without saying goodbye had dug a canyon wider than Grand Gulf between them, when once they'd been thick as thieves.

"Rebecca!" Earl called. "You're burning the home fries."

"I'm getting them, Papaw." Lilah unrolled the Gazette, set it in front of him and walked to the back.

Standing in front of the cooler, she eyed the contents. Smoked salmon. Leeks. Cream cheese. Feathery green of fresh dill. A crate of farm fresh eggs. She pieced today's special ingredients together, though the real hope of her heart filled her thoughts. Jake was probably still asleep. She hoped he was coming to the diner.

The front door jangled. Two rumpled-looking young men entered. Maybe carnival folk, but not likely by the close-cropped hair and muscular builds. Military. Must be passing through on their way up north.

"Good morning," Lilah called through the window. "Have a seat anywhere. I'll be right with you."

"I got them, Rebecca." Papaw pushed back from his seat, ambled over to the coffee pot.

Lilah blinked, looked to the men at the side booth, staring at menus, and Papaw approaching with two coffee mugs.

"Morning, boys." His stubbled chin reflected the morning sun. "Coffee?"

They both mumbled thanks as he poured them each a cup without spilling a drop.

"My daughter'll be out with the cream. No getting any ideas. She's this year's Queen of the Reunion Carnival." He shuffled back to his spot, then reached behind the bar for a cup of his own and settled down to read the sports section.

Lilah was entranced as she rounded the corner to sketch out the day's special. "Morning, Papaw."

"Hey, sweetie." He kissed her cheek, his whiskers scratching. "Gotta get crackin'. Gonna be a busy day when the carnies get here."

"You want the carnival people here?" Lilah palmed the counter with both hands.

"Every year they bring us some of our best receipts, save for the hatchery meetings, a'course." He shook his head. "Your Nana thinks they're riffraff, but someone's gotta feed them. Gotta show them God's good grace and welcome. If not us, who?"

Lilah finished "Smoked Salmon Omelet" in her flourishing script and propped the sign against the wall. "If not us, who," she repeated. "Hey, what year is it, anyway?"

"What're you? Soft in the head?" He chuckled. "Nineteen-eighty-seven."

The year before she was born.

"And Rebecca?"

"Carnival queen, light of my life, apple of my eye." His pride welled with the straightening of his spine. "Can't believe that little girl's seventeen. Where do the years go?" His voice trailed, his focus fixed in the middle distance. Then the light behind his watery gaze slowly, steadily extinguished and replaced with something else. A waterfall of fear overtook him in rapid blinks. His lip quivered as he turned, saw her for who she really was. "Lilah?"

"I'm here, Papaw." She pushed around the bar and took his hands, gave them a strong rub. His fingers were ice cold.

"Something's not right." He could have been a little boy in trouble, the tone in his voice, the way he twisted to face her. "I was doing something...and now..."

"I'll go call Nana."

"No." He inhaled, deep. "Get Mr. Hackleberry."

"The pharmacist?" Lilah gaped. "You need to go to West Plains. To the doctor."

"You mind your papaw, now." He wrapped shaking hands around the mug. He seemed steady again. "Now, get him."

Lilah untied her apron strings and headed for the door. She hesitated a moment by the soldiers. "I'll get your orders in just a sec. Don't let him cook anything."

The blond-headed one's jaw jogged, but he nodded.

Imagine doing such a thing in Los Angeles. What person even knew their pharmacist's name, let alone dragged one out or left a shop in care of the customers?

"How long's he been like this?" Mr. Hackleberry held the door as they pushed through and hustled back across the street to the diner.

"A few minutes." Lilah went dry mouthed as the door jangled. "Papaw slipped out of one of his memories and got, well...scared."

Mr. Hackleberry settled down beside Papaw. "I'll have a coffee, if you don't mind, Lilah?"

She nodded.

"Hey, Earl." He clapped the frail man on the shoulder, his hand remained, subtle, reassuring. "Special looks, uh, interesting."

"Lilah?" Papaw looked up, concerned. "See to the customers. I'm all right. Ron owes me a checker game."

The man her grandfather trusted more than the local doctor nodded. "I think checkers might be just the thing. Come on, Earl." At the door, Mr. Hackleberry hesitated. "I'll call his doctor. Give us about an hour?"

Blond-crew-cut waved her over.

Lilah plastered a pleasant look on. Too bad Eden wasn't here. She'd eat this up. "What'll it be?" she breathed. "Sorry about all that, by the way."

"Eden?" The tall, blond man's forehead furrowed in obvious confusion.

"No." Fighting the eye roll, she found her smile. "Lilah. I'm her sister. She'll be in at ten."

He glared at his friend. "Told you."

"Twins?" The dark-haired, dark-eyed man set the menu back in its chrome holder.

"That's right." Lilah cleared her throat. "Special today's smoked salmon omelet, with string potatoes, home fries, or fresh fruit."

"There's your solution." His heavy brows lifted. "One for each of us."

"Excuse me?" Alarms jangling, her pencil scratch stopped. "You are talking about the special, right?"

"Both sound awful good." Dark-haired guy wore a shark's leer. "But I'll have steak and eggs. Easy."

"Sausage biscuit and gravy for me." The other

shrugged. "Uh, my platoon commander, Eli here, and I've got a mutual—um—interest in your sister."

"You. Both of you..." Lilah fought the sick laugh in her throat. "You're Eden's soldiers."

They nodded in unison.

"This ought to be interesting." She unfolded a fresh page. "I'll get your meals started and call her." Phone on her shoulder, Lilah cracked the sunny-side-up eggs, got the rib eye sizzling, and informed Eden of her problem.

Eden's shriek and refusal to come down ended with a phone slammed in her ear. *You reap what you sow, kid.*

The ambulance pulled into the front spot outside. Luke and his partner pushed the door open and sat at their regular table. "Morning, Lilah." Luke waved, a sheepish look on his face, eyes shadowed from lack of sleep, face sallow, as if he'd had a few too many the night before. "Eden coming in today?"

"Ten."

He sighed, ordered up his usual, as did his partner.

Lilah kept busy as the morning rush filtered in.

Eden had a whole crop full of trouble scarfing down breakfast at the diner.

# 23

The back door to the diner didn't budge. Biting her lip, Eden raised a fist and knocked. Once. Twice. Three times.

It creaked open. Eyes wild, obviously frazzled, Raymond scooped her into his arms. "Eden! I thought you'd never get here. It's like a dance off out there."

"Lilah can handle it." She grabbed an apron off the stack. "I'm not serving today. I'll stay in the back."

"You're gonna cook?" He snorted.

"I can cook."

"Yeah. And I can knit." Raymond snickered. "Just not well."

"Very funny." Eden breathed a sigh. "So, they're both here?"

"Luke, too."

"Oh, Lord, have mercy." She rolled her eyes, held her breath in silent prayer. "This must be that sense of humor thing they always talk about."

"Oh, it's anything but funny, I'm afraid." Raymond let her through. "Your grandmother's at the hair salon. Lilah just set after your papaw. Had a spell this morning."

"Fine. I'll do it." She ripped the pad out of his hand and charged off. She hesitated, catching sight of her reflection in the pie case Plexiglas. Of all the days not to touch-up her makeup or hair on the way out of the house!

The men sat still as two statues, staring at her. Across the room, Luke sipped coffee in front of a scraped-clean plate. She bustled over, took up the dishes, slanted a smile, and leaned forward, arm around his shoulder. "You get on to work now, y'hear?"

"I wanted to see you." He swallowed. His off-shade revealed a hangover and his breath reeked. "I need to apologize."

"I don't need apologies. We had a misunderstanding." She tried to keep it light, sensing whispering at her back. She did her best to maintain focus on Luke's plight while her world crumbled at her back. "We're still friends. Now go away."

"Eden. I meant what I said. I just didn't mean for..." Luke saw her glance over her shoulder. "Oh, heck. Is that what this is about? You rush your way through my apology to get to another crop of jarheads?"

"Now, why would you think that, Luke?" She inhaled, fixed her most serene expression.

Hazel swirls of hardened stone stared back at her. He wasn't buying it.

"Look—"

"We could have had something, Eden." He pushed back and dropped a few coins to the table. "My pa always said tip the pretty waitresses a little extra. That ought to cover it." A nod to his partner, he hightailed it out to the ambulance.

She scowled at the coins but left them and gathered a jangle of cups, plates, and crumpled napkins onto her bus tray.

"Eden?" the dark-haired soldier spoke. "Eden Dale?"

"Be with you in a second," she snipped, stormed to the back. "Can you believe him? He left me a fist full of nickels. Nickels! Like he doesn't think I'm pretty." For emphasis, she dumped the whole tray, napkins and all, into the sink with a clatter.

"I know it." Ray looked over her shoulder, then back to her.

"Thinks he's so all that, just because he drives an ambulance. Wanna-be doctor." She tossed the now-empty tray into the sink water. "You know, that boy's been sweet on me since the third grade."

"Preach it, Edie." Ray saluted with his spatula.

Eden jabbed a finger to his chest. "You got something to say to me, too?"

He shrugged, waved his spatula toward the dining area. "Just that your soldier boys are leaving."

"What?" Eden turned to see them one man in, one out of the door. "Wait!"

"Eden!" Raymond interrupted. "Your eyes. You forgot your mascara..." He was right.

"Oh, crumb." She looked around. "Where's my bag?" She remembered her purse on the peg by the front door. At home. "Of all the dumb luck..." She hurried to the desk, pulled out and slammed every drawer. Pens rolled. Paperclips slid. A pink tube, the bottom said Brown Black. When on earth had she bought such a thing? She swept the gluey stuff on anyway. Better some eyelashes than none at all. "I'll be back," she called to Raymond and pushed past customers entering.

A young, pert-looking redhead gave her the once over, striding ahead of a tall, suntanned gentleman with a shock of white hair. "Go on and have a seat anywhere. Be with you in a jiff."

Two men bookended a fancy red car across the street. The morning air warmed to a low simmer. She waited for a truck to pass before heading over.

"Hey." Chin high, she managed a smile. "Sorry about that in there. Did you ask if I was Eden?"

"I did, indeed." The dark-haired soldier looked amused, larger than life there on the patio. Arms crossed, biceps bulging, he leaned against the post. Confident. Like an action film star. Eli. Had to be…

Her heart bloomed a bit just for knowing he wasn't lying flat stomached on some rock in Afghanistan. "Your tour over?"

"Yeah." He turned to his friend. "Both of ours."

Eden's heart almost broke on the spot. She'd have known him anywhere. Tony twisted a ball cap. White-blonde hair, a soulful look in those pale blue eyes, a million questions behind his stare. He towered over Eli, standing six foot three. "Hello, Eden."

"Tony...hey." Steps away from the rail, she reached up. He didn't budge. Her outstretched hand hung midair a beat, and she drew it back. She squeezed fingers hard to keep from screaming.

The three stood a triangle—them on the porch, she just below on the sidewalk. They couldn't have been further apart if the two boys were still overseas.

"Darndest thing, really." Eli plopped himself in one of the chairs by the checkers table. "The mail drop came through, and somehow our letters got switched. He got mine, and I got his." Eli made a show of unfolding the creased letter from his back pocket and read aloud, mimicking her southern drawl. "Tony. How I long to grow old with you. To count the stars together every night. To greet them as they blink into the night sky, one by one…"

Beside him, Tony coughed. His eyes, downcast, refused to meet hers.

"That's a far cry from the letters you sent me." Eli shot a sly smile. "Why don't you read her a line from the one you got, buddy?"

"I'd rather not." Tony stood tall, head straight. A muscle jumped at his clenched jaw.

"Oh, Tony...I..." Foot to the stair tread, she caught his eye. Seeing the full force of his embarrassed fury, she was rooted to the spot. "I'm sorry."

"What are the odds, really?" Eli cracked open a can of soda to take a long pull, still smiling. "Of all the soldiers in Afghanistan, you write to two of us, and Tony transferred to my platoon?"

"Small world, I guess." Her voice shook. She clenched the railing. "I'm sorry if I hurt you. Either one of you."

"It was worth coming all the way out here just to see the look on your face!" Eli clapped his buddy on the shoulder.

"Yeah." Tony swallowed, though Eli's easy humor didn't show in his expression. "Just about."

"With the tour ending, we thought why not come and meet the girl who's kept us company the past six months." Eli smirked. "Both of us. Seemed like a good thing to do before re-up."

"Re-up? You're going back?" She gaped at Tony. "Both of you?"

"That's right." Tony swallowed. "Don't have much to stay home for."

"Oh, no." Eden shook her head so hard her brain rattled. "Don't you dare lay that one on me."

"Tony didn't actually realize your mistake until we went on leave to Diego Garcia." Eli swept her into his arms, unfazed as she pushed against his chest with both hands. No question of his intent as he held her, trapped against him. "White sandy beaches, beautiful island, just the sort of place you'd love. We both thought so." He nuzzled a moment into her neck, mouth exploring where it met her shoulder as she jerked away. "Ah, Eden. It was nice while it lasted."

"If you say so." Eden gave him the force of her elbow to his midsection. "How long did you know I was writing to Tony, too?"

The glint in Eli's stare indicated it was a bit longer than he'd let on.

"So that's why you kicked things up hotter, is that it?" Eden fumed, jabbed her index finger into his shoulder. "You got some nasty ideas about what love is, Eli Jones."

"We had some laughs." He shrugged. "Just something to pass the time, a million miles away."

"You knew Tony was falling for me, didn't you?"

"That's right. I saved him a heap of trouble, because girl, you're nothing but," Eli said as he stood. "Hey, Tony. I'm grabbing a case of beer from inside."

"Good luck, pal." Eden shot a nasty stare. "It's a dry county."

"Well, Missouri's not, and Branson, here we come." Eli pulled his keys out. With leering gaze, he reviewed her head to toe as he opened the driver's door, unabashed, unashamed. "Sure you won't come with us?"

"I wouldn't bet on it." Eden shot daggers, keeping him trained in her sights. Her mind drifted to the notes she'd sent him, the casual words of intimacy, so easy to write to a man she never thought she'd stare at face to face. Like right now.

"My invitation wasn't a lie." Eli's voice resonated on her eardrums, sent tiny shivers down her spine. A wayward plastic grocery bag cartwheeled down the street on a gust of breeze, as a fast-moving cloud blotted the sun.

"You honestly expect me to hop in your fancy car and head off for a weekend with you?" She seethed. "After what you did to Tony? To me?"

"Please." Eli opened the driver's door. Collapsed heavy behind the wheel. "If both of you could lighten up a bit and see this for what it really was. No one got hurt."

"I'd as soon we said goodbye here." Tony's voice cracked.

Eden's eyes welled as she sat in the bookended chair, the checkers table between, gave the red and black board a little push. "I guess this means we won't be growing old together."

"Nope." His lips hardened.

The weight in her chest shifted to something altogether different. Anger. "You listen here, Anthony Atkins. Don't you dare pin your chance at life on a girl you never even kissed. You think of your mama. Your sisters back in Kansas. They need you here, don't they?"

Tony swept his attention back to the vehicle where Eli waited, drumming the wheel with his thumbs. "Eden. You hurt me. You need to know that."

She crossed her arms in a huff. "Well, thanks for coming out here to tell me in person."

"You don't get it, do you? Your words, your promises." His stare froze her. He continued, ice-cold anger spearing each word. "You can't do that to people. This stop wasn't just to say you broke my heart. We were passing through, anyway. Eli thought you'd find it funny, maybe even come with us."

"Goes to show he never really knew me at all, doesn't it?" Eden sniffed, dared a pleading look, and died a little on the spot at his solemn expression. "You did, though. Didn't you?"

"I looked forward to your...to your letters." He squeezed her hand. "It meant something. And the guys out there, they need something—someone—to look forward to when they're out there in the field. You never know when you start patrol if this will be the day your truck gets blown to smithereens, like your buddy's did the day before."

"Oh, Tony—"

"Let me finish, Eden." He took her hand, kissed its palm, and released it, bittersweet and slow. "When you come home, it's not all wine and roses that you let me daydream about. Especially when the girl you thought you knew, well—when she turns out to be just some chick with a sick hobby of leading on soldiers. The dream crumbles, but the nightmare sticks. Think about that next time you lead a guy on, Eden Dale." He pressed a kiss, dry and cold, to her cheek, then left her on the pharmacy steps.

In the driver's seat, Eli gunned the engine, his radio station tuned to the weather channel.

"...Thunderstorms, and high winds expected. Tornado watch in effect for the greater Thayer area." Eli's sports car drove down Main Street under the bridge, and off toward the greener pastures of Thayer and beyond.

The ambulance buzzed past a moment later, Luke at the wheel. Their gazes met through the glare on the windshield, but he drove by without slowing.

A blast of wind tugged a strand of hair across her face, obscuring her vision; in her mind's eye, that fistful of nickels still lay scattered on the table. She trudged back to work, wondering if she'd ever be able to mend that fence with the best guy she knew.

Tony was right about one thing. After the mess she'd made, she no longer believed she had the right to try.

# 24

As the lunch crowd faded to early dinner diners, talk focused on the growing storm. Outside, gray-green clouds bunched, massed together over the slice of valley.

"Twister's comin." Quentin Marshall, the high school principal, stepped to the register to pick up his to-go order, tugging a wallet out.

"Our trough doesn't get hit. Don't you fret now." Papaw spoke with surety from the back counter, but Lilah no longer felt soothed by those words.

She traded Quentin's twenty and change for his regular: club sandwich on wheat, no pickle. Keeping voice low, she asked. "You really think so?"

They turned to the small television mounted by the bar, set to a storm watch. A weatherman gestured over a blotch of red, orange, and yellow storm path; it swirled right to the boot heel of Missouri. Mammoth lay smack in the zone under tornado watch, and a shudder raced her spine.

Marshall stepped to the door. "If not here, close by." A gust almost ripped the door handle from Quentin's grasp. Dust blew down the street in a small swirl. "We'll be setting up shelter at the high school, same as always." Raising his to-go bag, the principal set off toward the water tower at a walk-jog pace.

The glass door shuddered, rattling at the hinge.

She pulled it tight. Maybe she'd lived in California

a bit too long, but the news station with its swirling Doppler maps of storms moving in had Lilah scared witless.

"Don't listen to Quentin. He just wants to use our budget to go to that emergency management seminar in Little Rock every year," Nana scoffed, placing tender fingers to Lilah's elbow.

"Sure about that?"

They watched the bruising sky together, Papaw silent at her elbow as they went out to the sidewalk and looked south.

"Something about that shade of gray-green, gives me the willies." Lilah gestured to the mottled clouds as they hot-footed it over the trees.

The breeze whipped leaves from moaning, wavering branches. Leaves whooshed down the street in swirling dervishes. Farther down Main Street, a wind chime jangled a mad tune.

Nana frowned at the chip bag that attached itself to her shoe and pushed it into a concrete trash bin. "No weather here. Storm'll skip us by."

"That's what you always say." Lilah choked on the nervous laugh in her throat.

"All the same, why don't we close shop early?" The crags of Nana's face softened. "You'll be all right, honey. Want me to come back, walk you home after I get him settled with his crossword?"

"No. That's silly." Lilah inhaled. "Eden's here. We'll get it sorted out and come home. Does she have a storm cellar?"

"No. Papaw didn't think it was worth the extra money. No need here, remember?"

"So that's why you dive in the hall closet, then?" Lilah's pitch sounded off in her ears. "Cover yourself with pillows?"

"That was just the one time. Keep your ear to the radio," Nana said, though she seemed to wrestle with herself. She sighed. "If you're that worried, there's a storm cellar at the church across the street."

Lilah turned back into the diner.

Eden paid out their last customer, handing him his to-go boxes, hustling the contractor along.

"Should be quite a blow." Tom stood, tugged his belt loops. "Best be getting home before the Mrs. locks me out of our root cellar."

Lilah's tongue stuck to the roof of her mouth. "Think a tornado's really coming?"

"Never hurts to prepare. Plus, with the kids off at college, it's like date night come early."

The door banged shut as fat raindrops fell, splattering the windows and sidewalk.

"That's it, then." Eden tugged the door tight and wiggled the keys in the lock. "Stormin' already at Hardy. That gives us about ten minutes to get home and batten things down."

"But, Eden, there's no cellar there."

"We don't need one, sweetie." Eden cupped her sister's cheek, her tone a reassuring reminder. "Tornados don't come here."

Lilah forced an inhale, exhale. Already, her pulse pounded adrenaline.

The streets were empty. The daylight faded from bright blue to an off shade, as color drained from the world.

The two hoofed it uphill, trudging into the wind like they had as schoolgirls.

"Maybe we should've asked Tom for a ride." Lilah shot her sister a look over her shoulder.

"You could drive, you know." Eden smirked. "I guess you only ride around with your new boyfriend in that fancy car."

"He's not—" Wind whipped curls of blonde into Lilah's eyes, obscuring vision. "I don't know what he is." She pressed on, ignoring the barking laugh from her sister and the vicious wind, concentrating on each step. No time now for questions without answers.

The river flowed in a swift mass of white-watered, gusting waves.

They hustled past the houses on the lower hill. A father cracked windows open, while the mother dragged kids and toys inside. Everyone prepared for the worst.

"Ever think maybe Papaw's wrong to not believe in basements?" Lilah raised her voice over the wind as stinging rain drove cold spears into her skin.

"Ever think maybe you should have stayed in California?" Eden shook her head and wiped streaming rainwater from her eyes.

"Yeah. Give me an earthquake any day." Lilah scooped drenched hair back from her face. "A minute of terror, then done. None of this 'early warning' business."

Eden withered a stare before she spoke. "I took you in. I give you room and free board, and all you do is complain about it."

"I complain?" Lilah shrieked back.

Across the street, a tree branch wrenched from its trunk. Wood splintered to kindling as it crashed to the ground.

"It's a wonder what Pastor Jake sees in you. C'mon." Eden pressed on, homeward.

"What about you? What about those soldiers you

led on into showing up today?" Lilah's temper got the best of her. "At least Luke finally got wise."

Eden pushed ahead. "That's just plain mean."

Lilah stepped toward her sister, heart dropping. "Eden, I—"

*Crack!*

The sky electrified with bright blue lightning—a fearsome glittering hand skittered under the clouds, its target exploding with terrifying accuracy. The oak tree illuminated with the charge, glowed against the blackness, then shattered in a splintering blast.

Lilah fell back as the air charged with smoke and burning wood. The hundred-year-old oak crashed to earth in a ripping explosion of dirt, disintegrated timber, and flame. The once proud tree blocked the road between them. Orange flames engulfed the dry, brittle bark in the howling wind, but rain doused the fire, fast.

Lilah scrabbled around the tree, taking in the horror of a crushed roof, caved in, pink insulation exposed. "Edie!"

"I'm here..." Eden sat on her rump, hands cradling her left foot. "I think I twisted my ankle."

Lilah saw the blue-black bruise forming above her white sock. "Lean on me."

They stumbled a few steps before she hesitated, turned to Eden. "Should we have checked to see if anyone was home?"

"Foreclosure. That family left town months ago."

Another tree was down along the slope. Below, the river rushed in a torrent of mud and rising water. Rain hammered down.

Outside the chapel, Jake dragged a small dining table from the donation's lot inside the shed, leaving two lonely stuffed chairs and a dilapidated dresser. Of all the harebrained, lunatic—

"What the heck's he doing?" Eden angled to her driveway. "Crazy Californian! Doesn't know a guster's coming."

"I'll get you inside then scream some sense into him." Lilah pushed her sister towards the door and headed across the street.

Dark curtains of rain took over the tree line as the storm edged closer over the hill.

He tugged a large chair toward the shed, at her approach he shouted above the wind. "I've gotta get these donations out of the storm!"

Lilah strode over, stood nose to nose in the stinging rain, "You knucklehead! Don't you listen to the weather?"

"Why do you think I'm in a hurry?" He set down a lamp and jogged back to grab an overstuffed chair. "Was that a tree I heard falling?"

"Yeah." She shivered, picked up the front of the upholstered chair and helped him haul it into the storage shed.

They ran back out, gathered up another, and piled boxes on top.

"We've gotta get inside."

"This first." Jake's hair plastered to his face. He lifted an end table and trudged forward, water streaming down his arms.

Lilah grabbed two more chairs and followed him, cursing under her breath with each heavy step.

He eyed a large dresser, the last piece. "Get the drawers out. I think I can move it."

"Are you absolutely insane?" She cast a worried glance back to the east in the direction of the wind. The swirl of clouds rushed low, so low she was sure she could touch them if she stood tiptoe. "Leave it."

"But—"

Lilah's attention shot to the flicker of lit windows at Eden's and Nana and Papaw's. All winked out at once. "Power's out."

"The sky looks so weird..." He closed the heavy bolt, tugged for good measure. "Done."

Her heart jack-hammered as the rain blew sideways, streaked windows. "Not good."

They needed shelter. Fast. No time to get across the street to Eden's. No time to race uphill and see if Nana and Papaw were safe.

~*~

Jake stood back, his eyes wide. "I've never seen a sky like that. The color of a three-day-old bruise."

"That's tornado weather, genius. Now that we saved that third-hand furniture we should save ourselves." She grabbed him by the sleeve and tugged. "We've gotta get to your storm cellar. Now."

"Do I have one?" He blinked.

"Come on." She pulled him around the back of the chapel. To the right of the storage room, the ankle-high wood door, set in concrete, lay between the church and pastor's house. She tugged on a ring, rusted hinges screamed as it flew open, the wind threatening to whip it out of her grasp. "Down there."

Jake stepped onto moss-covered cement steps and hurried down.

At their backs, wind banshee-wailed, the rain ricocheted through the open door, but in the depths of the earth all was muffled and musty.

She tugged on a handle and rusted hinges screamed as the doors slammed shut. A yank to the slide lock, and it jammed, frozen. "It won't stay shut! Find something to wedge it with."

Along the far wall, dusty mason jars coursed the shelves underneath a course of cobwebs. The other wall was bare earth and support beams. There was a lamp on the scarred wooden table in the middle, a couple of chairs.

He'd heard of storm cellars as a kid, but this was his first time ever in one.

Grabbing a stack of contractor pencils she hustled up the slimy stairs, jamming a handful between the rings and lock. "That might hold it."

He shuddered. Pencils versus the wind?

She sloshed the kerosene lamp and turned to him. "Got any matches?"

Jake shook his head. Ten years since he'd had a cigarette. No call for matches since.

Rattling. Sounds of resistance at the top of the stairs. The cellar doors flew open with a bang as if invisible, furious hands slammed them back and forth.

She started forward.

He held her back. "Find a lighter or something. I'll get them." Jake sailed up the stairs as air rushed around his body like a vacuum. The hairs on his arms stood on end; adrenaline fueled his limbs to keep moving as he grabbed the rings of the first door, secured it. The wind screamed a wild thing that tore at everything in reach. Rain sheeted by in blasts, he could only make out ghostly shapes. Giant oaks bent, snapped, broke in protest as limbs tore away.

No way the Revival tents would survive this. What of the carnival? Surely they'd closed their doors, but did those people have anywhere to go? Where would carnival workers hide out in a storm? Dodge a tornado?

He squinted in the direction of the spring, the fairgrounds, but visibility was next to nothing. The heavens unleashed their next fury. Lilah shouted at his back, urging him to hurry as bullet-sized hail zinged rapid-fire.

With a prayer for protection of this small valley, Jake muscled the second door shut, then shoved the slide-lock into place, secure, as their world went dark.

~*~

She struck the match. White flame shot to an orange glow as she replaced the glass hurricane. Shadows pushed to the shelf-lined walls. Jars packed with floating peaches, plums, and jellies glittered behind dusty jackets. Baskets of potatoes rotted where they sat. Must have been a few pastors since anyone had tended this place.

Jake eyed the contents, took inventory of the stock, and scratched his stubble.

"What are you concocting there, genius?"

"Stop calling me that."

"Furniture?" She shook her head, dragged out a cane bottom chair that looked reasonably sturdy, and sat. "You wanted to move furniture in a tornado warning?"

"I was doing my job." He glared. "Someone dropped it off."

"Let's not fight, please."

"Do you see a radio anywhere?"

"There should be one."

Together, they scanned the eight-by-eight room. No sign of a radio amid the clutter. Bibles, texts, and hymnals moldered on the long shelves beneath coats of dust; untouched for an age.

"Everything but, apparently." He snorted a laugh and dragged a finger through the dust. "And they said I'd have nothing to do here in the middle of nowhere."

"Everyone always says that about this place." She observed his profile in the firelight. Something about him being here made her feel warm and safe—even though she knew more about tornados and Ozark storms than he ever would. The thought fluttered, whirled, that she should be the one setting him at ease instead of the other way around. She pulled out the other seat and pointed. "Sit."

He placed hands on his knees, wiping away nervous sweat from his palms. "Earthquakes, I'm ready for. I thought storms like this didn't come through until August."

"Nothing weather-wise is the same anymore, anywhere, right?" She jogged her shoulders up trying to keep things light. "Climate change?"

Jake blasted a laugh, obviously less nervous now. Then, his worried look returned. "Do you think the others are safe? Your sister? Your grandparents?"

Lilah looked in the direction as if she could see through the earth into the spaces she'd spent many storms hiding under Nana's quilt as a child. In bathtubs, closets, and once even in the windowless hallway. The only one who'd never bought into Papaw's faith about Mammoth's trough. But she'd never let Jake know that. "They'll be fine."

Jake seemed steadier. Still, the rain had tossed his reddish hair to a wild mane. Lamplight gleamed in his eyes while shadows deepened the crags of his face, the line of his jaw.

They were completely, utterly alone.

Outside the wind sang an ominous, howling tune. A hum and snap as something uprooted.

Storms would bring Papaw to panic mode. She prayed Nana was holding him together. Strong, supportive, brave, and made of sturdy stuff. Her little grandmother had the deepest roots of all. She wouldn't be toppled in the storm of Papaw's illness. She would bend just enough to keep from breaking, and no more.

"What now?" His hand outstretched, he waited for her to meet him halfway.

She took it, allowing him to stroke her skin with a calloused thumb. She sighed through the shiver that his touch sent. Thrills ringed her blood like pebbles in a stream. "Now, we wait."

"Pray with me?" So hopeful.

She leaned toward him in a rush of rightness. In the low gleam of lantern light, she bowed her head for the first time in many years and prayed with another.

# 25

Pain radiated through right leg from foot to knee. Stupid ankle! Eden's cheerleading injury reared its ugly head at the most inopportune times. Her brief moment of glory at the top of the pyramid, the crash to the bottom. Never the same again, and for what?

Lilah disappeared across the street.

Eden dragged her injured self into the house, flipped on the television, squinted at the fuzzy broadcast out of Springfield. The warnings for Fulton County scrolled across the bottom in red, ordering residents to seek shelter.

Rain streaked in fat drops across the windowpanes, fingers of water blowing sideways across the glass. Not good. Below the river, dark sheets of driving rain obscured the moaning oak tree limbs swaying in swirling, growing wind.

Through the fury of winds and rattling of windows, her cellphone chirped from her purse by the door. Her own personal life raft. She grabbed it and screamed hello.

"Eden?" Luke's voice was high. Healing water.

"Where are you?" She clung tight.

"Are you all right?"

"I'm home. Sprained my ankle good..."

"...tornado...accident on the route." His words garbled among the static. "...safe...still there?"

"Don't worry about me," she urged. "Just do your

job. I'll see you when it's over. Luke? You there?"

The line was dead.

She stared at the phone, the no-signal indicator flashed. Always taken for granted, never on the receiving end of her affections, and still he called to make sure she'd made it home safe.

*Lord, what've I been playing with?*

The storm raged. Wind howled. Window panes shook furiously in their frames. The living room lamps flickered, then winked out, the television silenced. No power.

Eden hobbled to her bed, grabbed fistfuls of pillows, and headed to the bathroom and climbed into the cast iron, claw foot tub. *Help me through this and I promise I'll tell him I'm sorry. I promise I'll come clean with him. I'll tell him everything.* She scrunched down as the demon raged at the door. She waited. Prayed. Luke's disappointed gaze that night at the carnival watermarked on every plea to God for her safety. And his.

~*~

Luke shoved the phone to his hip pocket. The blue and red lights of the ambulance swirled, reflecting in the blowing rain. His fireplug of a partner, Jeremy Anders, gripped the wheel, sure she'd made it home safe. They slow-drove down Main Street, peering through windows in search of folks to help. "Looks empty."

"Only a fool would be out in this weather," Jeremy agreed, hesitating at the intersection. "Or us."

"What about the carnival people?" Luke scowled through the weather. The fairgrounds was obscured from sight by the darkening storm. "Think they got somewhere safe to go?"

Jeremy turned left to go toward the school, right to head to the fairgrounds. "We've gotta go see. Get them to the school. There's time."

"Let's do it."

"Your girl OK?"

Luke scowled deeper, then sighed, took the CB from its holder. "She's not my girl."

"Yet."

Luke called in their location to base. Waiting for a response, he turned and answered his partner. "We're done. And, don't ask." Luke rattled off their location to the West Plains hospital dispatch, suggested they check at the fairgrounds.

"Good call, Nine." After a muffled exchange, dispatch agreed. "You gather who you can and take 'em to the high school. Be safe now, Luke, Jeremy. You hear?"

Situated in the trough, the high school offered a natural shelter from the storm. Most everyone in Mammoth without Earl Dale's convictions would head there; everyone but Eden and her hard-headed family. The ambulance shuddered in a hard blast of wind. He turned to his partner and grinned. "Let's go to work."

He aimed the Maglight, slick under his palms, as Jeremy angled through the lot, devoid of cars. Then, in the shadows of the headlights, the flashlight, a figure hunkered down battening down tent flaps.

"Over there!" Jeremy drove down the empty midway, between booths and the strong man pole that wavered against its restraints. Dipping clouds spoke 'funnel' before the Klaxon sounded, but not much.

"Sounds like War of the Worlds."

"Feels like it, too." Luke jumped out as the man finished one, started another. "You gotta get out of here."

"Nowhere to go, son." The man in the dark green jacket continued wrapped another cleat. "No way to get there, neither."

"We're taking people to the high school." Luke dragged at the man's sleeve, feeling his thin arm under the coat sleeve. "You'll be safe with us."

The man slanted his attention back toward the ambulance and finally found some modicum of self-preservation at the sight of a thickening downdraft. "I'll go, all the same."

Luke opened the back doors. "Anyone else here?"

The worker glanced to the trailers, his gaze hesitating at the largest one. "They'll all be in there. Randall's the owner. Tell 'em Guthrie said it was time to go."

Jeremy maneuvered the vehicle as tires spun, then found purchase on the mud. They didn't have much time left. The fairgrounds were already flooding from the pounding rain.

"My turn." Wipers swished a metronome beat as Jeremy took off running. Within seconds, he banged his fists against the Class A trailer.

Luke scooted into the driver's seat and turned up the heat until a warm blast of air poured from the vents. His clothes steaming, Luke's yellow slicker dripped and puddled by his boots.

Jeremy remained on the small step of the bus-style trailer, pounding on the door with his fist, looking small, defeated. No answer.

"They won't come with you, you know," Guthrie spoke, rubbing absently at his whiskered jaw. "Not many, anyway. Even with my say-so."

"It's our job to see folks to safety." Luke watched through the rain-spattered shield.

Jeremy pounded again and the door opened a couple inches.

"Thought that was the poh-lice's job, son."

Luke slid a glance to the rearview, noting his rumpled passenger eyeing the bottles of water and bags of granola bars. "Go on and take some. They're for upping folks' blood sugar. Looks like yours could use a boost."

The man crunched a bar in three bites, folded the wrapper with his long fingers. "Can't say I recall a tornado ever coming through this early."

Luke flashed the brights, just as the storm klaxon howled its three-minute warning. "Yeah? It's comin' anyway." Luke's thumbs drummed in time to the wipers.

Jeremy argued with someone through the narrow opening into the trailer. Turtled into his slicker, Jeremy returned, followed by a teenage girl, a white-haired, lanky man, and a trio of bedraggled women. Jeremy slammed the bay doors after they huddled inside. He climbed into the passenger seat and shoved back his hood. "Let's go!"

"That it?"

"All that'd come." Jeremy shivered as he warmed his hands, rainwater dripping from his nose. "Think these folks never watched the storm chaser channels."

"Or they want to be in one." Guthrie's cackle from the back seat raised the small hairs on Luke's neck.

The odd bunch sat in the back benches of the ambulance while wind howled.

He traversed down the access road through the

fairgrounds, to the safety of the Mammoth High School storm center.

# 26

Wind screamed at the walls as dirt and rocks pelted the windows. In her cast iron cradle, Eden cowered under pillows clutched over her head, heart slamming in her chest. *Jesus, Jesus, Jesus.* Over and again—her only prayer, His name.

At last, the shrieking wind ceased.

She shoved the pillows away, sat up, and strained her ears for sounds. The tiny window at the top of the bathroom wall leaked weak light into the room. A flick of the wall switch indicated the power was still off. She flipped it again. Nothing. Her reflection showed hair standing in a million directions, thanks to static from piles of pillows clutched over her head. She stepped into the other room, breathing with relief that all walls and the roof were still in place.

Late afternoon gray light poured through the curtained front windows. Outside, wind and rain blew about in fits and spurts. The bulk of the storm looked as if it missed their hill, even the trough of Mammoth. North, toward Thayer was blotted black by the clouds and storm.

Papaw had been right. Papaw. Nana.

She limped toward the big house, past trees scoured of their delicate spring leaves. Limbs torn down, broken stubs from the trunks looked fresh and torn and bled sap. The river cleared of its mud from the rain, continued to flow by in silent witness of the event. Her grandparents' iron lawn furniture lay jumbled in a heap along the waterline. Not a single house seemed affected on Riverview Drive. Mammoth had once again dodged a bullet.

"Nana?" Eden called. She stepped through the door a little thinned of paint but no worse for wear.

Muffled voices came from within.

She glanced down the stairs to the extra room. Nothing. Down the hall, no sign. "Papaw?"

"We're in here!" Nana's frail voice called.

Eden followed the sound to the large hall closet, opened it to find Nana and Papaw much as she had been, surrounded by a nest of pillows, wrapped up in Nana's quilt.

"It's over." Eden breathed. "You can come out now."

"Did it hit?" Papaw's clear eyes were wide, worried.

"No. Not in Mammoth." Not on Riverview, anyway, but she didn't need to share her worries with them at present. "We're OK."

Nana nodded, dragged herself out of the windowless room, and then stood to fold her quilt with shaking hands.

Eden grabbed a corner, folding the queen-sized friendship quilt into a tiny square. "Thank you, Eden. You're a good girl."

"I'm gonna head to the diner to check things out down there." Eden inhaled long, exhaled deeper. "You OK?"

"Go on." Nana helped Papaw to his chair. "We'll be fine."

"Get the phone, Naomi." Papaw squeezed her hand, eyes going distant. "I'm in the middle of the crossword."

"He was with me during the storm a bit." Her grandmother's gaze drooped with exhaustion. Or grief. "We even talked."

Eden swept her up in a hug, tighter than Nana usually allowed.

"Don't worry about me, child." Bird light, Nana wrapped arms around, and held on. "I'm all right."

*Like hugging a ghost.* Eden forced her mind away from that horrible notion and released her. "You always are."

# 27

Jake sat on the quilt-covered earthen floor, Lilah's head on his shoulder, and stared at the crack in the overhead doors. Waning strands of daylight touched them through hairline cracks from up above. No sign of wind, the rain a subtle patter on the wood, he strained to hear other sounds of life.

Lilah dozed off. The soft, lovely bow of her lips curved up at the corners.

He wondered what she dreamed about. He wondered if he could ever make her smile that way. Or if, by some chance, his dream self was the reason.

A girl like Lilah was worth waiting for. His mind raced to Margaret and how opposite his former wife was when compared to Lilah's subtle beauty. Margaret, with her pulled together confidence. Even when caught cheating, Margaret had maintained the upper hand. Her voice rang in his head, *"You live too much in your emotions, Jacob; ever the optimist, only seeing what you want to see."*

Maybe that was true. Perhaps the storm was God's way of showing him he'd planned too much for this little community. But it wasn't as if he were bringing snakes to kiss, or planning a massive healing event. He simply wanted room for all. To allow the casual wanderer to drift in, see what all that music was about, and find Jesus waiting in the tents. Softening hearts of the faithful, opening the locked places of those who'd never witnessed such a gathering. And really, wasn't that what he wanted? God to manifest Himself in some miraculous, physical way? He'd heard about such things before—lay pastors at his home church often spoke of it. Pastor Pingry went on at length about seeing the Holy Spirit wash over his group of pastors in a wave of light.

Jake's heart surged. What pastor wouldn't want to see such a thing? To know, beyond measure, that the Lord was with them? Really with them. Beyond a subtle feeling, or a stirring in his gut. And wasn't that vanity in its purest form, trying to force such a thing into happening?

A cloud-strained sunbeam crossed Lilah's cheek. Cool, gray light stroked her gentle features. She sighed. One arm flopped over his lap, and her fingertip wove its way through his belt loop. Tugged tight. Her body, warm against his side, her head on his shoulder, curling hair tangled in his two-day growth of beard.

What had this poor girl gone through since she'd returned home? Persecuted for wandering and her failed marriage, yet saying nothing. She faced the masses on a daily basis with subtle strength and kindness. Sometimes sad, sometimes angry, but she always showed up, making her daily specials to please herself, if no one else cared to order them. Did she realize she glorified God just by her own personal act of creation, with the faith that perhaps one day someone might order what she'd made? Isn't that what had drawn them together in the first place?

Her eyes blinked open. Found him staring down.

"Whoops." She yawned, covered her mouth with the back of her hand. "Sorry."

"It's OK." He kissed the top of her head, gave her

a long squeeze, and then got up to stand at the bottom of the stairs. "I think the worst is over."

Behind the peace of the subterranean doors, her shoulders quivered in a shiver-shake. There was so much he still didn't know about her. About the town.

And now, they'd spent the whole storm together underground?

As if she read his thoughts, she shook her head and yawned. "Nu-uh, Pastor. The worst's just starting."

~*~

The power remained out, Nana's great room lit only by the fading light seeping through the paned windows, their million-dollar view leveled to downed trees, toppled patio furniture strewn across the lawn, and blown corrugated metal wedged into crevasses and rocky crags down the slope.

"Lilah?" Nana appeared around the corner, little brown glass in hand, ice clinking as she walked. Her hair was mussed, the only sign of anything wrong.

"Are you guys OK?" She swept her grandmother up in a hug.

"Fine." Nana pushed free from her granddaughter's grasp. "Papaw's resting. Just gave him his pill."

"Naomi!" he called from the bedroom. "Rebecca's not in her room..." His voice trailed off.

Nana met Lilah's questioning gaze, shook her head, and took a sip from the glass. "It's the storm. The weather. He's already having a time enough, and this—well. It makes things worse."

"Can I do anything for you?" She outstretched a

hand.

"He just needs rest." Nana's fingers clutched her glass. "He has an appointment in West Plains tomorrow. Maybe you can go with us."

"I'd like that." Lilah stiffened, lip quivering. She caught and captured Nana's faltering gaze. "I want to be here for you. It's why I'm back."

"Is it?" Nana challenged, voice shaking. "Where were you during the storm? Eden came to check on us first, and then she set off to see if she could help in town. Eden's never needed anything but her family."

So many comments flew to her lips, impossible to choose just the right barb to sling back. Fighting with her grandmother was as easy as breathing. Still, this wasn't the time or place. "I'll check on you later."

Turning on her heel, Lilah raced out of the house, over to Eden's, and found it empty. A bathtub full of pillows showed where she'd weathered the brunt of the storm.

Across the street, Jake yanked at a tree limb. It budged, but only slightly.

"Let me help."

"Thanks."

Together, they tugged, moved the branch, and freed up the parking shed. He hauled open the doors where his yellow, dusty truck sat, covered in a layer of globs of leaves and wet dirt dislodged in the wind and leaky roof. Mud streaked, but drivable.

"Cell towers are out, too." Jake frowned as he checked his phone. "Anyone across the street?"

"Eden's on her way into town." She frowned at Jake's dented, rusty vehicle. "Might be better to just walk down, see how everyone fared."

"Truck's got a winch." He dragged out a thinly

populated key chain. "Extra gas, water, supplies. Former Boy Scout." Jake three-fingered a salute to prove it.

"Always prepared?"

"Never hurts."

"They'll have gathered at the high school," Lilah guessed, joining him in the truck cab. "Anyone without somewhere to go heads there in time of trouble."

Jake stared at the ominous sky, a worried crease in his brow.

"Don't worry." She squeezed his hand. "The storm's not coming back."

"I'm not worried about that. But look where it's been." Across the river, she saw the source of his obvious agony. The carnival. The Ferris wheel remained straight and tall, as did the tents and midway structures. Up on the hilltop, however, was another story. The Revival tents were ripped to shreds. White canvas flicked, flags of surrender in a wicked wind.

"Jake..." Her heart sank.

All of their work, all of their plans now blown to ruin.

He nodded, swallowed, and turned the truck key. "It's just a tent."

"But your Revival..."

"My Revival?" He cocked his head, stared at her with hazel eyes gone stormy. "It's not my Revival. It's for Him. From all of us. Doesn't anyone in this crazy town understand that?" The engine revved and he backed out a bit too fast for comfort.

He leaned closer to see as the wiper blades smeared brown sludge back and forth.

She said nothing—merely hung on to the loose

armrest.

~*~

Luke blinked at the generator-run lights, their rattling muffled from inside the gymnasium walls. A crowd of about fifty people huddled on the bleachers and sipped water from paper cups filled from the orange power drink containers usually reserved for the basketball team. A group of Mammoth's seniors shot hoops.

The computer lab teacher, Mr. McPhearson, looked up from his laptop with a frown. "No internet. No cellphones, either."

Principal Quentin Marshall spun the handle on an emergency radio, twisted the dial until an AM newscast crackled out of the small speaker.

A trio of adults hunkered close to listen, and Luke joined them.

"What a difference ten years makes, huh, Luke?" Mr. Marshall clapped him on the shoulder. "Luke here was the basketball star, class of two-thousand-ancient-history. There was a time you'd be steering that game of 'horse' over there in your favor."

Luke ducked his head at the attention. "Time was."

The others jabbed about the lost state championship game—the one that got away.

Luke's thoughts drifted. Part of him still regretted the decisions made by a boy in love, the stupidity of youth, and all the dubious consequences that came along with one fateful choice.

He watched four high school kids jab and jeer at each other, wistful at how blissfully oblivious of the storm they were, ignorant at how quickly their confident little universe could end.

The radio found purchase, spat out a weather report through whining static. "...missed northern Fulton county...Thayer was hit hard by what area experts are claiming was a class four tornado. Damage is still being assessed..."

"Class four?" Quentin straightened and hitched his belt loops up.

"Yeah," agreed Scott, who matched Luke in size, but outweighed him. "Day I asked Emma to marry me? That class five came through. Took out farms and houses, tore through the Hardy theater."

"Probably God telling the angels to cover their eyes," Quentin ribbed. "As you two were off to overpopulate the planet."

Luke caught Scott's warning glare that no one else noticed.

"Thayer's built of strong stuff," Scott continued in even tones.

"Tell that to the folks who got hit." Luke headed over to the doors. "I'm trying dispatch again."

Outside the gym, howling wind still raged. He eyed the parking lot up the slight rise of hill, surveying trees knocked down. Cars parked every which way— the ambulance boxed in by folks in a panic to find shelter. Squinting into the wind, he pressed the button on the radio at his shoulder. "Jenny, this is Luke. Come back?"

Static.

"Anything?" Jeremy stuck his head out.

Luke shook his head.

"We may as well stay here, man." Jeremy scanned the massing crowd with bulldog intensity.

Luke nodded. "Let's see if any of the landlines have service."

"I'll go." Jeremy disappeared inside and Luke followed. Jeremy, in the graduating class behind him, knew as well as he did where the phone bank was located.

Inside, the gym resonated with innocent laughter echoing from the kids playing basketball. Their naiveté bounced from the rafters around the room. No worries past Friday's game.

He unclipped his walkie, laid it on a bench, sauntered over to them, and held a palm out for the ball.

"Give it to him, see what he's got." A kid in gym shorts seemed the alpha player. With shrugs and some "old man" comments, the lanky kid in possession bounce-passed it to him and leaned over, gripping an imaginary walker.

The leather filled Luke's hand, its rugged surface a familiar fit. He dribbled once, twice, three times, passing one hand to the other. He eyed the square above the basket, then one-move swished the ball through. "That's *H*."

He caught the ball on the rebound and winked at the kid who'd been walker-mocking. "I'll just be a sec."

He made it to "*S*" without missing a beat. Or breaking a sweat.

The boys exchanged surprised glances as he swished "*E*."

Luke dribbled out of the paint and back, and when he faced the bucket, the teenagers had shut their mouths and now gathered in a half-circle, cheering and waving their arms to distract. Luke held the ball aloft, eyeing the angle, when he heard a thud and shriek. He hesitated, ball still eye level.

"Come on, man," the short, heavyset kid called. "Shoot!"

"Just a sec."

Luke rolled the ball on his palms, spun around and surveyed the crowd, ears tuned for signs of distress.

"He just knows he's gonna miss," Alpha jabbed. "I'll give you five bucks if you make that shot."

Luke's chest brewed with the challenge, but his ears perked. Someone was crying. He scanned the room and caught sight of a small girl in the back of the room. Two adults—her parents, most likely—hunched over her. The mother looked worried, bordering on frantic.

"Be right back." Luke bounced the ball to the short kid and trotted toward the family.

"If you quit, you lose, man!" Short kid wedged the ball under his arm.

"Yeah," the other ones agreed, but their jibes died as they watched him hurry off.

Luke made it to the couple in quick strides. "Now what happened here?"

"Our Bethie slipped. Cut her head." The mother pressed a napkin to the wound already seeping with her daughter's bright red blood.

The girl sobbed hysterical gasps.

"Hey, kiddo." Luke knelt in front of the child. He turned to her worried mother with a nod. "I've got a first aid badge with your name on it, if you let me guess your name."

"You know my name?" The brown-haired girl hiccupped.

He dragged his bag over, assessed the injury, and

darted a glance at her mother, who mouthed at him. "Sure. It's—Mildred, right?"

"No." She frowned at him and hissed as he dabbed ointment.

"Gertrude?"

That brought a giggle. "Guess again."

He kept her distracted while he cleaned and dressed her sliced forehead, and then proceeded to wrap a sling around her arm.

"My arm's not hurt." She laughed, proving it with an elbow flex.

"Oh, then maybe it was your big toe." He reached a hand out to her foot, and her giggles doubled. A few minutes later, he wrote Bethie on a sticker and pasted it to her shirt. He pointed at his nameplate over his pocket. "Just like a real paramedic."

The girl threw her arms around his neck and squeezed, as did her mother.

Across the gym, the boys finished the game. Shorty won. Alpha spun the ball on his finger, shot, and missed another basket. A series of ribs and jabs met the air ball.

This was why he quit.

After that fateful night, witnessing three totaled cars at the bottom of Deadman's Curve, helping the medics on scene, how could he do anything else? No double-double could ever match the feeling of helping someone in need. He might not wear an army uniform, like the guys she favored, but he did his share of good in this world.

The gym doors opened and Eden appeared in a slice of daylight, dressed in pink shorts and a white work blouse, eyes wide, searching. She needed something. He steeled himself for the force of her, watched her scan the room, seeking familiar faces out and giving them a squeeze, celebrating together that the worst of the storm had passed.

She was a whirlwind of hugs and well wishes. The doors opened behind her, folks milled about, gathered their belongings and headed home.

The five carnies milled together. One poured a little something extra into her Gatorade cup.

Luke stepped to them. "Storm's over."

"Just like that." The older man raised an eyebrow. "We could have ridden that out in our camp, Maya."

"Better safe than sorry, Dad." The girl—sixteen if she was a day, with curves of a twenty-year-old and makeup to match—turned back to him. "Thanks for bringing us here."

"You never know with these storms."

"Still, I know how the townies feel about us." Maya dipped her gaze and then stared up through long lashes. "You're a good man, Luke."

"Thanks."

"What's all this about?" Eden marched up, hands on her hips. A little limp in her progress; he spied her wrapped ankle.

"I was just thanking one of Mammoth's finest." Maya stood tiptoe and kissed him full on the mouth.

Luke pushed the girl back, startled, and blotted his lips as if it would wipe away Eden's obvious disapproval. "I'm not a cop."

"Who said you were?" Maya swished her way back to her father and the rest.

His gaze remained glued to her backside, though it was the last place in the world he intended on staring. He hazarded a glance and met Eden's withering gaze.

"I'd ask who the blazes that was, but she's just a child, so it shouldn't bother me none."

"Shouldn't bother you none, anyway." Luke rubbed his jaw. Inside, his heart skipped just knowing Eden was safe. Outside, he fought to maintain an even keel to his expression. "You OK?"

She held out her foot, gave it a flex. "Just an old war wound." She blew at her bangs. A smirk tugged at the corner of her mouth, she reached and squeezed his hand. "We're still friends, right?"

"No reason not to be."

"Fine..." She inhaled a tirade, exhaled through it. "Sounds like Thayer got hit hard."

Luke scowled through the worry, scanned the crowd for Jeremy, and spotted his driver at an impromptu table covered with cookies and scattered paper napkins. "We'd better go out there, see what we can do to help." Luke scooped up his walkie and reattached it. Tested the squelch.

"Can I ride along?" Eden looked so hopeful. "I still have my first aid badge from your class."

"I'm sure I could use you." He took in the loop of worry at her forehead. The regal slope of her nose, the subtle pout of full lips, and drank in the long, cool sight of the girl of his dreams. Mammoth's should-have-been homecoming queen. The one he'd let slip away an age ago, the night she met her first soldier. The one who'd never let him forget what he'd lost.

Jeremy appeared at his side, cookie crumbs on his lip. "You ready?"

"Let's go." Luke held a hand out to Eden. "All of us."

~*~

"How much longer?" Jake asked as they bumped around another tree fallen across the road. Downed power lines lightninged across their path. He drove onto the shoulder to avoid the sparking wires and splintered wood.

"High school's down the hill, across that little bridge, next to the water tower." Lilah pointed the way.

Jake followed her finger down Riverview, across Main, on the other side. He scanned the oak-covered hill and the nest of neighborhoods he'd yet to visit. He bumped his truck back onto the rutted drive and along the direction that Lilah pointed.

From behind mottled clouds, fingers of sunlight angled down from heaven. The sphere of the water tower shadowed toward the high school.

"There it is." Lilah breathed, her relief evident by the curve of her shoulders.

Folks filtered out of the open doors, including Eden, Luke, and his partner. In the glutted parking area, the ambulance sat, boxed in by cars, a bus, and a crisscross of downed trees. Luke scowled over the puzzle of vehicles, as Jeremy wrote down license plate numbers.

"No way they'll get that mess sorted out any time soon." Jake wrapped his hands tighter around the wheel. "We've gotta get help."

"Eden!" Lilah called out the window, waving.

Her sister glanced up, then tugged Luke's arm.

"Anything we can do?" Pulling over, Jake stepped out just beyond the mess of hastily parked vehicles. "I've got a winch."

All of them stared at the ambulance, obviously

thinking on ways to extricate it from the crowd of cars.

The radio on Luke's belt squawked, startling them all.

"Base to Nine. Come back, Nine. Luke? Can you hear me?"

"Nine, here. I copy, Jenny." He spoke into his shoulder mike, staring at Jake, then back at the ambulance unit buried behind cars and debris that could take hours to clear. "Can we take your truck? Thayer's slammed."

Jake nodded and Jeremy jumped into the unit and began dragging out supplies as Luke listed what they'd need. "Neck braces. Spinal boards."

Luke shoved a large yellow container lettered across the top "AED," at Eden. "Remember how to use this?"

She nodded, eyes wide with worry, but she took the handles, obviously set with resolve.

Others came over, and they formed a human chain and ferried the equipment down the sidewalk from the blocked ER unit to Luke's truck parked on the road.

"We'll go with you." Luke straddled the gate, one foot in the liner, the other on the bumper, and rattled several cases onto the truck bed. Loaded up, Luke opened the king cab door and scooted inside, followed by Jeremy and Eden.

Jake matched Lilah's attention with his own determined look. "I'll drive, you navigate." With a twist of the key, the reliable truck chugged back to life. He followed her directions back to the road, to the rural route, as the voice on the radio told of the mess that was Thayer, Missouri.

# 28

Jake navigated the twist of the four-lane rural highway around downed trees. On either side, power lines drooped, sagged.

The white electric company rig cruised along the frontage road with the cherry picker doglegged up. Orange-vested workers stepped out into the misting rain.

He slowed the truck and rolled down his window. "How long 'til power's back up?"

"In Mammoth? Probably tonight." The barrel-shaped man apparently in charge tromped over wet grass in his rain boots and slid his hat back on his head. "Thayer'll be up in a day or two. Hey, Luke. Where's your ride?"

"Blocked in at the high school." Luke gave Jake's shoulder a solid pat. "Reggie Willis, meet Pastor Gibb. His ole truck can get through most anything. He's my chauffeur today."

"Head out to Steadman's farm first." He pointed over the rain-soaked hill. "Got hit pretty hard."

"We'll go straight there." Luke waved as the truck rumbled over the carved road, through the hills, past the scar of rusty Ozark boulders, stripped of their leafy-green kudzu by the wind and rain. Fences had toppled along the rural road. Long grass bent, sodden with water and blown leaves, even now fighting to right itself in the growing sunlight.

"There's a turnout ahead, to the right." Lilah pointed. "Across from the motel."

On the left side of the rural route, Jake saw the rectangle of the Star Traveler Inn. A broad section of the second floor rooftop gaped like an open maw, the main box of the hotel stripped into a cross-section, but the star-shaped neon sign remained untouched. Red shingles floated atop the muck and leaf-strewn swimming pool, along with half of a downed tree.

"Mercy..." Lilah closed her eyes and then forced them back open.

"Steadman's ranch is over across on the other side." Eden leaned across her seat. "Still no cellphone reception out here."

"CB works. They'll call when the ambulance gets towed out." Luke placed an elbow over Lilah's chair back.

Jake bumped the truck around downed trees and back onto the blacktop.

Luke continued, "Remember our senior year?"

A laugh, and then worry dusted Lilah's gaze.

"What?" Jake ran into a blocked path, backed his truck around, eyeing some downed power poles with concern. "What happened senior year? I'm a foreigner, remember?"

Through the mirror, Jake saw the seriousness behind Luke's gaze even as he maintained easy conversation. "Jeremy, you want to tell him about prom night or should I?"

"Stupid story, anyhow." Jeremy sniffed and turned to look out the window.

Luke laughed. "Jeremy here wanted to ask Rhonda Steadman to the prom—he and I played basketball—were pretty good at it, too. So, he decided to talk to her right after the big rivalry game with the Thayer Broncos and he'd shot the winning basket. Feeling pretty reckless that day, weren't you?" He elbowed Jeremy, then turned back to the others. "Anyway, so my boy here calls Rhonda up—"

"I was working the diner back then." Jeremy stood on one side of Eden, with cheeks brightened beet red. "It was noisy."

"Oh, sure. That's why." Eden snuffled a laugh into Luke's shoulder.

"Why what?" Jake steered along the dirt access road and looked both ways across the rural highway. No sign of cars or traffic, so he gunned it across the road. "Tell me more."

"So, when Mrs. Steadman answers, he asks for Ronnie—" Eden offered with a snicker, reliving the moment right alongside Luke with obvious enjoyment.

"Then he doesn't wait for her to say much and goes ahead and asks her to prom—" Luke continued.

"And never realized he was asking her kid brother, Ronald!" Eden finished the punch line with a hoot of laughter. She and Luke doubled over, enjoying the tale far more than Jeremy, who shifted uncomfortably in his seat.

"It was noisy at the diner." Jeremy jutted his chin and looked out the window. "Like I said."

"That wasn't even the best part." Luke reached an arm across Eden's shoulders. Luke's hand squeezed, then shot back, as if burned.

"Uh, the best part was the joke Ronnie and Rhonda played on our Jeremy on prom night." Eden cleared her throat. "You finish it, Jeremy. Luke and I were already in the limo."

"When I answered the door, they had little Ronnie

all dolled up in a dress and makeup, waiting for me. Everyone had a big laugh. Most of all, Mr. Steadman, who also put the fear of—oh, my Lord."

"He didn't look that bad." Eden frowned. "Ronnie's picture even made it in the yearbook."

"No, not that." Jeremy blinked, pointing. "Look."

The sign for the Steadman ranch, Barn Hollow, hung cockeyed, swaying in the wind. The sprawling, groomed lawn sliced with a wide dirt scar that led to a concrete slab; the tornado's path blazed as if it'd been on a mission. The house was leveled to the foundation. Cement, sticks of timbers, one brick and mortar wall with the chimney were still standing, the other three were just gone. Beyond, an enormous, shattered red barn, presumably the one mentioned on the sign, sagged in what used to be the backyard, next to the twisting splinters of an old oak tree.

*Lord, help us find these folks safe from harm.*

"Mr. Steadman!" Luke was out of the car and shouting as he scrambled up and over what used to be a wall. "Tom!"

"Careful!" Jake called as he eyed the teetering mass of lumber and crumbled drywall. "That doesn't look stable."

"Hey, Jeremy. You dated Ronnie awhile." Lilah turned a full circle, taking in the destruction. "Tell me they had a basement? Something?"

"Something." He turned to the road, then back to the main house as if trying to get his bearings. "By the little red tack barn. To the left of the peach tree."

Jake looked for the landmarks and failed. Shattered beams, tin roof tiles, splintered trees, a downed laundry line with a shirt still clipped to the cords. Then, he noticed the long, redwood line of fence far off on either side. He traced a line to something that could have once been a peach tree, roots exposed leaving a deep hole in the ground.

"Wind uprooted it." Luke stepped up. "There's the door. It's wedged shut by that beam."

The three men stepped up and gave a solid heave to the wood beam that once might have been the ceiling support for a tack shed. It shifted, but wouldn't budge.

The girls dropped the bags they carried and joined. All gave a solid push.

Finally, the beam groaned and gave way, revealing the hard metal vault door set into a concrete bunker, a sign with a trio of black triangles against a yellow square: The Steadman family's nuclear fallout shelter.

Luke knocked, sounding a gong. He knocked again, listening.

Thin sounds came from underneath.

Life.

Luke and Jeremy each hauled open a side of the door, revealing inner steel-lined doors underneath. The Steadman's storm cellar wasn't just dug out from the earth like the one at the chapel; it was set in solid concrete. Luke shook the handles. Nothing.

"They must have it latched from the inside." He gave it another shake, rapped on it with his flashlight butt.

Then, something clicked. The door whooshed as seals opened, and then pushed up.

Jeremy and Luke hauled back as the shaking body of Mrs. Steadman emerged like Lazarus from the grave. Concrete dust whitened her shocked face, raccoon-eyed from tear-drenched mascara. "Oh, thank you, Lord!" She called up a prayer, clasped her hands, and hugged each one of them in turn. "It's Tom. He's down below, but he's hurt."

"I'm fine, Earnestine." A voice sounded from below, still larger than life.

"You're not fine. You're bleeding," she bit back at him, turned an apologetic grin. "He's well enough to want to argue with me."

Luke and Jeremy trotted down the concrete stairs to do their work.

A generator hummed, light pushed up from below.

A moment later, the voices went professional, and then the tone shifted. Footsteps trotted up. "Aw, Mrs. S. That's just a scratch." Luke poked his head up like a squirrel.

"Told you, you old worry-wart!" Tom called up. "Let me go, boy."

Luke gave an arm to help his patient up to ground level. "You'll be fine. Let's butterfly close that gash, then we'll help you up."

"My...my..." Earnestine Steadman turned around. She surveyed the wreckage that she'd once called home. "I told him it was heading straight for us! He wanted to hide out in the closet and I said no way. Not this one. Tom couldn't find the cellar keys. We almost didn't get the doors..." Her voice trailed off as she sank to her knees amid the rubble of her former home. Tears came in a tidal wave; sobs wrenched her shoulders. "How could this happen?"

Jake viewed the wreckage, surveying the total loss of their home and property. His mind swept every available verse and scripture, but came up dry. Like the tissue from his pocket, clean, and folded. He unpocketed it, pressed it to her palms. "Here, ma'am." *What do I say to a woman who just lost a lifetime of earthly memories? What comfort can I give? I don't even know these people.*

Earnestine Steadman blotted her eyes, face, sighed at the black and grime she'd wiped away. "I must be a mess." A burble of almost laughter came from her throat. "Me and my house."

"I'm so sorry for your loss." Jake squeezed her hand, finding the cold clamminess of shock. He folded her slight frame in an embrace. "There are no words that can mend this damage. No scripture that can replace what was lost. But you still have each other. That's what matters most."

"God sent you here to help us." Earnestine blinked at him, her face, now clean from the chaos of her grief, shone in the subtle reflection of her faith. "We were trapped, and you came. You found us, and I don't even know how, seeing how we were in the fallout shelter. No one knows about that."

Jeremy paused in leading Tom up the stairs, coughed into his hand, shrugged sheepish, silently imploring Jake not to say anything.

Jake's gaze anchored on Lilah, gently freeing a flag from the rubble. Her face was dusty, determined, and absolutely beautiful. "God works in mysterious ways,"

"He does." Fresh tears spilled from Earnestine's sky-blue eyes. Her hands clasped Jake's, tighter with each word. "Oh, He does indeed." She turned to the group and stammered through her gratitude. "I was so scared, and Tom, well, he was just like an injured bear. Not even letting me come near him with the first aid."

"I did no such thing, Earnestine," Tom grumbled, rubbing his forearm, the sleeve of his shirt torn, dried with brown blood, a fresh bandage peeked out underneath.

"Hmph." She stepped to his side, wrapped him in her thin arms. "Couldn't even touch him to put on a bandage."

"Well. You found us," Tom growled toward Jeremy. "I can only guess how."

"A miracle!" Earnestine waved her arms at the heavens. "Thank you, Lord!"

Fear flash over Jeremy's face, there was anger in Tom's, and wonder in Earnestine's gaze.

"You know how we found you, don't you?" Jeremy dipped his toe in the situation.

"Of course." She cocked her head at her daughter's high school crush and then blinked back to her new pastor, her faith in their discovery unshaken. "It's a miracle."

"God had nothing to do with it..." Tom's face reddened again with anger as he turned his wrath on the paramedic who'd once dated his daughter. "You knew about this place?"

"Yes, but...I didn't—we didn't—"

"Oh, you go on and stop it, Jeremy. He's not gonna hurt you." Earnestine stepped in between her husband and the paramedic. "Her daddy might rail into Ronnie some, but you're all grown now. A few stolen kisses and whatever, that's water under a very old bridge." She set her hands on her hips, having a good laugh. "Rhonda's got three kids, living in St. Louis. You think I don't know she showed you our fallout shelter?" She turned to Eden and Lilah. "I made sure I knew what my teenage daughter was doing most of the time. And that's why I also sent her to college in the city. She needed to broaden her horizons a bit." She turned a sweet smile and patted the boy's cheek. "And so did you, Jeremy."

"Indeed." Jake couldn't help the laugh that bubbled out of his soul. "Miracles come in all shapes and sizes, don't they, Mrs. S.?"

"Why else would God have sent you all out here together?" She hooked arms with her husband.

Tom nodded in agreement, though his glum look indicated he thought otherwise.

Together, they walked through the wreckage of the former barn, the bulk of it now scattered across the back field, though half of the structure—one wall, the hay loft, the barn door still braced shut, and part of the roof—soared into empty space.

"That used to be the back door," Tom said.

"We'll have to change the name of the ranch, Tom." Mrs. Steadman shook her head, leaned her forehead to his shoulder. "Can't call it Barn Hollow when there's none there no more."

"Maybe we should call it Barn-A-Field." He swept her up in a bear hug with his good arm. "Or, maybe we should just chuck it all and retire to St. Louis, like you've been begging me since the grandkids were born."

She sagged against him, and they laughed like two people who hadn't just lost everything in the world.

# 29

Jake headed the truck back toward Mammoth at the end of the longest day he could remember.

Sunset painted the broken storm clouds shades of fuchsia, burnt umber, and amethyst as they turned on Main Street.

"Who's hungry?" Lilah asked, pointing to an empty space in front of Earl's Kitchen. The orange neon sign winked "Open," beckoning them inside for a dish of comfort and a cup of reassurance after their long day.

Jake parked and shut off the engine.

Jeremy, Luke, and Eden jumped out the back of the king cab.

Jake hesitated, hands still gripping the curve of the smooth steering wheel.

Lilah unlatched her seatbelt, but made no other move to leave the cab.

"Quite an effort today." He cleared his throat. "Well done."

"You, too." A smile touched her lips. "It meant something to those folks, you know. Your being there."

"I didn't do anything."

"You. God. Whatever." She emitted a strange-sounding laugh.

"Me, God, whatever?" He repeated her callous words, a shard of worry slicing his spirit.

Where was this flirtation going, exactly? If he

followed this relationship through to fruition, what sort of comfort would she be as a pastor's wife?

"I told you, Jake." Her gaze went cold. She shrugged, as if in answer to his silent question. "I'm the wrong girl for you."

His thoughts dusted to Margaret—the perfect pastor's wife—all but raised for the part by her devout family. Charitable to a fault. Sweet. Good-natured. Understanding about the time required to help those in crisis. Or, at least, so she'd seemed on the outside. Looks were deceiving...

"I'm going in." Lilah's hand hesitated on the door handle.

"Wait." Jake captured her hand, thumbed a circle caress on the back. "I just wanted to say thanks. For not giving up on me. Not yet."

"I'm not giving up on you." She blinked. "I'm just telling you I've got emotional baggage. Like enough to travel around the world without doing laundry. Twice."

"You and me both, kiddo." He drew her close, kissed those bow lips. Inhaled her subtle strength, her silent warmth, until at last, she stopped fighting him. She fit tight in his arms, pressed against him, as if they were two halves of the same whole. Their kiss, sweet, the need behind it grew clear. He focused on that and let the rest fall where it may. "Don't let me fool you. I've got no idea what I'm doing."

"And yet, you keep doing it." She opened her door and slid out.

He remained in the truck cab with eyes closed, reviewing the day's events with amazement. Seeing God so visibly at work mentally brought him to his knees. Every pastor should go through crisis, to see the strange beauty of coincidence play out, how God lifted ordinary people to angel status by helping each other, by just being there to offer a shoulder, a smile, make someone laugh, or help them stop hurting, begin to heal. A ragtag quintet of helping hands put together, seemingly for the sole purpose of finding and freeing the Steadmans from their own shelter.

His mind drifted to the plains of Thayer now lay to waste alongside the remains of Barn Hollow. They'd followed the scar of that tornado from the Steadman place through Thayer, lending help where they could, prayers where they could not.

Inside the restaurant, the dusty group edged into an empty booth, all tables and the seven stools at the counter full of customers. Four lifetime friends, high school buddies and twin sisters who had probably been at that same diner for sodas and fries after every hometown Friday night football game.

Folks shuffled into the diner, shell shocked, and lined the waiting area until a booth or table opened up.

*Where do I fit in with this, Lord? Will I always be the one on the outside, looking in?*

A muffled tone from the glove box brought him to blink. Cellphone. He'd thrown it in there—when? Couldn't even think the last time he'd made a call on it. Amazing it was still charged at all. Caller ID read Hot Springs Regional Ministries, the head office.

"Dad?"

"Jake!" Margaret's voice cannon-blasted across the miles. "Are you OK? I asked your dad if I could call—I hope that's all right." She clipped at the end. He could almost see her manicured fingernails rat-a-tatting on the cherry wood desk of her office.

"We're still here. If that's what he's wondering."

"Well, of course he's concerned—"

"Then, put me through." A breath, then silence as she transferred the call. Calming, wordless hold music chimed in his ear. Jake inhaled, no more words left to fight her, but no forgiveness in his heart, either.

"Son?"

The phone *booped* its battery level warning.

"Better hurry, Pop." He eyed the red bar. "Phone's dying."

"We saw the news." His father's pastor-tone soothed. Just like it sounded over the radio. He knew the warmth could fire to brimstone just as easily. "They're saying you got hit hard."

"Class four. I hear it could've been much wo-rse." Jake cringed through the crack in his voice. Suddenly, he was the little boy with the black eye who'd broken Timmy Ryan's nose on the playground. The star of the baseball team who'd struck out at the state finals. The grown man telling his father—the head of the largest church in the southland—that his marriage was at an end. And the endless well of disappointment in his famous father's pale, blue eyes.

"Hold it together, son—with the storms up and down the whole eastern seaboard, it's making folks panic a bit. We need to be a rock, son. We need to be His rock."

"I know. Dad, I—"

"I'm sending a news crew out to get your story. Could do wonders for the ministry, son. For the church."

"No!" Jake curled his fist around the phone. "These folks don't know who I am. I won't capitalize on their pain, Dad. Not like last time."

"We did more good than harm, Jake, and you

know it."

Across the miles, Jake knew they thought of the same thing. The San Diego fires. Parents who'd lost a daughter to the blaze, his shame of not knowing what to say...his anger at the destruction, unable to offer God's comfort to ones who'd lost everything. And the unspoken, bitter disappointment in his father's steady gaze.

His father bridged the gap first, in his low, pastoral tone. "It's your chance, son. And, maybe enough now to bring you home."

Silence dragged as Jake's gut churned with his father's dangling proposition. "These people don't need the media. They're hurting...they're—Dad?"

Silence.

The phone was a brick in his hand, worthless as a stone skipped on the river.

Moments later, a subtle knock startled him out of his quandary. "Pastor Gibb?"

Jake blinked into the round, wind-weary face of Tom Steadman. He rolled down his window with a squeal of gears. "Tom!"

Hand to Jake's shoulder, his contractor smiled. "We needed somewhere to go for the night. We're headed down to the bed and breakfast and saw the lights on at the kitchen."

"No dinner at the mayor's B&B," Earnestine chuckled.

"Join us?" Tom opened the door, apparently not one to take no for an answer.

Jake stepped out, and amazed by the swiftness of the Lord's answer, followed them into the restaurant.

# 30

Lilah woke before her 5 AM alarm. Scents of brewing coffee wafted to her room and roused her better than a screeching clock ever could.

Yesterday was a memory. The gray light of the storm cellar with Jake. Watching as he ministered to the Steadmans, to the people of Thayer, just by being there. He offered the strength of his back or the steadiness of his shoulder when someone needed it most. Today, they'd have to investigate the fairgrounds and see how bad things really were.

Last night, she'd served not just the crowd from Mammoth, but the folks from Thayer and the traveling carnival workers. All packed together under the roof of Earl's Kitchen, in some kind of misfit family driven together by the chaos of the storm.

There was that white-haired man, Mr. Randall, the one the carnies called "boss." A shiver raced up her spine. His daughter, with the dark, exotic eyes, makeup and clothes that aged her well beyond her years, knew she had the high school boys' full attention. To drag a kid from town to town, with no real home, no real school, or friends. What sort of life was that?

Lilah rubbed her eyes.

Oh, to be young, with no regard for what came before or worries about what comes next.

Her mind drifted to the finalized divorce papers in

her dresser drawer. Her do-over. In her naiveté, she'd mistaken Ryan's secretive nature for brooding interest. She'd never have guessed in a million years that his deep, dark eyes could flash with such ferocity. Such brutal anger. That his palm could hurt that much when slapped across her cheek, or the sound it made, like firecrackers, as it ricocheted in her ears.

And her, ashamed to go home. Scared to leave him. Not until Eden needed her did she find courage to go. If only she'd known what Eden was up against in running the restaurant, ministering to Nana and Papaw—she would have come back ages ago.

Now, her sister's soft snores came through the cracked door. For the first time since they were children, she and her sister finally were back on solid ground.

The ringing phone startled her up from her nest of blankets. Lilah jammed her feet in slippers and headed out into the kitchen. She blinked at the caller ID and shuddered. Not possible. Her hand lifted it to a numb ear. "Hello?"

"You all right?" Ryan's voice grated every nerve. "I just saw on the news."

"We're fine." Her voice rang hollow. Flat. She wrapped her hand tighter around the receiver.

"CNN's reporting from Thatcher. That's close to your grandparent's place, right?"

"Thayer." Hang up. Just hang up. Instead, she poured a cup of coffee. "We're fine."

"Good." Ryan's worried tone switched to relief. As if he really cared. Always with a plan. Always an angle. "Lilah...listen. I know it's over, but I need you to do something."

"What?" The phone went hot in her hand.

He cleared his throat. "I got a call this morning. Word got out where you are…This could be a press opportunity for our restaurant."

"You mean your restaurant. I've got my own place now." She grasped the counter's edge to keep her knees from buckling.

"If you want to call that hole of your grandfather's a restaurant." He snorted, all pretense of caring for her safety, gone in a snap. This was the Ryan she'd left. "Now, look. You owe me big for agreeing to your terms. I'm having a reporter contact you. I need you to say—"

The force of her fury no longer containable, she interrupted him. "Still capitalizing on other people's anguish? Don't call me again. It's done. I'm not your punching bag anymore." She slammed the receiver down as she pushed the button to end the call. Shuddering, Lilah inhaled, exhaled her fury, her anxiety, her panic the same way that she had driven across the country. Every mile, she'd felt the connection between her and the idiot she'd tied her soul to stretch like a rubber band, and finally it snapped. Lilah sank her head in her hands with a sob. All the pain raced to the surface. His need to hurt her breeched even the dissolution of their marriage, as if he wanted to reach out and strangle her from two thousand miles away. Her emotions ran the gamut, but fear won the race with icy persistence. She sank to the floor, cradling head in her hands.

*Have courage.*

Calm swept over her. Shuddering wonder raced across her shoulders as she stood. Whether moved by the still, small voice in her head, the Holy Spirit, or the ghost of her mother speaking from beyond the grave, she realized that what was done was done. She was finally free.

"Only one person can make you that crazy," Eden's sleep-slurred voice warned from the doorway. Her hair mussed from slumber, she padded straight for the coffee pot, filled a mug full of brew, poured a generous dash of half-and-half. "How'd he get your number?"

"Ryan? Nothing a computer and twelve bucks can't buy you. He's overly concerned for my well-being." Lilah snorted. "Wanted some free advertising."

"Good riddance. You don't need him. Never did." Eden's mug sloshed java onto the counter, and she wrapped her sister in a warm embrace. She pushed back and gave a slight rub to the center of Lilah's eyebrows.

"What are you doing?"

"Quit your frowning, you're making lines." She massaged a small circle, kissed her as only a sister can, smack between the eyes, and then mopped up the counter spill. "No sense starting Botox before you reach forty. Don't think the pastor would want a wife wearing a nest full of wrinkles around her face."

Lilah blinked at her reflection in the oven chrome. "You marrying me off again already? You just helped me get divorced."

"Yeah, maybe I should take my own advice." Eden hopped on the kitchen counter and lifted her mug. "Did I mention what happened yesterday after you left? My soldier debacle?" Eden filled Lilah in on the gory details. "Here's to hoping they made it to Branson before the storm hit." She breathed a sigh. "Not that I'm gonna go calling. Can you believe Eli? He suggested I go along for the ride! As if that would have made it all one big happy how do you do."

"Can't say I blame him. You're a hot ticket." Lilah hopped up on the counter, settled herself next to Eden. "Luke seems to have forgiven you."

"Luke." Eden stared into her mug, as if the swirl of cream held the answers she sought. "Like forgiveness is his to dole out in the first place."

"He's a good man." Lilah squeezed her sister's arm, warm and reassuring.

"Too good." Eden sniffed and stared out the window. The river flowed its constant current over rocks and reeds. "I don't deserve him, so I kicked him to the curb. For his own good."

"Like I should with Jake." Lilah sighed.

They watched a light come on and fill the front window of the pastor's house. His shadow bustled about against the closed curtain in his own morning routine. The first day of the Revival.

"He's not too good." Eden slurped her mug empty. "Just enough tarnish to spark your interest, I'd reckon."

"He's not tarnished." Lilah hopped down. "Just a bit rough around the edges. Doesn't matter, anyway. I'm not preacher-wife material, Edie. God's truth. Don't you ever just get the feeling we're supposed to be alone right now?" Lilah pulled her hair back into a tail and leaned shoulder to her sister's. "Just the two of us?"

Eden's silence was answer enough.

Maybe so.

Or maybe, just maybe, they'd finally made a perfect cast and hooked their limit.

# 31

Lilah followed at a respectable distance as Jake surveyed the Revival site damage. The tent rental company declared a total loss.

Shoulders stooped, his hands dragged through hair of fire as he picked his way through the wreckage. His heart obviously as heavy as the tent's center pole, now wedged between a stand of oak trees. The old school house collapsed, into a dangerous game of pickup sticks. How could this hilltop be devastated, while so much of the carnival below remained intact?

She sat on a boulder, rubbing the hole in her belly. This was God, destroying the very structure they'd built to honor Him. This was the fire and brimstone Savior drilled into her head as a child. This was the fierce, unforgiving Lord who reached out and smashed lives just because He could, like some sort of obscene puppet master. Lilah closed her eyes and faced the wind, imagining the ferocity of the storm that could shred this spot into so much chaos.

Jake sank to his knees amid a shamble of blown chairs and twisted tent poles.

Drums and speakers smashed, blown off the stage, sections of the raised floor gone, and the rest strewn over the grassy knoll as if some giant had dealt them in a wicked game of fifty-two pick up.

"What now, Lord?" Jake spoke, face upturned to the cloudless sky. His arms splayed out, palms up to the heavens.

She watched his prayer send off on the breeze, unanswered. Wondered if she shouldn't join in somehow, and then focused on the tips of her mud-smeared sneakers instead. Praying with him now, when anger brewed in her gut, felt more akin to lying. What God would do such a thing to a man so overwhelmingly faithful? Who would destroy the Steadmans' house and that beautiful old, redwood barn? And then send so many innocents to the hospital?

Lilah drew a squiggle in the mud with the toe of her shoe, then glanced up to see Jake sitting cross-legged on his remnant stage; head in his hands, hair disheveled as he scrubbed a hand through, a low, feral groan filled his throat.

"Did they call? From the head church?" She hazarded a step closer. "Surely your headquarters saw the news."

"Saw it," he said, then snuffed a mirthless laugh. Jake dredged his gaze to hers, green eyes welling with sorrow. "They want to capitalize on it. To prove that God is in the aftermath. You hear that?" His voice crescendoed as he fisted the sky. "The aftermath?"

She didn't see worship in him, but anger, awe, and utter frustration as he kicked a corner of the riser, hobbled his big toe. Jake crumpled to the mud. "Where are You in this?"

Lilah looked away from his display of frustration. She'd never imagined he could lose control, seem so utterly lost. Her heart swelled like water from behind the dam at his private moment of despair. She shouldn't have come, and drew breath to tell him so. "Jake—"

"I had all these dreams, these ideas, this fire! But, after Margaret..." he held up hands, shrugged, "...after she wrecked me, our marriage, and my ministry I couldn't find the message anymore. Couldn't see Him in any of it. I went into my—into the head office to resign but, my d—Pastor Bill handed me a dart, pointed at the map, and told me to throw it." He dragged a hand through his mop of hair. "I wanted to quit, and he gave the choice. One last hurrah, and then I could hang it up for good."

She tilted her head and watched him heave a sigh to the floor.

"That's how I ended up here. This is my aftermath." His voice started low. "I stood in that office, and threw a dart at the map. Dead center."

Lilah blinked, a bubble of laughter rose, but he looked so distraught, she fought it down.

"I deserve all the criticism and concern that your grandmother and the deacons feel about me." Jake's confession had his face twisted in remorse. "What I don't deserve is whatever faith Mammoth's given me."

Wonder surged as she waited for him to finish.

"Sorry I brought you out here." His words fell gruff, his voice betrayed the pent up bitterness. "I'm sorry I promised anyone I could help change things. I can't even help myself."

"It's not you, Jake." She shadowed him with her body, wrapped her arms around his hunched shoulders. "It's this place. It doesn't want to change any more than it wants to grow. In spite of its name, or maybe because of it, Mammoth is just what it's always been. A blip. A place people drive through—the middle of the map. Bull's-eye."

He jerked to meet her gaze then slid his attention

back to the shattered floor.

"Sometimes you just have to let a dream die, you know?" She touched his jaw with gentle fingertips, and reeled him back to her. "It's time to wake up, and deal with the cold, hard reality. Who cares if God intended you to come here, or sent you here in a crazy game of chance? How you handle it is your choice." Lilah sidled up next to him and elbow nudged. "I'd have aimed at Hawaii."

He tilted his attention down to her waiting gaze.

A wave of warmth washed over her, the total focus he had on her. This was their moment.

"Pulling out all the stops to make me feel better, huh?" He dusked a hand through her hair, cupping the back of her neck. "Because, if so, you're doing a lousy job."

She pushed back, made space between them though remaining in the protective circle of his embrace. A jolt of longing, a magnet pull drew her mouth inches from his. His breath warm, scented vaguely of mints he favored, mingled with her cherry lip balm. "I'm so wrong for you, Jake. Why are you the only one who doesn't see that?"

He was warmth and light and fire. She sensed his need for her. Theirs was a loose connection, a live wire, sometimes solid, other times, vapor. She couldn't let him go or it would fall cold, fizzle to embers as everything else in her life had so far.

"So, what now?" His green eyes flashed with heat, as much as confusion, and consequences. They were both free, and yet, shackled to the choices they'd each made in their mutual journeys.

"I'm telling you, even though you might not want it to, life moves on. You get a do-over, and it's what you do next that counts. So, Pastor Gibb. What do you want to do next?"

"Can't I just sit here and mope?"

She shook her head, drew him to stand. "You organized this party, got more of a crowd coming than either one of us could have hoped for after yesterday."

"So, where are we gonna put them, oh, Miss Party Planner?" He fought a growing smile and cupped her face. "Yesterday you insisted you were all wrong for me, for the church, for everything. Know what I see today?"

"No." She kissed his mouth closed. Shivers ran head to toe as her arms draped his neck. "And don't you dare tell me."

"Why on earth not?" Jake's gaze heated her to the soul. "I know mistakes. I've made more than my share. This doesn't feel like one."

"Whoa there, cowboy." She pushed back against his chest. "We've not even been on a proper date yet, there, Pastor Gibb."

"I took you fishing." His smile jogged her heart, but she stood firm.

"I seem to recall it was the other way around."

"What about the carnival?"

"Just your attempt at slaying the spirits of the faithful into joining your revival crusade." She pouted. "I had to win my own panda and everything."

"Fine."

They slow danced to the music of the breeze. Clouds raced.

The tattered tent waved its surrender as he spoke again. "I promise, when we've dissected your brilliant idea and put it into play, then I'll take you out to a real restaurant. One without spinning stools and Formica tables."

"Before you go waxing rhapsodic..." She turned toward the carnival grounds, even now bustling with visitors in spite of yesterday's storm. "This might be the biggest hare-brained idea since putting a couple of tents on the hill."

"Yeah, that one didn't go so well."

"Hey, you thought that w—"

He silenced her with his mouth, their arms anchoring each other from the storm that already passed, and the one yet to come.

# 32

Lilah trudged downhill toward the carnival, Jake following at her heels.

Off the beaten path, he let her lead.

She headed straight through the scatter of trucks, around the back entrance, and past the ticket-takers, not even pretending to purchase entry into the Reunion grounds. A large bouncer with "Security" in block letters across his pocket, munched on what she recognized as an Earl's Kitchen Panini sandwich. "Can I help you?" He wiped his chin clean of what looked like her garlic aioli sauce.

She took a step forward. "We need to get in, please."

He halted her with an incredibly large hand to the shoulder. "Entrance is around the other side, ma'am."

"I'm not here for the carnival." She eyed the towering security guard with a hooded stare. "I need to speak to Mr. Randall."

The guard wiped a hand over a stubble-covered jaw, checked his list. "Your name?"

"Lilah Simp—I mean Dale. Lilah Dale." She cleared her throat. "I won't be on your list, though. He doesn't know we're coming."

"Go buy a ticket, like everyone else, then." The guard straightened, closed his silver clipboard, and picked up soda can.

"How're you enjoying that?" She stood tiptoe,

observing the combination platter. "It's better if you order it with the roasted peppers."

"They said you were fresh out."

"Of roasted peppers?" She sniffed, turned to Jake. "Eden just didn't want to melt her nail polish roasting them." Hands on hips, she stared down the guard. "I tell you what. I'll send you another one tonight, with an extra serving of sweet potato fries. And, if you love it, another one for every day you're here."

"Who are you again?" The burly man considered his sandwich, as if imagining it as described.

"Earl's Kitchen? That's where your lunch came from, right? It's my place."

He shrugged. "OK. Go on in, but I warn you, Mr. Randall's none too happy with those Mammoth folks who dragged him away yesterday. Not by a long shot. He's thinking of pulling stakes up, early."

"Thanks." Lilah hurried inside, Jake on her heels. She turned as he fell into step beside her to the large RV. "What do you suppose that was about?"

Jake shrugged. "I don't have a clue. Luke took him and the others to the gym, yesterday. I doubt he dragged him, though."

She trotted up the small staircase and rapped on the door. Hollow footsteps trod from the back, paused. The lock flicked, and the teenage girl she'd seen at the diner the night before leaned out. "Can I help you?" The girl dragged an errant camisole strap up onto her shoulder.

"I'm looking for Mr. Randall." Lilah cleared her throat. "Is he in?"

"He's passed out." She shrugged, stepped back. "I'll see if he wants to talk."

They followed her up the steps and into the grand

looking room. To the right, the steering wheel and dashboard was hidden with a large cover, the windshield drawn tight with matching gray shades. The left was a mansion on wheels. On the hardwood floors, a scatter of rugs, and long hallway to the back. The walls were graced by framed artwork—photographs of landscapes, devoid of people. A low-lit chandelier hung over the dining area, a splay of expensive furniture in the deceptively large room. A spicy candle licked the air, filling the trailer with scents of amaretto over acetone.

"Sit down if you want." The girl pointed to a leather couch.

The television was tuned to a daytime talk show, volume low.

Lilah noticed the remnants of a manicure in process at the dining table. Beyond the galley kitchen, the girl stepped through to the back of the trailer, holding her hands out, freshly painted fingertips splayed. She blew on them as she walked.

"What are we doing here?" Jake whispered.

Lilah shrugged, sat gingerly on the seat as directed. "Give me a second. I'm thinking."

"...OK. I'll tell them." The girl's words drifted ahead of her. She stepped across the carpet onto the hardwood, sat back at her manicure station, and propped a foot up onto the seat. "He'll be out in a second." She brushed her toenails a bright shade of pink.

"Thanks." Lilah cleared her throat, failing to remember the last time she'd given herself a pedicure.

"So, where'd you two spend the tornado?" She dipped her head, viewed them from behind a curtain of her hair.

Jake cleared his throat. "We were, uh, in a storm cellar."

"Together? Sounds cozy." She painted another stroke on her pinky toe. "Dad wanted us to stay here. Said it was safe enough. Then, the ambulance came and took us to the high school."

"That was Luke." Lilah screwed her lips at the sharp uptake from the kid. Luke was a looker, after all. Interesting. "So, Maya, is it? What grade are you in?"

"Don't go to a real school." She thumbed toward a stack of binders and texts on a small desk. "If I did, I'd be a senior."

Her wistful tone got Lilah thinking. "You rode out the tornado at the high school gym?"

"Yeah."

"See any cute boys?" Lilah picked up a bottle of green polish, unscrewed the cap. She painted her thumbnail with a long swipe.

"Yeah." A secret smile shot to Maya's lips. The slice of girl-talk jogged something within her. "There was one shooting hoops. Tall, built. I'll keep my eye out for him on the midway."

"Sounds like Andy Phelps." Another fingertip painted emerald green. The color of Eden's prom dress. "He's not dating anyone right now, is he, Jake?"

"Um." Jake crumpled his forehead, and turned back to Maya, his own face blank. "I don't think I know him."

Lilah smiled back to Maya. "He just moved here. Barely knows anyone."

"You two got together quick, then?" Maya looked from one to the other.

"We're—um—hey, you thinking about college?" Jake interjected, obviously a bit out of place with the nail polishing and girl talk.

"Nice idea." Maya shrugged again. "Carnival's a family business. No college I couldn't do online, anyway. Already got twenty credits toward my degree."

"That's great," Lilah offered. "So, if you want, I can let you know if Andy's coming tonight. Wait, that's right." She tapped her teeth. "Tonight's the Revival."

"Revival?" Maya blew her tips. "Like a cult thing?"

"No!" They answered in unison. Laughed together.

"No." Jake finished with a long breath. "Just a gathering of like-minded folks, praising God with prayer and music. Revival as in renewal of spirit. Of hope."

"Not a lot of that going around these days." Randall stepped from the back room and settled his lean body into the leather chair across from his daughter.

Jake stood and they introduced themselves, shaking hands.

Randall eyed them as if viewing alien beings. "Not every day I get a pastor in my trailer."

Jake grinned. "Not every day I go trolling for a favor, either."

"I'm listening." He kicked his legs out, grabbed a deck of cards off the table, and set to shuffling one handed.

Lilah cleared her throat and explained her plan. The carnival had the large midway tents, bleachers, and sound system, untouched by the storms the day before. The Revival promised to bring in folks by the thousands, due to the media coverage and calls for help for the homes destroyed in Thayer. They could work together, as a team, and everyone would benefit.

"Or..." Lilah's shoulders did a shimmy in the chill of the Randall's air conditioning. "We both suffer. Ours from lack of location, and you, for want of a crowd."

"So, what do you suggest?" He paused, mid shuffle, forming a bridge. "We just let folks into the carnival for free?"

Jake leaned forward, elbows on his knees. "Everyone wants to win the big prize for their girl. They'll shell out at least a twenty to try their luck, especially if admission is free for storm victims."

"So, you just want to use the main tent?" Randall remained skeptical. "For how long?"

"Tonight." Lilah slid a glance from Randall, to his daughter, and back again. "Tomorrow. And the mayor won't rush you all out of town if you want to stay another week."

"Any other time, I'd say no and don't let the door hit'cha." Chewing his lip, Randall leaned back, considering. "But after last night...I'll say, yes. We'll give it a try. Just for tonight. No promises for tomorrow."

"All or nothing, I'm afraid." Jake stood, hand to Lilah. "Both nights. Or it's a no go."

"He's right, Dad." Maya stood, too, shaking a bottle of clear polish. "The people have to know they have a place to go."

"If it means that much to you." He considered Jake, looked him up and down. "Fine. Both nights it is." They shook on it, then scratched out a quick agreement.

Randall and Maya saw them to the door.

"Tent one's yours. Set up any time."

"Folks will arrive around dusk." Jake pumped the carnival owner's hand. "You're welcome to come, too, of course."

Randall barked a quick laugh and set for the main ticket office, spoke over his shoulder with a wave-off. "Don't count on it."

"You'll tell me, won't you, Lilah?" Maya's voice held a slight tremor of excitement. "If Andy's coming around?"

"You bet." Lilah smiled and hugged the teenager. "We'll see you there. Spread the word, OK?"

"Sure. Whatever." Maya waved a dismissive, perfectly manicured hand and turned to banter with the security guard.

Jake wrapped his fingers around hers, a nod back to the teenager and the swollen-muscled bouncer. "You're seriously setting Andy up for that? Pretty sure we could both go to hell for that one."

"Everyone deserves a chance." A flash of premonition skewered her gut as they exited out the back the way they'd come. Thoughts of Randall and his ever shuffling hands, she wondered how long they could keep their house of cards from toppling.

# 33

The figure waited on his worktable. His creation, spun from nothing but brittle glass and fire. A girl with windblown hair, face upturned to the sun. Her clear curls lifted by an unseen breeze. Her fingertips outstretched, lips parted in a slight smile. Guthrie observed the statuette and sighed, her likeness emblazoned on his brain. Closing his eyes, he inhaled the bitter ache—the brutal punch that came every time he let the image of her out of his thoughts and into the glass. At least, now, he saw her as she was.

A note or two rising above the calliope, lifted through the pendulum swinging boat and tilt-a-whirl, beyond the gong of the strong-man tower, the sweet melody rose, and wove a harmony unlike any carnival clatter. Sweeter than a siren's call, it lifted in a rhythm that wouldn't be denied.

He pushed himself up to stand, frowned at the lack of crowd. Whatever the reason, the slow night gave him time to brood.

The thin liquid in his vest pocket sloshed from its glass cage. Reminding, always reminding of its presence. His damnation was just a sip away.

One more bender and he was out of the carnival, Randall warned him. But Guthrie knew the sober truth about Randall's misdeeds, so he was allowed to stay on. His neck hairs bristled at the memory of his mentor, who was now nothing but bones in a shallow, unmarked grave. Every time the carnival neared Heber Springs, Guthrie made a point to make scarce, as if Randall might turn that murderous temper his way, and be done with the worry once and for all.

The two men were deadlocked in a bitter standoff. It was no secret the carnival master simply waited for him to screw up again. Men like Guthrie always did, he so often said, and then he'd kick him out just for the sheer joy of it.

He took the bottle out of his breast pocket, viewed the clear, brown liquid as it sloshed in his hand. It beckoned in its wave, promised to quench countless sorrows.

The music from the main tent reached crescendo. A voice, pure as silver, captured. Captivated.

*Come to me...*
*For my yoke is easy,*
*I'll take your pain.*
*I'll give you rest.*

He tightened his fingers, unscrewed the cap, and tilted the bottle, at last, allowing the contents to splash around his feet. Lid tossed in the trash, he shattered the bottle onto the recycling pile to be re-melted, renewed for a purpose more worthy, uplifting. Relieved, he returned to the moment and followed the music across the midway. Pocket lighter, and heart along with it.

He ambled, steps scuffling under the insane twirling lights, but through the tent flaps was another world. Inside, the press of bodies, sawdust scents greeted—on stage, a teenage girl angel sang, eyes closed, arms raised in worship. He stepped into a throng of folks with their hands palmed to heaven; men and women, with kids in arms, even the babes singing along. Eyes closed. Some clapped. Smiles.

So...peaceful. So joyful. All of them, singing that beautiful song, knowing each word by heart and he, the only one on the planet who didn't.

*Come to me...*

*For my yoke is easy...*

*I'll take your pain...*

Not after what I done...his throat filled with a lump that wouldn't be swallowed away. A rush of cool to his eyes.

*You want my pain, Lord?*

Smiles and warm hands reached to touch his shoulders, and he shrank away, stared at his shoelaces. The hands remained. He didn't look up as the tears rose in his eyes. Didn't meet anyone's gaze. He didn't deserve that sort of recognition. He remained a stranger in this crowd as he was in every town. No one knew him, so why were they looking at him? Smiling at him? He'd been a ghost in this world, waiting for the next, ever since the night he lost control. His fault, and no other. Then, he saw her at the side of the wide stage, a smile on her face as she gazed at the musicians. Standing by an old man and a withered, white haired woman, the trio's arms linked, singing praises with the rest of the crowd.

*For You, You are my king...*

His heart lurched.

She glanced up as if drawn by the weight of his stare. Their gazes met, and her face softened in some crazy recognition as they had when she'd brought him food in that alley. Like outside the diner where he'd spent his youthful hopes and dreams on the vague hope of winning a girl's heart, once upon an age ago. On the side of the road, covered in blood, broken glass, spearing headlights.

What had Randall said? He was the only hope for Guthrie. Without the carnival, he'd have been thrown into jail years before, rotting in prison, waiting to die there. Waiting for hell.

*Come to me...*

But Guthrie took a step back, bumped into someone. A woman yelped as his heel struck the toes of her tennis shoe, broke the revelry with her scowl. Why was he here? He didn't belong with the faithful. He was the outcast.

The loner.

The murderer.

"'Scuse me." He pushed, fought against the throng that surged toward the stage.

They moved as one: the faithful. He shoved his way back out, panic rising in his throat. Toward the tent-flap door, each step was like swimming upstream toward the falls. He knew without turning that her eyes bored a hole in his back. Though every ounce of energy pulled, he fought just as hard to get away.

Now, out the door, into the night, into the fresh air and the crazy lights, the zinging of the games, the whiz-bang of the shooting gallery, he raced out of the carnival and up on that hill behind. Away from the music. Away from the call he had no right to heed.

Away.

# 34

Lilah searched the crowd for Jake, still praying with the family from Thayer.

Donations filled the truck with clothes, food, toys. They didn't even need to ask. On stage, Raymond sang, his guitar slung across his back as he led the worship. Behind him, the drums continued their steady, shaking beat matching pace with her pulse.

She sagged shoulder to shoulder with her twin sister. Eden, stood firm, though Lilah's feet and legs ached after hours of standing. She could only imagine how Papaw and Nana were faring.

"I'll get 'em some chairs." Eden read her mind, hustled to unfold a few, and Lilah drew them to the back of the red and yellow tent, away from the speakers.

For once, it was Papaw's grateful smile she received, as he wrapped a protective hand over Nana's.

A rush of tears filled her throat as she embraced his paper-thin frame and drank in his scent. Tobacco. Cinnamon, from the mints he always pocketed. How much longer would Papaw's lucid moments last? Her throat constricted at the thought.

Eden tapped her on the shoulder. "You look pale, sugar. Why don't you get some air?"

"I'll be back." Lilah beat a quick path, pushed open the tent flaps, and charged outside. The humidity, close bodies, the unrelenting heat from the tent structure all mixed in the thud of the deep bass notes.

Outside, all was still, as if after that prayer for the tornado victims, God granted a reprieve from even the slightest breeze.

Rounding the red and yellow striped structure, Lilah eyed the crowds and their reaction to the Revival signs, with thumbs up graphic, tacked up on posts all over the fairgrounds.

A group of college aged men in fraternity shirts ambled by. Three laughed, pushed each other toward the doors, and then turned and headed to the beer garden. One lingered, looked through the door flap, and then ducked inside.

Ray and his worship band continued to out-sing the music drifting from the Ferris wheel and Flying Dutchman.

The Revival change of venue had startled some, intrigued others. In the end, it resulted in the media frenzy that she predicted.

The camera trucks parked at odd angles, their satellites pointed heavenward just outside the chain link fence on the dead-grass lot. Vans emblazoned with news logos. Reporters and cameramen, floodlights, and microphones appeared out of nowhere to tell the same story from many angles. An old fashioned Christian revival held at the hedonistic fairgrounds, days after the largest tornado to hit southern Missouri in fifteen years.

She heard them seeking out the pastor, but knew Jake wouldn't come out. He was dug in, tighter than a tick, hiding, almost. Camera shy, maybe.

Even now, Tom Steadman pitched his contracting

business in front of the microphone cone held out to him. He rocked back on his heels with thumbs hooked in his pockets as he explained the depth and breadth of God's work here. Most of his comments would probably end up on the cutting room floor. That wasn't the story those reporters were after.

And still, Jake avoided the spotlight.

Lilah skirted the edges of reporter's row—each heavily made up reporter illuminated in their camera mounted spotlight, dressed to the nines from the waist up, wearing shorts and flip-flops out of viewing range. Stories of rescue from sparking downed power lines. Pets found. Livestock spared. Not one story of misery in the devastation—just praise and thankfulness, celebration with new friends and their expanding church family.

"And that's exactly what we see here." A brunette reporter's blunt observation interrupted Lilah's thoughts. Pausing, she listened as the thirty-something reporter spoke in that sing-songy cadence of well-rehearsed news. "A bizarre joining of saints and sinners tonight, where hope's revived in one place, and then lost at the game tables, in a tiny town called Mammoth. Back to you, Steve." The spotlight dimmed. She waved a finger in a circle. "Wrap it up, Benjie. Let's get the heck back to civilization." Eyes darting up, she met Lilah's bemused stare. "No offense."

"Of course not." Lilah crossed her arms but didn't budge from her spot.

The news lady scrutinized, up and down. "You with the saints or sinners?"

"Pardon?"

"Bad joke." She shucked her jacket, accepted an icy bottle of water from her assistant, and drank deep.

"Just wondering how late that's gonna go." She stepped closer, gaze on the tent at Lilah's back.

"Could go all night. Never can tell."

"I got a tip through the wires that Pastor Bill's son—Jacob?—saved a few folks in Thayer? Do you know anything about that?"

"Pastor Bill?" Lilah blinked. "You mean Hot Springs Ministries Pastor Bill?"

She unearthed a handful of Channel Seven business cards and shoved them at Lilah. "Now, that's a story I'd love to scoop. Do you know Jacob Gibson? Can you have him call me?"

Lilah took it, ears thudding her heartbeat.

Jacob Gibson.

Jake Gibb.

The sounds and sights of the carnival left streaks of light behind her growing realization.

The reporter hopped into the passenger seat of her van, not waiting for her crew, as if she couldn't get back to Springfield fast enough.

Her camera man dug into his pocket and drew out a ten dollar bill. "Hope it helps some."

"Thanks." She folded the bill neatly around the business cards.

He packed his gear and walked around to the driver's side door. The news van left the fairgrounds in a trail of dust. The remainder of the reporters and their crews packed up and drove away as well, but still, Lilah remained rooted to the spot.

Pastor Bill was Jake's father.

It punched. Deep.

Another deception, another lie.

Back inside, money in collection box, she rejoined her family, Nana's voice trilling her favorite hymn.

Jake stood apart, watching the crowd. The resemblance of the famed Pastor Bill was there in his shape of face, his smile. Now she saw it.

Nana's hand found its way into hers. Warm, dry, gripping strong. How could such a small woman be filled with so much strength? Lilah sang along, imagining the cabin in the song, wishing she were anywhere but here.

At last, the evening wound down as the faithful left with spirits high, offerings generously gifted, and prayers of thanksgiving lifted.

Lilah took the chance to sit heavy in the folding chair as the band wrapped up.

Deacons stood with Jake on the edge of the stage, their heads bowed, arms wrapped around each other, some with hands laid, others raised high to heaven, their murmuring voices filled the room with prayers.

She'd never seen so many people, so many hearts softened by the words and music. Like no church service she'd ever witnessed. A shiver ran up her spine. She hugged herself, hands clasped on her upper arms. Though the humid, warm tent no longer surged with people, a few lingered, not wanting their experience to end.

The baskets and bags of collected items for the affected Thayer families overflowed. Food, clothes, toys for the children, all promised for distribution after services tomorrow at the main church. They'd gathered, more than a thousand strong, under this makeshift church and prayed for the lost, the lonely, and the forsaken.

The songs that Raymond and his band played that night were handpicked by Jake, designed in a careful church service of music and light, to go along with the shared testimony of the church members. Every detail, overseen and planned, had gone off without much of a hitch. Jake—as Pastor Gibb—held quite a party. His father taught him well. So why hadn't he told anybody? What did it matter?

She turned to face where Jake delivered his message under the white hot spotlight. With heart, soul, and reverence—the depth and breadth of his belief in salvation, in renewal, revival of the spirit, of the "do-over" that their Savior allowed, encouraged, even in the wake of nature's destruction.

His sincerity spoke to the gap in her soul, where love bloomed. But he wasn't just a pastor. He was Pastor Bill's son—famed, lauded on radios across the country, the world. Heir to that ministry, a national stage, and once he decided Mammoth was too small for him? What then?

"You ready?" Jake's voice called her thoughts back to the here and now.

"Sure." She glanced at her watch. "Wow. Almost midnight. We should put the donations in the truck. "

"In a minute." He held a hand out, pulled her to stand. "I want to show you something."

She followed him out into the bright, strung bulbs swaging the midway.

Folks walked about, greeting each other, some riding, others playing games, but unlike the night before, it seemed like a true reunion. Family camaraderie filtered from the Revival and spilled out into the carnival grounds. For one night, perhaps, angels and demons called a truce.

"Did you see Maya? Or Mr. Randall?" Jake asked as he led her by the hand, up the rocky hillside.

"No." She turned to the moon swept field, the

garish carnival circled by a stand of high-reaching old oaks. Leaves glinted with moonlight, rustling in the breeze, chilly on her skin. A brisk cloud dusted the earth in its passing shadow. "Lots of news cameras showed up, though." She offered, but he ignored her bait.

"I thought they'd come. Maybe they stayed at the back." Jake trudged around a rocky outcropping to a flat spot at the crest overlooking the fairgrounds. "Guess he figured just offering the location was enough."

Lilah swallowed the barbs of her discovery, savoring them a moment as Jake spread out his flannel shirt on a flat rock.

Below, laughter, music, and the whoosh of the Sea Dragon ride ebbed in carnival chaos. Up on the hill's apex, overlooking all of Mammoth, the black-blotch of Thayer to the north—still without power—and Pastor Jake, setting a pallet up on the self-same spot where Wayne O'Neill once planted an unripe kiss on her, at the age of thirteen.

"What are we doing here, Jake?"

"Sit." He reached a hand, drew her to his side.

"What's going on?"

"I thought you and I needed a minute alone." He dipped his gaze to hers, wrapped an arm across, warming her shoulders.

"Why?" She dared, the moonlight flashing in her eyes. "Got a deep, dark secret to share with me, Pastor Gibb?"

He opened, shut his mouth and tilted his head toward her. "What's bothering you, Lilah?"

"Lots of reporters out there tonight." She crossed her arms tight around her chest. "I wonder why you didn't want to talk with them."

Jake just looked away. "Just, didn't seem right. I'm not advertising anything. We didn't call the media."

"They love a good, juicy story, hmm?" Lilah prodded, even though her guts weighed with guilt. "One was asking lots of questions. About Hot Springs Ministries. About you."

"What is it you really want to ask me, Lilah?" His gaze questioned, stars sparkling in their inky blackness. "No time like the present. There's no one else around."

"You're wrong about that, Jake." She bit her lip, fighting the welling laughter. "Look around."

He darted a glance over his shoulders. Bushes rustled. Low voices murmured, most of them in fast, hushed, worried tones.

"I wanted to give you a birthday present—it is your birthday, and Eden's. Right?"

She nodded, throat filling with that familiar guilt, and palmed a pebble. "It's not something we celebrate…so much confusion, guilt, sorrow wrapped up in it."

He nodded, as if he understood growing up in a house with no birthday cakes or princess parties. Even with Ryan, her birthday slipped by without notice.

Jake cleared his throat and continued. "I didn't know what you want, or need, so I figured—fireworks. We could share them."

"Ah, Jake." She leaned her head on his shoulder, but his back remained ramrod straight.

"I was told…" He used his pastor voice, projecting so all within earshot would hear. "…this was the best spot to watch them."

"Who told you that?" She tilted her head as he

spied the huddled, whispering forms in the bushes. The first bloom of pyrotechnics exploded over the carnival below.

There was a reason that kids came up to this spot to hold hands, kiss, and play that dangerous game of chicken with bodies, hearts.

The darkness bloomed with green, blue, and bright white sparks. The air screamed with rockets, boomed with explosions of light and color, tinged with sulfur and phosphorous smoke. Shadows lengthened. Shrubs danced as a young couple did their best to pull themselves together, shushing each other with hurried whispers.

Jake scrubbed his head, realization reaching his eyes along with a flash of anger, a scattering of humor. "Your sister."

"Well, she'd know. Spent her share of time up here. She and Marty—Luke's best friend. Back in the day, they were quite the item. She probably would have married him if he hadn't died in action..."

The words hung in the air along with a splash of light, a huge circle of exploding white, faded to quick-falling in streaks of orange embers. Trails of phosphorous smoke lingered in the humid Ozark night.

From the thin cover of bushes, Lilah heard a feminine sob.

"Should we say something to those kids?" Jake whispered. "Or just go?"

"Give them a second." Lilah suggested, wrapping her hand around his, they leaned shoulder to shoulder.

Fireworks boomed, one after another. The show blossomed with searing whistles, and twirling rockets, the firework-induced clouds low enough to brush with their fingers.

"We all make mistakes," Jake said, after a while. Her hand curled in his. "Maybe that's why we're here. To keep those two from making one."

"A reason for everything, hmm?" Lilah glanced over as a girl's voice whispered, hushed and hurried in the darkness, heading the direction of the carnival.

Feet beat down the hill, followed steps behind by the lanky teenage boy she recognized as Andy Phelps. The basketball star. Responsibility bloomed, as she'd dangled that carrot for Maya, and ultimately Mr. Randall's approval to have the Revival here.

"That the last of them?" he whispered.

"One more, other side. We'll wait them out."

The fireworks continued as her mind flipped from Jake's deception, to thoughts of her mother. The tragedy of their beginning wove the fabric of her life. Her mother's death was the yardstick by which every choice she'd ever made had been measured. From her first date, to Eden's prom, to canoe trips down the river with the senior class and getting caught puffing a cigarette on Emma's dock. Nana's disapproving stare and keen eyes missed nothing, promising to forgive, but never willing to forget. Especially after Ryan, and the crescendo of her lasting mistake, she knew Nana's heart, even if her grandmother never uttered the words out loud. She'd come back too late for forgiveness to matter. She stared into the dark, rustling hedgerow.

"Hey, y'all!" Lilah called out. "We suggest you get home quick! And think twice about coming up here next time, OK?"

"OK." The feminine voice at last leaked out of the darkness from the opposite side of the hill.

A quick shuffle of feet and scrabbling of stones,

the teenagers scuttled down the opposite side of the hill. In the intermittent light from the fireworks, Lilah thought she saw a familiar outline. Charla, Emma's daughter, and a shadowy boy high-tailed it ahead of her.

"That was nice of you." Jake squeezed her hand. "Looks like your plan worked. That was the basketball kid, right?"

"And not with his sweetheart." Lilah shrugged as bright blue sparks bloomed overhead, pungent smoke drifting. "So Andy and Charla escape the Mammoth curse." At his non-understanding blink she added. "Seems like every kid in this town thinks they have to marry the first person they fall in love with. Look at Emma and Scott. Eden would've done it with Marty. She didn't get the chance."

"And you."

A swallow, she nodded. "He was so exciting for a good girl like me. Eden had the spotlight since day one. I figured I'd take the diner over after Eden started popping out kids. But Eden lost her love to the war, her light shut off awhile. Ryan buzzed through town like a man on a mission. He wanted me. Whisked me away. How could I say no? No one had ever looked at me that way, touched that place of longing in my heart. Then, everything changed." She cleared her throat and turned to him. "Your turn."

"Margaret. She was perfect for me. Always there, saying, doing the right thing...like I didn't have much of a choice. We just fit." A sad smile graced his face, matching her own. "Look. Can we skip that part where we share our past regrets?"

Lilah viewed him through a curtain of her hair, tears threatening to spill "OK," she said, at last, even though questions, accusations lay just below the surface. "For now."

"For now." He brought the back of her hand to his full lips, pressed a warm, lingering kiss, aching sweet, to seal the deal.

She swept her hair back to view another screaming, swirling rocket spear the heavens, all thoughts to her planned accusation on whether Jake Gibb was Jacob Gibson—Pastor Bill's son, and why he was hiding out in Mammoth, left to burn inside like a sizzling rocket fuse.

If Margaret was perfect, she was the polar opposite. This was a glimpse at what might have been, a dream, and soon she'd have to wake up.

Silence fell between them, replaced by the grand finale of the fireworks show, his fingers wrapped over hers as they leaned back in alternate light and shadow.

# 35

Jake finished reviewing his sermon notes as the parishioners filtered in from the streaming light of Sunday morning. He'd been late returning from his early run, chasing inspiration just beyond his reach, like the mist that blanketed the river. Today he'd gone farther than before, up the steep hill leading to Mammoth's cemetery, tilting headstones, flat polished markers, flags and flowers. He'd paused and watched as doves lifted from tree limb to grass and pecked at seeds on the freshly churned soil. One landed on a flat, glossy stone, etched: Dale.

The opening sounds of the day's hymn brought him back to the here and now, Raymond and his little band of worship musicians softened their Christian rock to mesh with Marilee on the organ, a compromise.

Jake peeked through the crack in the door, eyeing a full to capacity crowd. He stood in the back room and adjusted his hair, spiking and smoothing in the small, round mirror. Checked his breath. Popped a mint from the tin on the table.

He stepped from the antechamber into the sanctuary and smiled at the parishioners. These were the faces, the reason he'd been needed here. The men, dressed in all manner of clothing from suits to golf shirts, the women, garbed in everything from sundresses to slacks in the thick, humid Ozark morning.

All eyes intently focused on the podium as they promised to gather at the river, their melodious tune blended into another hymn, the same songs they'd lifted heavenward for fifty years set to a new beat.

Next week, he'd talk to Raymond about teaching Marilee a contemporary song, or two. Next week. That was presuming they wouldn't boot him out by then. Jake gripped the podium.

*Imposter. Deceiver. Liar.*

Time for truth telling. Again. Jake closed his eyes a moment while he finished singing along with the congregation. *Lord, help me share Your word. Help them hear what each needs to hear this morning.* He prayed, sermon notes thick in his hand. Then he stood up to begin. Jake inhaled deep, soul tingling with the presence of the Holy Spirit as he quoted Acts 13: 38-39. "All of you, my fellow Israelites are to know for sure that it is through Jesus that the message about forgiveness of sins is preached to you; you are to know that everyone who believes in him is set free from all the sins from which the Law of Moses could not set you free." He closed the book. "All of you. To know — for sure. Not just some of us. But everyone. Everyone who believes will be free from all of the sins. All. Every single one."

Jake took his time to tick through the list of impossible laws as he traveled across the stage, away from the podium: The proper number of knots on a robe; the right prayers to say before eating; how or what to eat for that matter. This always was a good one, to share the differences between Old Testament rules and New Testament freedom in Christ.

Nods. They were nodding. They weren't taking him out to the proverbial stockade. For the first time since he arrived in Mammoth, Jake inhaled the sweet vapor of their approval. At last, could this really be his church?

"Baptism is the time for renewal—a new member of the flock, showing their faith and trust at being dunked by their pastor."

Chuckles.

*Keep them with me, Lord...*

"It's a renewed pledge for all of us who witness. We're re-baptized, just by being there. Watching, lending a hand, or a towel. This Wednesday, come back out at sundown, and let's show our support for our brothers and sisters who are ready to announce their new-found faith."

~*~

Jake's voice boomed in the small building about his baptism plans.

Sandwiched between Eden and Papaw, Lilah's heart was full for his profound words, and the willing ears of the faithful as he preached.

"Someone has a good case of revival fever," Eden's whisper tickled her ear.

"Stop it." Lilah brushed at her hair and shot a glare to her twin. "He'll settle down."

"Just trying to impress his new girlfriend, maybe?"

"Shhh!" Nana glared at them from the other side of Papaw, then returned her gaze to Jake, at the podium.

Eden shot a grin. "Our Nana's supplying her own brimstone this sermon."

Burying laughter, Lilah focused hard on the

offering envelopes until it subsided. Across the aisle, Luke lasered his attention to the stage, ignoring them.

"I should have known to separate you." Papaw leaned to whisper around Eden, a grin brightening his otherwise pale face. His hands reached out to clasp both of theirs. "You two girls always did get into trouble in church."

"Sorry it took me so long to come back." Lilah squeezed back.

His skin, cold, clammy.

"You're here now." His gray eyes went sad, watery behind his freshly cleaned glasses. "That's what counts."

"You OK, Papaw?" She rubbed heat into his palm.

"Juss let me rest a spell." Papaw's head sagged forward.

Fear welled in her breast.

Around them, the music started again, the church rose to sing in one voice.

Lilah frantically tried to wake him, to no avail.

"What's wrong?"

"He's collapsed!" Her gaze met Eden's, fast with worry. "Call an ambulance."

# 36

Lilah traced the hospital wallpaper design with her fingertip. Loops and whorls, over, up, down, back again. She relived the church scene.

Papaw was teasing them, right before the sudden pallor that swept over his skin.

Luke was at his side almost before she realized what happened, inspecting airway and pulse, calling for the ambulance that took them away.

Everyone sorry. Everyone praying. So many concerned folks touching, hugging, reaching that she had to race outside to even breathe.

Somehow, she'd driven herself and Eden, while Nana rode in the ambulance. Now, here in the long hallway with whispering nurses and doctors with soulful eyes, she waited, tracing the bumpy pattern in a vicious, tangled circle.

Through the propped open door Papaw's breathing apparatus clicked, hummed, and whooshed air into her grandfather's lungs. His chest rose and fell in forced, awkward motions. Robotic. Unnatural. She brushed past memories of him dozing in his chair, the river running out the window.

*This is no way for him to go, Lord...Not here, not now.*

A tear leaked down her cheek, followed by another.

"Hey." Jake walked down the corridor from the nurses' ward, fingers quick-combing his shaggy, red-gold hair.

Lilah hurried to meet him, falling into his ready embrace.

"How is he?" He breathed into her ear.

She couldn't speak around the knot, just shook her head.

He cocked his head, "Want to go in with me?"

"No. That's OK. Now that you're here, I'll go get coffee for everyone."

There were hushed greetings with Nana and Eden as he entered the room. A nurse buzzed past Lilah on her way to the cafeteria. Garish lights, plastic-wrapped sandwiches, burnt coffee.

For hours Papaw was poked, prodded, carted here and there for tests, his body frail, thin, fragile. Hanging on to this world by a thread. And, to what end? For what purpose?

She prepared a tray, busying herself with the mundane process of caring for others, as Papaw had taught her an age ago. Her mind's eye swept to those burnt orange booths, the Formica counters, Papaw's confident, competent hands teaching her how to cook. How to serve. How to greet folks. Coffee for four, creamers, sugars. Snapping lids atop the fourth cup, she blinked back tears. Papaw. When had he gotten old? How had she missed everything, following her own foolish aspirations?

She sagged into a chair at one of the empty tables, her clutched tray clattering to the surface. A cup bobbled, then righted itself as Lilah inhaled, exhaled in rapid streams, unable to catch her breath. Too much air. Too much breathing. The world tunneled, and, at its core, she saw her grandfather's handsome, lined face, concern darkening his gaze.

"Miss?" A voice called from beyond the darkness.

She blinked, looked up.

"Are you OK?" The weathered man from the carnival—the glassmaker—adjusted his dark green jacket over a bandaged, sling-cocked right arm.

"N-no." Shaking her head, she at last admitted the truth. Her soul revealed. She wasn't OK. None of this was.

An unsettled look marred his rugged face. The carnival man turned to the row of coffee machines and condiments and left her side.

Her tears came hot, fast, and unstoppable. Memories, remembrances of childhood that she'd forgotten. Simple things. Little things. Learning to thread a hook. Practice a perfect cast. Train a hunting dog with nothing but a bunch of turkey feathers and a fly reel.

Papaw there, in the background, all the while.

But none more potent than the motorcycle pulling up in front of the house. Riding away, hands clamped around the waist of a stranger. Nana's disapproving gaze from the upstairs window. Papaw remained down, fishing at the river. Not even turning for a wave, or her pausing to say goodbye.

Sobs wracked her shoulders. Lilah's heart wrenched, her soul churned with an ache that couldn't be soothed. How could she apologize for shredding the fabric of someone's life?

"Breathe."

A paper bag crinkled over nose, mouth, catching her off guard.

"In. Out. Slow. On purpose." He directed with a shaking hand, replacing his hand with hers.

She held it in place and did as she was told. The

air tasted of paper, warm, and something peppermint.

"Good."

She concentrated on inhaling, exhaling. Coughed, but kept going. Time stood still until her mouth warmed, her breath intoxicated and slowed by the carbon monoxide, she removed the bag and wiped her face with a weary hand. "Thanks. It all just hit me. My grandfather's upstairs, they don't know if he's gonna make it. It's been a long day."

He nodded, shifted in his seat, and hugged his bandaged arm closer.

"Everything OK?" They both glanced up as Jake joined them. Jake studied the two of them, the tray of coffee cups in between, and then made quick work of a napkin, mopping up the splash.

"Had herself a panic attack. Had myself a few over the years. Got her calmed down, I reckon."

"Thanks for…"

"None needed."

She flattened the rumpled paper bag. "I think I'm OK now."

She stood, retrieved the coffee tray, an eye to Jake. "You coming?"

"Be right behind you."

~*~

Jake watched her leave and slid a gaze to the bandaged arm. "That looks painful. What happened to you, friend?"

"Ah. Had worse." Guthrie sighed, looked at his bandaged elbow. "Some workers didn't take kindly to the church taking over the carnival tent. I set 'em straight, though. Doc said it'll be fine in a few days."

"God doesn't need you fighting for Him, you know."

He nodded. "Actually, it was for you. And the others. Good folks in this town. I used to live here, you know."

Jake kicked back in his seat. "Is that right?"

"Grew up not too far away, down in Hardy." Guthrie continued. "Declared my love to my girl on top of the carnival Ferris wheel." His face brightened, the creases all but vanished. A much younger man hid there, beneath the weathered surface. Memory must have swirled Guthrie away, taken him back to that moment in time. Wherever he went, it was far from this bustling hospital cafeteria.

Jake glanced around and caught sight of a doctor he'd seen upstairs. Time to get back to his own girl. "That must have been something." Jake smiled, tried to bring the man back to the present.

"Got myself saved with her at a tent much like yours that same year." Guthrie's gaze lasered on his, all hint of smile lost to the solemn, brooding hood of his brow. As he spoke, the lines in the man's face seemed to deepen, a shroud of remorse wrapping around each word. "I done asked for forgiveness again and again. I've been baptized in the water, and in blood. But there's nothing that can save me from what I done."

Silence brewed. The hairs at the back of Jake's neck soldiered to attention as he prayed for the right words. "Sounds like you've got a wrong idea about salvation."

Bright overhead lights gleamed down on the polished table and glared off the metal spoons, as though it all shone dim through a filter of darkness.

Guthrie wadded up a napkin, stuffed it inside his cup, and stood. "Don't you go fretting over me, Pastor Jake. I'm happy to stand at the gate and watch the ones I love squeak through."

Jake watched the carnival man in the army jacket push through the span of blue and white scrub suited doctors, nurses, and spattering of visiting families, the darkness following with each step. A shadow, disappearing around a dark corner then gone through the glass doors.

*Lord, cover him. Help him see You through that dark cloud he's wrapped himself inside.*

Upstairs, Lilah needed him. Nervous energy powered through Jake's blood as he took stairs to the fourth floor, turning quick by the nurses' station. Three blue-scrub-shirted nurses circled around a cake box and chatted. One glanced up.

"Pastor to the Dales." Jake offered, huffing past at a trot, heading straight to the room across from the station.

"Go on in." The blonde, spectacled nurse pointed to the open door. "Doctor's with them."

Earl Dale was pale as the white sheets up to his chest. Wired and monitored, IV in his sun-blotched arm, pallor over the tan of a man who'd spent his entire life in the sun. He sat up, the respirator no longer forcing air into his lungs—an oxygen tube along his upper lip, eyes open, limbs outstretched, clamped with devices that would alternately squeeze and release his legs for circulation.

The girls stood, arms linked, on the window side, their faces grave. Their grandmother, Naomi, stood opposite, alone, clutching the bedrail.

Jake walked to her, wrapped an arm around her

frail shoulders. He'd never realized how slight a figure she was. How fragile, under all the fanfare. Even accounting for the top of her perfectly set white curls, Naomi Dale barely came up to his shoulder.

"He's breathing on his own." Her thin voice rose above the beeps and whirrs.

Jake nodded, clasped her hands in his own. "How're you?"

"I'm tired." She blinked, stared at him with cloudy blue eyes, a sad smile. "So's Earl."

The sheets rustled, and Earl's thin arm rose. A mumble at his lips.

"What's that, hon?" Naomi leaned forward.

"Na...omi..." Voice slurred, his fingers curled into a hook.

"I'm here, Earl." Her forehead crumpled in concern, she patted his hand.

"That." He dragged his hand away again, pointing. "See that?"

Jake looked the direction Earl pointed, seeing nothing but the empty doorway, the bright hallway lights. He knelt at Earl's bedside, heart slamming. Was this it? He'd seen death call before, but... "What do you see, Mr. Dale?"

"White." Earl blinked, ran his tongue over his lips. "So beautiful."

"Not now." Tears slid down Naomi's cheeks. "Not yet."

"White. Beautiful." Earl cocked his head at his wife. "Go ask 'em for a slice."

"A slice?" Jake blinked, looked again to where Earl pointed. Outside, a quartet of nurses parted, revealing the white frosted birthday cake, sparkling under the incandescent lights. "You want cake?"

Earl gave a nod, a slurred smile. "Lord, I'm hungry."

"Earl Dale!" Naomi sat in a heap. "You done scared me to death."

He blinked. "Ask 'em."

"Come on, Jake." Lilah walked around the bed to the door, laughter escaping her pursed lips. "Let's go see if he can have some."

"I'll come with y'all, if you don't mind." Eden followed them into the hallway, her voice a shaky laugh. "Cake? I thought he was seein' angels, or his mama, or ours."

Eden and Lilah's gazes locked. Their laughter died as fast as it came.

"Hey, you all." The short, bobbed brunette smiled from behind the counter. "There's plenty for everyone. Be sure and grab a piece."

Laughter began anew as Eden stepped up for her share.

Jake took Lilah's ice-cold hands in his. "You holding up?"

"They don't know much yet." She nodded. "His vital signs aren't good, but he's stable."

"And hungry." Jake smiled, turned to Lilah. "I'll give you a ride whenever you want to go home."

"We're gonna stay." Her smile failed to reach her eyes. "I'll go home with Eden, later."

"Family first." He pulled her around to a small waiting area, glanced to see that no one was around, and encircled her in a tender embrace. With lips soft and warm, he kissed the creases from her forehead.

Lilah sighed into his shoulder, tears dampening his shirt. "Thanks."

"I wish I could do more." Jake combed her

ponytail through his fingers.

"Just pray." She stood stock still in his embrace, as if any movement would splinter her to a million pieces.

Two ships in a storm, they stood fast as the hospital sounds whirred around them.

# 37

Luke hauled the second stretcher from the ambulance into the buzzing emergency room. The bright lights fused in a flurry of action. Doctors dragged the gurney from his grip. He rattled off the condition and the treatment they'd administered since picking up two teenagers, cut from the wreckage of Andy Phelps' pickup truck.

"On the road to Hardy?" the mid-twenties-if-he-was-a-day doctor asked as he tied on a yellow paper trauma robe.

Luke nodded. "Need to call his folks. Andy took the curve about twenty miles an hour too fast. His, uh-friend, there, was unconscious on scene. Pulse thready."

The doctor shot a look at the other table where a trio of his peers worked on the young girl with rich, fire-red hair.

Intubated and bagged, they squeezed breath into her bleeding body as the monitors jangled and clanged with alarms.

"Do you know her?" The doctor asked as he adjusted his grip on the teenage boy's broken arm.

Luke seemed to recall seeing that rich, red hair before, but her face—so swollen. "She might be with the carnival folks." He offered, inside saying a prayer of thanks it wasn't Emma Thompson's daughter, Charla, then swallowed that burning, guilty thread.

In silence, they stared at the nameless girl, and went back to work.

Andy and Charla'd been darkening the back booth at Earl's Kitchen for at least their four high school years. Set to follow in her mother's footsteps, until—well, until now.

Luke wiped his hands on his coverall pants and nodded to his partner. "I'm off shift. Gotta make the call." The nurse station phone heavy in his hand, he dialed Andy's parents.

~*~

Eden turned the corner toward the exit, fiddling with the strap of her purse. The doctors weren't telling everything. Nana might buy it, and Lilah was too trusting to ask. But Eden knew there was more to her grandfather's condition. She reached inside the pocket for another stick of gum, foil crinkling in her hand. The back door of the hospital bordered the emergency room. She watched the bright red box of an ambulance drive away, lights blazing. Her heart gave a tug as the vehicle vanished over the hill, sirens blaring.

Luke.

Somewhere, somehow, he'd know how to find out what was really going on with Papaw. The doctors never told one everything. They whispered around stacks of charts and files and shot comforting glances as they sent the nurses to run interference. Luke was relatively in the know about things. He should have gone to med school but settled on being a paramedic, staying close to his mama.

*Would you look at him differently if he were a doctor?*

Eden swallowed at the small voice rattling in her

thick skull and dragged her chain from around her neck. She stared at the ring suspended on it; felt more like a millstone than a testament to her failure at true love, all the while, with Luke just waiting. She had to be the biggest blooming idiot this side of the Mississippi.

Her back to the chaos of the emergency room, she dialed Luke's number on her cellphone, gum snapping with her new resolve. Luke would know what to ask, what to do.

He always did.

Maybe it was time to tell him she finally realized that.

# 38

Rather than leave, as promised, Jake knelt at the small altar of the West Plains hospital chapel, staring up at the vacant cross. A stained glass panel lit it from behind for the illusion of outside.

At his back, the chapel door squeaked. Jake swiveled to see Mammoth's pharmacist enter. "Evening, Mr. Hackleberry."

The large, balding man shuffled down the narrow aisle, bowed to the cross, nodded at the preacher. The right front pew creaked under his girth. "Thought I'd pay my respects before I go home."

Jake stood from his kneeling position and sat across the aisle, silent.

"Does something to a man, seeing his friends laid low." Mr. Hackleberry sighed. "Earl—he's had his difficulties for some time now."

Jake threaded his fingers and stared at the multi-hued stained glass panels. "Lilah told me."

"I've been his pharmacist and friend for nigh-on forty years." Mr. Hackleberry wiped his face with a cloth handkerchief then returned it to his back pocket.

"That's a long time." Jake said and leaned forward, attention focused on the man he'd seen play checkers with Earl Dale nearly every afternoon since he'd moved here. "In any town."

"Thick and thin. Saw him and Naomi raise their sweet little girl, stood by them when they buried her.

Watched Lilah and Eden grow up. Seems like the longer you live, the less you know."

"The more you have to trust." Jake returned his glance to the empty wooden cross. Its black shadow obscured the crisscross of light fired blue, red, gold, and green glass. "Like a child we come to Him, as a child we return home when He calls us."

"Easy for you to say, son." Mr. Hackleberry laughed, deep, throaty. "You're what? Thirty?"

"Thirty-three."

"The closer you get to knocking on those gates, the more what-if's creep into your head." He wiped a hand over his thinning strands of hair, absently brushed them back into their place. "But not Earl, though. He's never been anything but faithful. Always trusted the right thing would happen. Even when Rebecca ran off with that boy."

"Tough on a parent, watching your kids make mistakes."

"Oh, that's for sure." He shook his head. "Earl and Naomi went to battle when she up and married him and moved up to the river house."

Jake sat up a bit straighter, unable to stifle his gape of surprise. "She married the boy?"

Mr. Hackleberry's brows lowered and hooded his brown eyes. "I'm speaking out of turn."

Jake shrugged, turning his attention back to the cross. It wasn't his job to seek out gossip, but if news that could help Lilah and Eden came his way, that was another matter.

After a beat of silence, the pharmacist's confession began in a slow rush of words. "Rebecca came to see me one afternoon. Bought that little test kit, and don't you think that didn't take some guts. To not just steal the thing like other girls did. She wasn't that way, though. Not Rebecca. Smart. Honest to a fault. I knew by the look on her face it was positive."

"She was upset?" Jake kept his façade cool, merely cocked his head though his heart kicked up rhythm.

"No." A pensive smile rested on Mr. Hackleberry's doughy face. "Quite the opposite. She was glowing. Even hugged me. The boy was waiting outside in that little black Pontiac. She hopped in and off they went. Got themselves hitched someplace out toward Branson, came back and told her mama. Naomi about blew a gasket. I was filling her Valium for months after...but I've said too much."

Jake splayed out his hands. "Goes no further."

"I've not spoken on this in thirty years." He blew a sigh. "Weighs on a man."

"I'm sure that's true."

"Near eight months later, she and the boy were heading back out to the river house her daddy let them live in. During a storm...well, you know the story about the curve. I don't think Naomi's ever forgiven Earl for that. For letting those young-uns live out there. For the accident that took her little girl."

"And gave them two others."

"Now, Earl's up there, wrestling his demons before he can pass on to glory." He frowned through a quivering smile. "I've missed him, you know. Hard to mourn your best friend when he's not yet left this world."

Jake sat, silent. Praying for words that would heal. Help. But nothing came.

Mr. Hackelberry raised his bulk, clasped a meaty hand on Jake's shoulder. "Thanks for the ear, Pastor."

The chapel door opened and then closed behind

him.

Jake remained, dragging his hands through his hair. He'd married people, laid folks to rest before. Baptized the faithful, and dedicated the young. Never in his few years since seminary, had he ever felt less of a shepherd.

How can one soothe someone waiting for their best friend to die? Or a grandfather? Or a husband? *What do I say, Lord?* Jake dropped to his knees and bowed his head before that vacant cross. *What should I say?*

*Why are you trying to say anything at all?*

His mind rattled as the truth speared his heart.

In all of his attempts to be brilliant, to bring hope and promise to this dying little town, he'd forgotten the most important part of being a pastor. Allow God's words to filter through him. Get out of the way of His message.

He closed his eyes, face angled heavenward. *There's nothing I can do here. It's all You. Please, help me remember that.*

~*~

Lilah sat at Papaw's bedside long after Eden took Nana home for a shower, rest, and change of clothes. The room was bathed in the blue glow from the desk-lamp. It was never really dark in a hospital. Never really quiet. She took a breath and picked up the small leather-bound Bible that Papaw always carried in his shirt pocket.

Onionskin crinkled, torn and taped from years of reading and rereading. With a red marker, he'd underlined favorite passages on nearly every page.

She smiled, cheeks heating with a fresh wash of tears, thumbing through. The whole Bible was his favorite. She'd never read more than a verse or two at a time outside of church. Had memorized the names and order of the books to win a prize in school—but had she ever really read the book to see what God had to say? Closing her eyes, she held the crumbling leather to her lips, smelled the ancient leather. "OK, Lord. Talk to me."

The Bible fell open to the middle, and she let her finger find a scripture. Isaiah. Screwing her lips as she read the angry words of a vengeful God, her heart stayed quiet.

"What did you see?" Jake's voice startled her.

"Nothing." Lilah looked up to see him watching her, pulse racing. "Just something about smiting someone. Death and destruction. No salvation for sinners."

Jake dragged the other chair closer to her side.

Papaw slept across from them, the thin blanket covering his legs.

"It's not a magic eight ball."

"I thought you believed God spoke to you through this." She wagged the book at him.

"I do." Jake held out a hand and took the small Bible from her with the same reverence she'd seen Papaw use. Lids closed, he opened the book, pointed, dragged his finger across the page, and cleared his throat to read aloud. "For by grace you have been saved, through faith. And that not of yourself. Ephesians two, verses eight and nine."

"Nice." She smiled. "See. It works for you."

"I know where to look." He winked, handed it back to her. "No pointing and guessing."

"Papaw taught us all that stuff, you know. How to live by the word. Be a faithful servant. All that..." She viewed her grandfather, the dripping IV bag, the tube in his thin and withered arm. "Do you really believe that God's watching from afar, waiting for Papaw to die?"

His smile pensive, his words gentle. "I've learned," he held the book up in both hands, for her to see, "Heaven's always with us. There's a thin curtain between this world and the next. God's not out there—he's here." Jake touched his breastbone. His hand went to her, just below the throat, with tender fingers, pressed warm. "Inside me. You. Him."

"And the angels?" Lilah tilted her head. "What about them? You believe that they're here?"

"They're everywhere..." Papaw's thin, quavering voice interrupted.

"Papaw?" Lilah leaned in, heart slamming, searching his half-lidded eyes for any sign of lucidity.

Her grandfather reached his arm to the ceiling. "How do I? How do I get up those stairs?"

"Don't. Please don't go yet..." She took hold of his hand, weathered with age and time. Hot worry shot through her veins as she glanced between her tenuous hold on him and the call button, ready to rouse the nurses.

"Gone again." He shook, turned his head, sighing into the pillow. "Maybe next time."

"What's gone?" Jake leaned closer, still, laid his hand on top of hers. "We're here, Mr. Dale."

"Papaw," Lilah smiled through her tears. "I'm here with Pastor Jake."

"Good." Under the tubing, Papaw managed a lopsided grin, tired eyes blinking into focus under the low, antiseptic light. "You two go on down to the river dock tomorrow. Catch me a stringer-full. Rebecca's makin' hush puppies."

Lilah nodded. Throat too thick with tears to speak, she cleared it. All focus rested on the lined face of the man who'd raised her. "Do...you see her, Papaw?"

"Your mama'n others...out in the hall." He blinked at her, pale eyes distant, cloudy. "Hear 'em callin' me?"

She released him in a flash. Gooseflesh shot shoulder to wrist, worry replaced with a healthy dose of chills. Lilah rubbed her exposed skin, then tilted the mauve water pitcher over a paper towel.

"Shh." She blotted Papaw's hot forehead, his bone-dry cheeks. "I'll get the nurse."

"No." He shook his head once, sighed back into his pillow. "Mama's singing. I'll just listen a spell."

Lilah turned to the empty doorway, the silence deafened. "What do you think he hears out there?"

"Maybe everyone. Everything." Jake's expression was locked in childlike wonder. "I have no idea. But, I think I'd better take you fishing tomorrow. By the restaurant?"

"No. He's talking about the place at our dock." Lilah inhaled, barely able to believe it herself. "At the river house."

Jake's eyes widened, though he said nothing. He turned his attention back to Papaw.

Hands clasped in silence, they listened for angels to come to call.

# 39

The next afternoon, the truck pulled into the parking area in a cloud of red dust.

Lilah guided them down the stone stairs, carved into the hillside, and pointed to a picnic spot, above where the river pooled above the falls. Tiny ripples showed a deceptively strong current. "It looks exactly the same."

"You've not come out here since you've been back?"

Lilah shook her head. "Nana didn't want me to. Said it was dangerous. Like a good girl, I tried to listen."

"It's good they closed the diner today." Jake spread out the polka dot quilt on bare ground where she directed.

Lilah squished her bare toes into the muddy earth. "Everyone's dropping over to West Plains, to see him there." She stopped on a broad patch of grass above the dock, and then settled herself down on the quilt along with the wicker basket. Jake cast the lines where she directed while she checked Eden's latest message. No change.

The family dock sagged from lack of use; the boards Papaw hammered together, now weathered gray and warped. The landing lay just above the rapid falls in the pool of rippling water.

She spied shadows of unattainable bass and

rainbow trout that swam slow circles in the deep swimming hole, away from the murk of reeds and algae; this secret cove on the hidden bank was the family fishing hole. The best place to catch the limit in record time. He'd fed the masses from this spot. Gifted everyone up and down the river with all the rainbow trout and small mouth bass that they could eat.

The dusty silver of Papaw's small, upside down skiff remained chained to an enormous oak tree trunk, the motor gone, the jagged edge of a paddle peeked from underneath. Lilah couldn't remember the last time anyone had used the boat.

Fizzy soda tickled her throat. She traced a quilted white circle with her fingertip, thoughts drifting to when Nana gave her and Eden the fabric scraps to make it in a futile attempt to teach her twin granddaughters the art of quilting. Laughingly, they'd all three shoved it in the closet, pronouncing the "snowball quilt" the ugliest coverlet in history. "Life isn't always beautiful."

"True." Jake spun the reel to his satisfaction, jammed a y-stick in the mud, and laid the rod between the forks. Sitting beside her, he trained his gaze on the rocky cliffs above. "River house, huh?"

"Nana only agreed because it was too high to wash out in a flood."

Not more than a singlewide trailer, it perched on a sheer cliff, the rockiest stretch of riverfront property from here to Memphis. Nothing grew here but stubborn weeds and ancient oaks with lichen covered trunks. Red rocks burst from the pebble covered landscape, crushed under years of truck tires and bicycle treads.

The train tracks glinted immediately behind the

shanty, too close for Nana's comfort. Each town had their stories of children stuck between railroad ties, or struck by locomotives, losing limbs, or worse, their lives. Those stories never stopped Lilah and Eden from sneaking out and laying pennies on the rails, leaning an ear to the vibrating rail to listen for the next train to smash the coins into thin bits of copper. The thrill of the danger, the power of the locomotive pulling the cars, clackety-clacking, past their quiet lives into places they merely dreamed of visiting some day.

If Nana knew the truth, she'd have sold the place long ago, rather than merely forbid them to go near the shack, so close to the dangerous tracks.

Lilah's palms suddenly itched to see if her emergency runaway supplies remained under the shack. Something no one knew about. Not even Eden.

"What do you know about your father?" Jake's innocent question dug a deep groove in her heart.

Lilah pulled in her knees. "He was just a kid, barely eighteen. I don't even know his name. They never told me."

Jake tugged the line, checking the float for resistance. "Why not?"

"Nana always said he was no good. Just biology, anyway. Rebecca is, for all practical purposes, good or bad, my mama. Though I don't suspect Nana ever saw it that way."

"It takes more than birth to make a mother." Jake settled back and took her by the hand, brushing his thumb a slow circle across her palm.

Waterfalls of sensation erupted at his touch. She tilted her head down, studying his face through the curtain of her hair. The fullness of his mouth, the concern in his bottle-green eyes, to the hard line of his jaw at his obvious disapproval of what her grandmother had considered what was best for her.

"Do we need to talk about them?" She rubbed her arms, skin dappled and warmed by sunlight raining through the oak leaves. "Can't we just fish?"

He glanced to the silent rods, slanted a grin, and edged closer still. "Apparently not."

"What else did you have in mind, Pastor Gibb?" Lilah blinked, brows raised.

"Fine time to start calling me pastor." His laughter ricocheted off the rock steps. He shifted toward her with full, smiling lips, and touched hers with the softest of kisses.

Every cell in her body focused on the sweetness, the subtle charge of heat, longing, wrapped in the embrace of a man intent on understanding her. Something no one else in the world had ever bothered to do.

As if on cue, the fish started to bite, interrupting any chance of a romantic interlude. Two hours later, with the time to relieve Eden of her duties weighing on his mind, Jake heaved the tackle, rods, and cooler of filleted fish in the truck bed. A stringer full, just as Papaw promised.

"Hot." Jake shook the near-empty water bottle. "Fill this up?"

"Here." Lilah unscrewed the cap, stepped to the hose bib by the boxy river house. Paint peeled off the sagging front porch, under which no less than twenty litters of kittens had been born to this world.

Water gushed. Filled, she handed it to him, then filled another, giving a peek through a gap in the under-house latticework. Choked with weeds, nurtured from the slow drip of a water spigot. Life found a way, even in the harsh, rocky hills of the Ozarks.

Her ears perked at the slight sound beyond that of rushing water. High pitched, sporadic. Then, silent.

"Ready?" Jake slammed the truck gate.

Cotton candy clouds spun overhead in the painfully blue, late-afternoon sky.

"Just a second." She tilted her head, listening, then ducked down to the hole of the fading lattice, and spied under the porch. "I think there's something under there."

Jake knelt and brushed back his tumble of bangs. "Too dark to see. Got a flashlight in the glove box."

But she'd already wriggled her shoulders and torso underneath by the time he returned. Cobwebs, dust, and something else, something familiar. "Hello?"

"Lilah!" Jake tugged her ankle. "Should you really be under there?"

She saw the old box, a wood crate with a dark green lining. She had to stretch but managed to drag a corner. The mewing grew louder. "Kittens! Look."

Commando crawling, she backwards-dragged the box of skinny, scrawny creatures out into the waning daylight. One suckled the tip of her finger, its gray eyes blinked up at her.

"Better check that we got them all." She took the flashlight and headed back under the porch.

"What about their mother?" Jake frowned at the malnourished kittens she'd shoved at his midsection.

"Abandoned them, probably." Her heartbeat kicked up a notch, thinking on how many litters of kittens didn't make it. Instantly, she was back to river girl again, fishing until dark, presenting her grandmother with lost dogs, stray cats, even injured birds. Each one, taken in, loved, and brought back to good health by Nana's subtle grace. How much about this place had she forgotten, chosen to ignore by blocking with bad memories?

"Great." Jake snorted. "We're going home with trout and a box of cats."

Back under the porch, the beam of light aimed at dark corners, light overtaking gloom. Pipes, dust, block stacked to level the floor above. No animals. Nothing. Except...She angled her beam to the propane tank, the gas line attached to it.

That was new. Her heart jogged. "Someone's been here."

Jake's reply was muffled as she disappeared back underneath the porch, headed to the tank, and spun it closer to her.

She frowned at the label. Milton's Gas 'n' Go.

Dragging herself back out, Lilah hoofed it to the front door. The knob turned easily in her hand, lock broken. "Squatters."

"Wait." Jake returned from the truck, cats properly stored. "You can't just go barreling inside. What if..."

"It's my house—my family's, anyway. Hello?" She pushed her way inside, anger swelling in her blood. "Anyone here?"

Darkness pressed against the threadbare, fully drawn curtains.

Jake halted her forward attack, his hand firmly on her shoulder. He shoved past, voice authoritative. "Me, first."

She followed as he swept room to room, mimicking what he'd probably seen on cop shows.

The counters were swiped clean of dust. Furniture, undraped of the white sheets. A dog-eared, weeks old

*People* magazine rested on the coffee table. In the kitchen, a pan, plate, and dishes, washed clean and dried, lined the dish rack.

Jake returned from the small bedroom, hand in his hip pocket. "Someone's staying out here."

"They're trespassing!" she spat. "We'll go tell the sheriff."

"Now, wait." He took her by the wrist. "They're not hurting anything. In fact, it looks like they're taking good care of the place. Maybe they'll listen to reason."

"Jake!"

"Let me handle this, will you? You've got other things to worry about."

He edged her back to the truck.

They could be anyone, growing pot or cooking up worse, using the place she remembered the most joyous for heaven knew what purpose.

"Think about it. Your papaw told us to come out here. Maybe this is the reason."

Jake's sincerity dispelled all the fight from her heart. Just like Papaw, to give all strays shelter. "Fine." She sat with a thump and looked over at the mewing kittens. She stroked the tiny, yawning orange tabby's back, it stretched tiny claws into cardboard. "I'll get these guys settled and go back to the hospital. You get until tomorrow to figure out what's going on here, and put a stop to it. Any longer, I'm calling the cops."

# 40

Eden pocketed her mobile, no news to offer Lilah. "What the heck's she doing out at the old river place, anyway?" At her right, Papaw's monitors beeped and hummed. The numbers didn't mean anything to her, only something for the nurses to frown at, then jot down on Papaw's chart.

Where was Luke? He'd know...if he'd speak to her. He'd never answered her message. Not even a text back. Nothing. Here, in her hour of need, Eden was completely alone.

"If Nana knew where she was, she'd tan Lilah's hide." Eden straightened the thin white blankets over her grandfather's frail form. "She's always hated that house."

The *whiz-shush* of the leg balloons squeezed and released, keeping blood clots from forming, they said. Some sort of medieval torture device.

She sniffed, swiped and smoothed over the covers yet again.

Still and sleeping, her grandfather snored with his mouth slack like a child in deep slumber, yet there was nothing childlike in that husk of a body he clung to. Like that river house.

"You loved that river place, though." Eden crossed her arms, fingernails clacking. "Was it the little dock we worked so hard on? Or happy memories, maybe? Why'd you keep it, Papaw?"

But, she knew the answer.

The river was everything to him. Eighty-some-odd years of fishing those waters, he knew them better than anyone. Its moods. Its dangers. Its blessings. The river house was testament to a time before, filled with hand me downs and cast offs. He'd threatened, many a time, to go out there and cool off when Nana had one of her tirades. "Nothing like the river to cure all ills," he'd said, whether it was running beyond the house, or under the cliffs, he'd told her once while they'd watched the sun set over the falls, amber light behind misty oak and boulder dotted hillsides. They'd watched the cows on the opposite bank drink from the quiet spot, just beyond the little island where she and Lilah spent so many happy summer days as children. Where they'd sneaked off to as teenagers when they wanted to be alone.

His words echoed in her mind as she ran a thumb over his calloused hand.

"God gave us this place to remind us how beautiful life could be, to remember where we came from, how little we really need to survive, and how much we all need each other."

"I need you, P-papaw." She wiped her tear-damp cheek with her shoulder. "I'm no good at being alone. How many times've you told me that?"

A nurse padded by in the hall without pausing.

"Can you hear me?" Eden leaned in close, whispered, chills floating over her arms. "Do you even know I'm here?"

What was a man so bent on meeting his Maker doing clinging to this world? She dared, for the first time, to ask the question that haunted her for months. What if the Alzheimer's robbed that peace that passes understanding from Papaw, along with everything else? A spear of worry pierced her heart. Her mouth had gone dry as she knit her fingers through her grandfather's, pressed her forehead to his flesh.

Lord, if you're listening, he loves you. He just might not remember...

She blinked up at Papaw's rattling breath. Still nothing.

Her throat clutched and she rubbed it. So hard to watch the man who'd been strong enough to lift timbers, build barns, set fences, and wrangle cattle one step from six feet under. Eden's shoulders did a shimmy-shake with the notion. Her fingers brushed that golden cross so often buried in Marty's ring. Papaw gave it to her the day they'd full dunked her and Lilah in the spring. Full of the spirit, dripping, all of ten years old, and loving every minute of it.

A knock at the door. She glanced up, startled to see Luke's tall blond form leaning against the frame.

"Hey." Eden backhanded the corners of her leaky eyes. "Wondered where you'd gone off to."

"Busy night." He rubbed his jaw. "Just came in on a stork run and wanted to check on that accident victim."

"Prayer chain's been texting about it all day. The girl with Andy?" Eden's curiosity got the better of her. "They know who she is yet?"

"Someone recognized her from the carnival. It's Maya Randall, the carnival owner's daughter. Nurses called him. He laid into Andy right good. Not a pretty picture from what I hear."

Her mind spun. She'd seen the sassy looking teen, and the way the town boys watched her walk. Teenagers did what the teenagers will do.

"Here we all thought Charla and Andy were one step from the altar."

Luke's silence spoke volumes. At last, he cleared his throat. "They're kids, Eden. Not that it does that poor girl any good. It wasn't anyone's fault. A big rig came around the curve too fast...you know the story." He shook his head. "Folks said they hadn't seen an accident that bad since your mama's."

"Sweet Jesus..." Eden closed her eyes, saying a quick prayer for that poor girl. "She's what, all of sixteen?"

"About that. What a mess."

"Is she gonna be alright?" Eden's heart raced as she grabbed out her cellphone, quick texted the prayer chain into action. "We need to call. We need to pray for her. Maya?" She squeezed her eyes shut, heart surging with her fervent prayer. *Lord, save Maya.*

Luke shrugged. "She's in surgery. They're taking her spleen. I don't know much else." He shifted his weight, one foot, then the other, seemingly undecided about whether to go or stay. "Everything else all right?"

"I took Nana home hours ago, and the nurses just come and go." She sniffed. "Can you tell me what's going on?"

Papaw stirred, muttered under his breath.

"I've asked some questions." Luke stepped into the room, looking like a skittish colt rather than a uniformed paramedic. "Not many answers to be had. Even if he does wake from this, he'll be—well..."

Papaw's frail arm lifted, pointed to the ceiling tiles, and fell back to his side, limp.

"But, he does that." She pointed at Papaw's restless slumber. "He tries to talk. He reaches."

"It's reflexes, from what I know."

"They've got all that danged stuff all over him. What if he wants to tell me something..."

"Even if he did, it wouldn't make any sense." Luke wiped a hand over his face, and then met her gaze. "They've told your grandmother. She's coming back in the morning. They've called in hospice. To let nature run its course."

"Wh-what?" Eden choked, mouth desert-dry.

Luke hitched his belt, fiddled with the knobs on his walkie.

"Don't people just die? Like in the movies?" Eden pushed out of the chair, anger surging at her breast, pointing at her grandfather. "What kind of a way to go is this?"

He laid his palms on her shoulders. She wanted to pound at him. Scream and cry. Instead, she allowed him to anchor her in this storm.

Warmth radiated at his touch, from shoulders to her core, where she'd been so frozen. Eden leaned her full weight against him and let him prop her up. Her rock. Guilt surged through her with an oily wave at all she'd done to him, all she'd said. How could Luke have possibly forgiven her? How could he still want her?

His hands slid around to her back, holding her close, her tether, lest she float off into the blackness of despair. "Eden, it's his time." His words broke the spell.

She shoved at him. "N-no. Don't you say it."

"Someone has to." He clung tight, his words floating through her hair, soothing through her tears. "Your Papaw's lived. He's loved. He knows where he's going. Isn't that enough in this life?"

"What's gonna happen?" She looked up through a wave of tears, her breath hiccupping, grief surged, rocked her shoulders. "What happens next?"

Luke just shook his head, but made no move to step away.

Together, they watched the machines and prayed.

# 41

Jake pulled into Milton's Gas 'n' Go off the state route into town. Milton, he supposed, was the man whose boots stuck out from under an old seventies station wagon, spouting "dag-nabbits" and "cotton-pickin-foreign-cars!" Jake cleared his throat, bringing the mechanic to pause.

"Kin I help ya?" The man rolled the low cart out from under the car. A greasy orange shirt with straining buttons covered the mechanic's paunch-belly.

Tucking hands into back pockets, Jake quick explained his reason for being there. As he spoke, Milton's face ran the gamut of emotions. He and Lilah were on to something.

"Yeah, I still deliver out there, got lotta folks at Taylor's place." Milton stood with an *oomph* of breath. "No gas, you know, not on that rocky top. Danged hard to get to in the winter time. That's why he comes out this-away. Picks up tanks hisself."

"Who?" Jake attempted to spy over Milton's stooped shoulder as the man smeared greasy fingers across yellow bills of sale.

"That carnival feller. The one who does the glass figures. Here it is." He rattled the fingerprint covered page for emphasis. "Sam Guthrie."

~*~

Lilah tromped up the hill having left the box of kittens safely under Dr. Underson's watchful care. The tabby had yowled at her, as if she were its mama. It tugged her soul to walk back out of that swinging door, even as the vet tech cooed over the warm, wiggly bodies. She wasn't any good with living things. The last thing that tiny life needed was her to watch over it.

Still, she wondered. Maybe she would find a place of her own, somewhere within throwing distance of Eden's house. They needed space before they killed one another. Another sign of God's cosmic sense of humor, she supposed: The need to be near the ones who've known you forever and the undeniable notion that you'll be driven slowly mad the longer you stay together. She trudged to her driveway with a glance to the chapel. Jake's beat up old truck was tucked neatly in its carport.

Pastor Jake Gibb.

Or was it Jacob Gibson? As if that even mattered anymore. No sad stories. He was the man who'd stolen her heart. The first one who'd ever done the job proper. All it took was a touch here, a look there, and a handful of kisses that shot her over the moon. Guilt doused her joy. Should she be so happy when Papaw was dying? When Eden had been laid so low by her pitiful mistakes?

*Love is all that matters...*

The still voice spoke to her. Cured her of the mire she'd dragged with her for so long.

Love.

She loved Jake. Hand hesitating over the mailbox lid, she glanced back over her shoulder toward Jake's place. At that moment, she couldn't wait to tell him.

A hollow sound emanated from the pastor's

apartment. Was that Jake singing? She paused to listen. His living room windows flung wide, the shower water rushing, she could hear his baritone rough-belting out an off-key Third Day song.

Yep. She'd fallen for a pastor who sang in the shower. A furious blush heated as she spun back toward Eden's bungalow. Laugh bubbling out, even as the rich tones of his gravelly voice melted her soul. So far removed was Jake from her ex. Night and day. She slow-strolled down Eden's walkway, between the fragrant geraniums and begonias, she headed to the front porch. A hand-painted sign requested shoes be left at the door. Her sister made a nice little life for herself here, quaint, country, in the shadow of their grandparent's home.

Eden never once asked her for rent, or grocery money, or anything else for that matter. She'd merely taken in her wayward twin, tucked her under her stable wing, and asked nothing at all. Neither, for that matter, had Nana. Almost as if everyone in the whole blasted town expected her to come back with her tail between her legs.

Just the mere hint of judgment for her wrong choices, through the telling of her personal drama with the prayer chain. Gossipers. That's all they were.

Her cell chirped in her pocket, and Lilah palmed it, spying Eden's prayer partners' names on the quick-sent list. Lilah's heart seized. Papaw?

*Pray healing for Maya Randall. Accident. In surgery.* Eden's text read. Her prayer chain, activated.

Guilt surged. "Oh, no…"

Texts and prayers blooped back.

One after another, Eden's friends and prayer warriors chimed in, lifting up the stranger in words and prayers. No one asked for more information, just charged in, prayers blazing.

*Healing!*

*God's grace to all who love her.*

"We're in heaven...heaven...woah..." Jake's voice crooned with the radio, gravelly, on key from across the street.

She didn't want anyone going to heaven today. Not right now...

Lilah sank to her knees there amid the waxy, red begonias, felt their damp petals, pollen stained like blood. His creation. Just like she was. Just like Maya.

*Lord, save Maya.* Lilah prayed. She added it to the reply text, for good measure, pressing send.

Responses back came fast, charging with encouragement.

*Welcome back, Lilah! Rita*

*Missed ya sister. <3 Eden*

And so many more...she scrolled through the continuous stream of replies. So, this was Eden's prayer chain she'd railed against? Some sort of crazy extended family. The church elders, the few remaining families she'd known since birth, the fellow storeowners who knew their plight. Not an invasion of privacy, or gossip, but honest, sincere hopes that the power of their prayer would be magnified by sharing. Now, the sweet incense of their prayers lifted up for Maya. For Papaw. For Nana. For all of them.

A wash of remorse swept head to toe. What must they have prayed while she made the biggest mistake of her young life? Hand to ponytail holder, she shook her hair free and sat on the Astroturf front steps, unlacing her tennis shoes and calling Eden for the scoop on Maya. This time, they prayed together over the phone.

"Jake should know. Maybe he can offer comfort to her father." Eden said.

"Right. Not sure Randall is the kind who wants a pastor's assistance." Lilah sighed, but she hurried across the street to paste a note on Jake's door, anyway. Maybe he would try and offer support to the carnival master after all.

He'd moved on to a secular song. Just like a preacher, only seeing the best in people. She'd seen enough of the other side to know the world wasn't as rosy as all that. Whether blind or hopeful, with Eden's insistence, she'd stay away from the hospital until morning. She intended on doing some checking of her own. Lilah slipped out the slim yellow pages, letting her fingers do the walking all the way to Propane. A phone call to Milton's Gas 'n' Go couldn't hurt.

After all, his wife already was praising Jesus by text that Lilah was back in the fold.

# 42

Randall flexed his raw knuckles as he walked past the roar of the Mammoth waterfall. Measured steps along that shoulder-wide bridge toward town. The still, languid lake on his left was at odds with the endless, cascading curtain of water on his right just like the cool, practiced expression he wore concealed the rage within. Each crunch of concrete under his shoes brought him closer to his destiny. Maya made her choice, but he'd allowed this to happen. Let the preacher and his lady talk him into opening a door that should have stayed shut. Sealed. He'd made his bed. Time to lie in it.

Mist churned from below, dampening his face, mingling with tears that now obscured his vision. His shadow chased him as he went, lengthened from the last light of day.

The fickle sun dipped below the tree line, like raging fire.

Fool. After years of being in charge, of calling the crowds, hawking the midway, he'd at last been the biggest mark of all.

They'd sat in his trailer, laid out the plan, and all he could think was the fools would come, spend their money, take home their trinkets, and leave their paychecks. Instead, all they'd done was destroy his life. Destroyed everything that mattered.

Maya.

Because of that church. The pastor who brought the audacity of belief to his little girl, had made her think of something other than what he'd given her. The white church was a beacon on the hill, ever since his return from the hospital, across Riverview Drive.

Why had he listened to them? Randall didn't listen to fools or suckers. He swindled them, got his way, and earned his coin from their pitiable dreams.

Either way, she was just a kid. And they were responsible for laying his daughter so near death. That was all he needed to know.

He adjusted the revolver, heavy in his belt, an emptiness rattling in his heart. Maya was in surgery. His only proof that possibly something bigger than himself and his dealings existed, or mattered— could've died. May still. Because of the boy. Maya clung to life by a thread while the boy who'd caused the accident sat in shock, mere bruises and butterfly band-aids over his mild injuries.

"Sorry," the boy, Andy, had muttered while the trauma room doctors worked, his daughter's blood smearing the fronts of their yellow paper robes. So apologetic. He was sorry he'd driven off the road. The rig had startled him. More than likely distracted by Maya's curves, her flashing eyes, or her rich flame-red hair. The boy must have taken his eyes off the road. Perhaps he'd been blinded by her persuasive smile, her full lips, amber eyes, or her velvet voice.

The boy wasn't responsible.

It was the preacher.

He flipped open the thirty-eight special, eyed the full chamber. Snapped the weapon shut, the bright lights streaming through the checker-curtained windowpanes. His steps carried him along the river's edge almost of their own volition. Randall stuck the pistol behind his shirttail, hiking up the hill the rest of the way. It wasn't the first time he'd pull the trigger, but surely, it would be the last.

Time to meet the devil on his terms. His way.

# 43

Lilah stared at her grandparents' home. The red light burned in the kitchen window. Who was Nana shining it for tonight?

The girl who'd crashed on the same curve as Rebecca?

Herself?

Papaw?

The weight of this secret she'd stumbled upon spelled out by the gas company, and now the bank. No wonder they hadn't wanted her to go there. The thought of her grandparents' deception plunged into her soul as she stormed out into the orange light of dusk, batting her way under the weeping limbs of the willow. How could they have sold her sacred spot? The need for answers propelled her up the hill.

The breeze gusted, the arms of the oaks above rattled and waved as if in warning against her growing tirade. She pounded steps up to the screened-in porch, tugged to open, but the door remained. Locked. Lilah knocked a furious beat.

Nana's zipper-robed form outlined against the blue-green of the television flickering behind her, thin scowl quickly replaced itself with worry. "Where's Eden?"

"Hospital, I guess." Lilah shifted her weight, one bare foot to the other. "Can I come in?"

Her grandmother stepped back and led Lilah into

the room where a highball glass at the side table declared it was time for game shows and cocktails. She settled herself into one of the two thrones of retirement. The other sat empty. On the table in between, Papaw's black glasses rested on top of an unread, folded newspaper. For a moment, Lilah could almost believe he'd trot in and demand that she change the station to the game.

"Have a seat."

A lump thickened in Lilah's throat as she settled on the velvet settee. She forced her full attention on Nana, wasting no time with pleasantries. "I've been to the river house."

"Why?" Nana dialed down the volume, and then tossed the remote onto the table. Papaw's glasses skittered off their perch. "Showing that pastor your old stomping grounds?"

"Papaw told me to go." Lilah rubbed her crumpled forehead, gathering composure before she met that icicle gaze again. "He said the fish were biting."

"He always says that." Nana pressed her trembling lips together.

On the television, someone bet five hundred dollars on a question of what foods start with the letter Q.

"What is a quince?" Nana answered out of habit, turned back to Lilah. "He loves this show. Maybe Eden has it on for him at the hospital."

"Maybe." At last, Lilah cast the question making her heart a sinker-weight. "Why would Papaw have sold the river house to that carnival worker, Mr. Guthrie?"

"Carnival worker?" Nana blinked up, adjusted her

wire frame glasses. "How do you know about him?"

"He came by the kitchen. He makes glass figurines."

Nana stiff-armed herself up out of the chair. It rocked in her wake as she stepped to the window, past the bookcase shrine of pictures of Rebecca, to look out on the river, the architectural focal point of the room. In the growing twilight, a heron dipped, settled on the falls to fish. "You've met him? This Guthrie character?"

"A couple of times." Lilah leaned forward, elbows on her knees, watching the array of emotions skitter across her grandmother's face. "Who is he? How do you know him?"

Nana sipped, and then set down, pushed aside her ice cube glass. "Your Papaw is the most gracious, asinine man I've ever known. A heart of gold and head full of rocks. Comes through every year, driving that big ole rig..."

"He gave me a figurine. I watched him make it. Very talented, really."

"Talented, but a drunk." Nana's nostrils flared. "A drunk, a heathen, and a murderer. He was driving that night. Thirty years ago. On the curve that killed your mother."

"The night we were born?" Lilah sat back, rocked. It explained the man's sorrowful gaze, his inability to look her in the eye. Her heart stabbed with half-formed questions. "Why would Papaw sell our special place, our favorite...to..."

"To show God's love. Forgiveness. I'm not that gracious." She jangled ice. Set the cup down before speaking again. "What did he make for you?"

Lilah joined her at the window, eyes on the river. "A heron. Just like your big bird out there."

They watched the long-legged creature land, saunter across the rocks to the tumbled oak to the best fishing hole at this bend. "Is that how Papaw always knew where to fish? He watched the birds?"

"Watches, you mean." Nana smiled, gaze fixed on the heron, poised, waiting for a fish to swim near enough for that lightning fast swoop. "He watches them."

"We need to bring him home, Nana."

Tears spilled from Nana's eyes as she clutched Lilah's hand. Dry, bony, thin, yet her slight grandmother overflowed with inner strength though her voice cracked. "You're right, of c-course. Tomorrow. We'll bring him home tomorrow."

"I'll call Eden and Luke. We'll make all the arrangements." Lilah wrapped Nana into her embrace. "We'll take care of everything."

"I suppose you should call your Pastor Gibb, too." Nana's head weighed heavy on Lilah's shoulder. "Seeing how he's all we've got."

# 44

Lightning bugs did their winking dance around the great oaks as Lilah backed her red convertible from Eden's carport. It growled down Riverview Drive.

Once upon a time, she'd chased after them, leapt and caught their fragile bodies with determined hands, placed them in jars to watch them glow. Now, there was no time to waste in confronting the man responsible for her mother's death.

She pulled into the carnival's now empty dirt lot in a wave of dust. The tromped field marked the grounds, now scarred by crisscrossed scars of parked cars and tramping feet. Ghostly memories thronged the empty midway; the ridiculous image of Jake, shouldering the giant panda she'd won on his dare, the molten, liquid glass that Guthrie stretched and pulled into her heron.

*I stared into the face of my mother's killer, and never knew. Lord, I even fed the man.*

Fingernails dug into her palms as she headed toward the dismantled glass booth. His big rig idled as he backed up to hitch itself to the wagon, a high, thin beep warning its intentions.

"Hey, there!" Lilah waved her arms, shouting to his rearview mirror.

The figure inside balked. Hesitated. Then the diesel chug-rattled to a halt. Guthrie exited with deliberate steps, paused in front of her. "Evenin', ma'am."

"Don't ma'am me. I know who you are. I—"

He nodded. "I thought you might."

Pulling work gloves from his hands, he spoke in low tones as he reached into his back pocket. "You look just like her, you know."

Lilah took a step back, looked left, right. The park was empty. All other carnies seemed to have evaporated in the dimming light. "Like who?"

"Your mama." He opened his dingy wallet to reveal a tattered picture. The same picture that Papaw and Nana had perched on their Rebecca shrine by the river view window.

"Where'd you get that?" A cold rush of adrenaline flowed from her neck to fingertips.

Guthrie blinked. "I thought that's why you were here..."

"You killed her. That's why I'm here." Fists clenched, unclenched. "You were driving the curve the night she died."

He stared at his shoes, the picture floated out of his fingers, settled like a leaf by the steel toe of his boot where she snatched it up.

"She's dead cuz of me. This...this is my penance for what I done."

"And my Papaw let you live in our house. He sold you the property. Why?"

The man went hunch shouldered. "He didn't sell it to me. It were a gift."

The very notion slammed into her and stole her breath. "When?"

"A few years back. I come to town. We had a long talk before he..." Chin dipping, he turned toward the last bit of light from the setting sun. "Well, before."

"I can't hear this. I don't understand it and I

can't...you, him..." Lila smoothed dust off the picture, kept it as she stormed back toward her vehicle.

Forgiveness like that made no sense. Was Papaw trying to prove his place in heaven by loving his enemy?

A glance over her shoulder proved the man didn't follow. She'd shamed him. That was good. She had no time for cowards, fools, or thieves. He'd stolen everything from her that was precious.

"Delilah Dale!" he called to her back.

She skidded to a stall, hand out for the door handle. Turning, she walked toward him with slow hesitant steps. Heart jack-hammering, she stared down the man who'd murdered her mother. "How do you know my real name?"

~*~

Jake stepped, hair dripping from the shower, a blue towel hitched around his hips.

The message light on his phone blinked angry red, but for once, he needed to shelve everything. Focus on what really mattered. Lilah. How could he tell her what he'd learned? For now, he'd opted not to do anything. To wait. To keep the knowledge hidden. *A truth unspoken is by definition a lie.* Isn't that what he'd said to Margaret right before he'd ended their marriage? Isn't that what he was doing now?

Steam wiped from the mirror, he reviewed the crags in his face, and stared down his reflection. Could he live with himself knowing what he discovered, and not sharing with Lilah?

She didn't hesitate to save those abandoned kittens. A girl who cared so much about living creatures surely would be more forgiving of someone in need squatting in the river house. But, the history behind the man who'd changed the course of her life forever? Could he expect her to forgive that? Could he?

He knew the story of the curving road, the car driving too fast around a hairpin turn. But the driver of the rig, ultimately responsible for the crash that killed her mother, had chosen to climb inside a bottle of alcohol. Jake knew Guthrie would never find redemption in the liquid. Numbness and escape? Maybe. Redemption and forgiveness?

Never.

Her grandfather, in the ultimate example of Christian charity, invited a murderer into their world. Allowed him to live on his property. Now, in Earl Dale's infirm state, Jake stood poised on blowing the whole thing wide open.

For Lilah.

Her name, the very thought of her, clutched his heart. She'd entwined herself to him, all of him, mind, body, and soul. A love like he'd never experienced in this world. A soul-mate love, like Margaret longed for, as she claimed they shared to anyone within earshot. Even while both of them knew she lied.

He owed it to Lilah to make good on his promise to her, but doing so could destroy the very foundation on which she'd been raised.

Dressing quickly in jeans and running shoes, he hurried from the house, not until standing at his truck did the thought hit him. Didn't lock the door, or even think about it. What's more? It didn't even worry him in the slightest. Maybe Mammoth would be home for him, after all.

Jake didn't notice the shadow until it was almost

too late. "Wha—?"

A slamming fist caught him in the jaw, spun him around.

Hands up deflected his attacker. He flinched at the sight of the gun and the familiar hand that raised it. The butt-end slammed his neck, hard, and the world went dark.

~*~

He woke with a jabbing pain to his jaw, ear, and head. Jake struggled to regain his focus. Ribbons of light played through heavy eyelids as ruby, amethyst, emerald, sapphire, gold, burned his wavering vision. He worked the hinge of his aching jaw from Randall's right hook. Not broken. *Thank you, God.*

Right shoulder, screaming, throbbing, damp. Was that blood? Jake pulled himself off the carpeted floor, in the thin, yet vibrant pool streaming through the church's stained glass window. He stared at the shape of his Savior, shepherd's crook in hand; a lost sheep found and tucked in the safety of His arm.

"Welcome back, Pastor Gibb." The towering, thin form of the carnival master, Randall, stepped into full view. "Wondering if you'd come around before dark."

Jake sat up, rubbed the bruise on his shoulder. "Why'd you jump me?"

"Why do you think?" Randall held a hand out to the downed pastor. "It was your idea to have the Revival on our grounds. You introduced her to that boy. If she dies, what does it all mean?"

So, the spider-like carnival master doled out a father's anger, mixed with grief? But why? The puzzle pieces jarred and jumbled in his rattled head, but the ache in his lower back left him in need of assistance, even of this potential enemy. Hoisted up, he stared at the man, obviously stronger than his years would suggest, and hobbled to the front pew. "Thanks."

Randall stood with his back to Jake, just underneath the cracked stained glass window. "I've read the Bible, cover to cover a couple of times. Bigger fan of the Old Testament than the New."

"Is that right?" Jake rubbed his jaw, now down to a dull ache.

"Good stories. Seems more real to life, if you ask me." The vein at Randall's temple bulged as he clenched his jaw. Steeped in shadow, Randall's anger emanated from him in a wave. "There's lust, deception, scandal, murder—"

"Redemption, salvation, hope." Jake sized up the white haired man across from him. The empty chapel. Wasn't tonight the deacons' weekly meeting? Or the evening the Ladies Guild changed centerpieces? He winced at a fingertip touch to his swollen jaw. "I've read it, too."

"That's the trouble with this corner of the world." Randall turned his back on the window, away from the steady gaze of Jesus. He focused the full force of his icicle gaze on Jake. "Get your nose out of that book and look at what's happening to the world around you. Everyone's high and mighty on Sunday, but by Saturday night, they'll be darkening my door again. Here, or in some other town."

"Maybe." Jake shifted on the hard wooden seat. "But I don't think that's why you're here."

"No." Randall sat heavily next to him, gaze locked on the sharp edge where rug met altar, not looking him in the eye. "Maya survived the surgery, but...the doctor took her spleen. She's in ICU. All those tubes, monitors. They call it a medically induced coma." Randall's eyes smoldered to charcoal pinpoints. "She had her reasons for going off with that boy. He had his for taking her." Randall reached round to scratch his back and returned both hands to his lap, weighted by a shining .38. "Do you think she'll be forgiven? If she dies in that hospital?"

Jake dry-swallowed, gaze glued to the polished nickel surface. "That's between her and her Savior, Mr. Randall."

"Her Savior." A sneer touched Randall's razor thin lips. He slow clicked the chamber one at a time. "I'm her father. No one knows her better. The girl's learned the trade, you see. She's a con artist, just like her old man."

Jake kept his gaze on the man's gloved fingers. The slow, deliberate turn of the cylinder and the sound it made, so loud in the hallowed sanctuary.

"What is it, son?" Randall lifted an elbow to the back of the bench. "You worried about this, here? I've a license to carry a weapon. I'll show you if you like."

"No need." Jake put his hands up, palms out. "I believe you."

"Not for this particular one, though." He proffered the weapon. Satin metal winked in the lights.

Jake's mouth went sandpaper dry. "Sorry?"

"Found this one behind the glass man's counter. He's packing it in, sold his rig, decided to stay. Ain't that a hoot?" An eerie smile touched his face as he angled the weapon. "So, I liberated this. Can't be too careful in our business. Never know when someone's gonna stab you in the back."

"Guthrie?" Jake blinked. His thoughts churned to

the trailer, the river, to Lilah.

"It's only the start of summer, and I've already lost my daughter to this town. Now, Guthrie seems intent to stay here, as well." Randall dipped his chin, his eyes remaining on Jake's blank face. "You know anything about that, Pastor?"

"No. I haven't seen him, not in a while."

"He came from these parts, you know." A subtle *snick-snick* as he cocked, then slow-released the firing pin back to a benign position. "Back near thirty years ago."

Jake's heart thudded, his gaze locked to the subtle play of Randall's long fingers on the polished weapon. On the thin leather gloves the man wore. No call to wear gloves like that on such a hot, summer day, his mind screamed. He sat stock-still and listened.

Randall continued, "Guthrie had an accident on that same stretch of road as my Maya."

"Lots of accidents out there." Jake cleared a tremble from his throat, searching for a way to get up, to move without the man leveling that weapon on him. His left hand searched blind, felt leather, and dragged the Bible onto his lap. Jake's prayer shot to the heavens. *Lord, help me find something to say to this man.* Following Lilah's method, Jake stared down at the words of the prophet Isaiah.

I will smite thine enemy.

Always Isaiah.

Just like Lilah said. Eyeing the pew, he gauged how many steps it'd take to lunge to the door as he spoke. "Many souls've been called up on that stretch of road."

"Called up?" Randall snorted a laugh, crossed one leg over the other, pistol dangling between two fingers.

"Kind of a pretty way to describe such a gruesome scene."

Jake moved to stand, but Randall grabbed his neck at the shoulder and gave him a solid, excruciating push down. "Stick around. I'm not through talking yet." He lifted the weapon again, this time, leaving it cocked and locked. He angled the short barrel of the pistol to the side of Jake's head.

"Our friend, Mr. Guthrie, thinks he's gone sober. He thinks he's gonna come back to Mammoth and stay. That this town will forgive him for the sins of his past. Ain't that the limit? The same town that ran him out on a rail."

"Crazier things have happened." Jake glanced to the door, then back to the black hole of the weapon and the man who threatened to end his stay in this world. No chance he'd miss from this range.

"They'll find you, here with his weapon. Then, they'll trace the bullet back to a shallow grave in Heber." Randall's eyes went crazy. "Anonymous tips are unique weapons. All Guthrie remembers is, he's the one done the digging," Randall continued. "My greatest con? Convincing that poor sap he's a murderer, just like I did on the night his wife died, all those years ago."

"Rebecca Dale." At once, Jake stopped. Listened. Randall had his full attention.

"Driving her to the hospital. Big rig crashed into that little car. He never forgave himself for her death, abandoned his babies for a bottle of his own. Spent his life on the road with me and mine."

Jake clutched the heavy Bible, heart racing. He'd talked down drug addicts, alcoholics, even helped a man from swallowing a fist full of pills. He'd never once tried to save himself. Not like this. Never like this, as Randall leaned forward, so obviously enjoying the unveiling of another man's sins.

"There's no redemption out there for us. God's not gonna sweep in and save you, me, or anybody else, for that matter."

"Maybe not." Jake's head ached, his shoulder throbbed, he'd have to get his wits together and make a break for it. His only chance. God helps those who help themselves, Jake. "But, I trust in Him." Jake's words gathered strength as he wagged the heavy, leather-bound book. "I trust His word. What do you trust, Mr. Randall? What do you believe in?"

"This." Randall pulled the trigger.

The chapel echoed with the boom.

The heavy book pitched up and out of Jake's hands as the projectile slammed through the pages. Paper exploded with the force, drifted around him like confetti as bullet and Bible crashed into the stained glass window.

The window crumbled, collapsed, and ribbons of lead and colored glass rained upon them.

Jake lunged, tackled, and plowed his attacker into the altar. The communion table overturned, further smashing the wasted work of art. Jake balled his fists and pummeled a boxer-worthy right-left combo into the carnival man's side and chin.

Randall crawled to the window frame, tilted his bleeding nose back, groping blind for his pistol.

Jake saw it under the pages of the pulverized Bible and lunged to scoop up both. Power from both surged through his hands.

Outside, the river ran. Twilight sky spilled with crystal stars. Motion lights whirred on in a blinding flash.

Randall stood amid the wreckage, glass dust in his hair, glittering on the shoulders of his clothes.

"Get going and I won't press charges." Jake gestured with a chin. "Unless you want to watch your daughter recovering from behind bars." Jake dumped the cylinder, allowing brass bullets to rain onto the floor. "And don't come back."

Jake watched until the man was out of sight, and then collapsed on the altar steps. No thoughtful prayer sprang to mind, just a jangle of "hallelujah" and "thanks be to God." His hands vibrated with nerves that only now showed themselves. He glanced to the front pew, the destroyed window, the confettied Bible, and wondered how he'd avoided getting blown to smithereens. His Savior. His Savior was right there for him.

"Jake!" Lilah's voice reached him before she raced through the courtyard. Her steps crunched over the broken stained glass. She knelt at his side, inspecting his wounds with careful fingers. "I heard a shot. Who did this?"

"Doesn't matter."

"Yes, it does!" Fire in her eyes, she turned the force of her fury on her pastor. "I've had it with this love thy neighbor nonsense bull. Sorry, Guthrie."

"No sorry needed here." Guthrie knelt at Jake's other side. "I'm afraid she's right in this case. Forgiveness can only do so much. Sometimes the law's gotta step in."

"It was Randall." A throbbing ache commenced in Jake's shoulder, head, and the raw meat of his knuckles from pummeling the carnival master. "He was going to kill me, frame you." He massaged the backs of his hands.

Guthrie wiped a broad hand on his stubble-covered jaw, shrugged under his jacket. "Some sins just ain't forgivable."

"He told me your story..." Jake winced as Lilah grabbed his hands and examined the cuts. "You're Lilah's father?"

Lilah merely nodded, her gaze hooked on Guthrie's empty, folded hands.

Head bowed, the glass man closed his eyes. "Heaven forgive me for driving that road so fast. The rain. The tires got away from me. I was fine, but Becca...the babies were comin'...I was a coward then...not much better now."

"If you loved her like you say you d-did..." Lilah's pain revealed in her trembling voice. "W-why didn't you stay?"

"I couldn't." He turned to his daughter, grief painting his features. "What could I tell you? After a few years, I tried to come back. To see you for myself. To hope the words would come." He shook his head as tears rolled from his welling eyes, and trailed through the valley of his cheeks. "You and Eden just got older, more beautiful. Just like your mama. When your Papaw got to ailin', your grandmother made no bones about having none of me. So, I just disappeared. Still use the river shack when I get back this way. Keeps Becca close."

"Lilah was ready to call the cops on you." Jake cautioned. One could almost see the wedge that kept this family apart.

"It's yours, and Eden's, too, a'course." He averted his gaze back to the door. "If'n you still want it, that is."

"Apparently, Papaw deeded it to him years ago." Lilah half-smiled at Jake. "He must have figured we'd make amends someday." The cellphone buzzed at her hip pocket. She flipped it open and stutter-sighed a long breath. "It's Eden. Be back in a minute."

"I'm ready to come back now. Rejoin the living." Guthrie watched her hurry to answer the call. "I always loved that river place. It's where Becca and I shared our life. Where she was so happy."

"Lilah, too." Jake said.

Guthrie directed a long, suddenly scrutinizing stare his way. "You love her, don't you, son?"

"That I do, sir." Jake dipped his attention to the ribbons of metal and glass. Could anything so broken ever be made right? "I love her with my whole heart, but I don't think she's ready to hear it yet."

The situation had turned suddenly off kilter, as he realized Guthrie now looked at Lilah with a father's eyes. "Well, that's alright, then." Guthrie turned back to the shadows from whence he came and glanced back over his shoulder. "Sorry about your window, there, Pastor."

"Me, too." Jake gazed out at the stars, an idea forming in his mind of how to mend three broken hearts. "Know anyone good with fixing glass?"

# 45

Naomi sat by the window, worried the locket on her chain, and stared at nothing. Back and forth, the grating of gold on gold made just enough melody to mask the whispers and long silences from the kitchen. Not enough to hide the beeps of the monitors now taking up residence in her parlor. And thankfully, not enough to cover the sound of Earl's raspy breathing.

Luke and Eden piled out of the ambulance as the hospice workers pulled in to find Lilah and Jake in final preparations in the living room, arranged as they'd discussed. Everything went according to plan.

She stood back and allowed her adult grandchildren to go about their business, attending to her husband as the bitter reality set in. They'd brought the man she'd loved since girlhood home to die. She barely recognized Earl inside that skeletal, withered frame on the hospital bed. Her mind refused to admit that this was the same cowboy who'd rode by on a cattle pony while she'd strummed a new tune on her guitar. The one who'd stood across from her at church and pressed his lips to hers when the preacher said "kiss the bride." The one who'd held her baby daughter, dipped a kiss to that fussy baby's cheek, and calmed her with a slow "shush."

The paramedic team rolled him inside on a gurney. Eyes closed and sunk with shadowed hollows beneath, he'd slow-blinked awake and looked at her as if he was seeing her for the first time, then, recognition washed his features. Earl Dale shot her a half-cocked grin and stole her heart for the millionth time. "Told you I'd be back for you, Naomi," he whispered in a sandpaper voice. And he'd even winked.

That was hours ago. He'd fallen into a fitful slumber and she'd sat down to watch. To wait. Her hips and back screamed from settling on that chair they'd dragged over for her. Her mouth pasty, her throat overcome by a powerful thirst. She gave a loud rattling clear to shake it, but nothing would. "Be right back, honey." She got up, satisfied the monitors were steady, quiet. Naomi squeezed her husband's hand and set off in search of a drink.

Overheads too bright, she switched on the red shaded hurricane lamp she favored. The double glass hooded antique was the only thing her mother had ever given her. The last thing.

Naomi closed her eyes, empty as the brown glass on the counter. *Lord? What am I going to do without him?*

Voices filtered into the kitchen, hushed tones of her angels in the other room. Eden, Lilah. So much like their mama, as if two halves of her daughter had been shorn and given to each. And she'd been given the opportunity to do things right a second time. Every way she went wrong with Rebecca made right in raising her orphaned twins. Ice clunked. Hollow, she spun a splash of water. No matter which way she sliced it, Lilah and Eden would always be her girls, right along with her Rebecca. Sweet Rebecca, the daughter born of her body that'd left her with two daughters, born of her heart.

Eden with her powerful faith and little girl dreams, now all grown up.

Lilah, her runaway, finally home, the gap that kept them apart for so many years, bridged at last. Thanks to young Pastor Gibb, of all things.

And it was Lilah, ultimately, who was there when Naomi couldn't breathe. Couldn't think. Because thinking meant the end of all she'd known since the tender age of nineteen. And thinking meant it was time to let Earl go. It was right for him to be here.

Eden appeared in the u-shaped kitchen, stepped to her grandmother's back, and squeezed her from behind. The girl certainly hadn't gotten her height from the Dale side of the family. It was from Samuel's, of course. The Guthries towered over everybody.

"You OK, Nana?" Eden's voice, so low it was barely a whisper.

Naomi just shook her head, tipped the cup to her lips, and clattered it back down again. "I-I don't know how to be today."

"You don't have to." Eden hugged her. "We're here to help."

Help. Naomi searched her granddaughter's tear-stained face. In a blink, Eden was six, caught playing with the makeup. Then sixteen, crying over that Reynolds boy. She shook her head to clear the images. *Earl's not the only one skipping through time. Where do the years go?* She gave her girl a kiss on the forehead. "Go wipe your raccoon eyes, honey. I'll be back out in a minute."

Eden gave a nod and padded her way down the hall to the bathroom as ordered.

The visitors vanished sometime during the night, just as they'd promised. The hospice workers didn't even speak with her beyond knowing looks and encouraging hand-squeezes.

That breathing apparatus off Earl's face, he looked more peaceful, if still out of place in that blasted hospital bed. Why hadn't Earl just taken a last fishing trip down to the river, cast his line for the last time, and...just...

One couldn't order up their way to go to glory. Not Rebecca on her fateful, final journey. Not their countless friends and neighbors, parents, and siblings that they'd laid to rest in that cemetery on the hill.

Someone had pulled a chair over and Naomi made use of it, sitting at Earl's bedside. She patted his fingers, wove hers in between. "I'm here."

Their hands. Hers stacked upon his, withered, wrinkled, and old. The bluish ropes of her veins startled her as thoughts dipped and churned from the days at the ranch, to Becca as a baby, to the newborn twins. A girl in each arm and a hole in her heart. *Sweet Jesus. The years snatched away like a thief in the night...and now, lost.*

"When'd we get so danged old?" Earl read her thoughts, his thin voice reaching her ears.

A gasp, she stuttered a laugh. "It's a blur, isn't it?"

He nodded once, breath whistling like wind through the reeds. "I'm tired, Naomi."

"It's OK, honey." Tears welled, spilled over her lips as she patted his hand, releasing the sea of tears the only thing that could quench the ball in her throat. "You can go rest, now."

"I'll go find us a nice little place...wait for you..."

Tears pricked, heated her eyes even as an icicle of fear clutched her heart. "I'll try not to be too long."

"You be watchin' for that big bird, now..." He sighed, worked for a breath and turned his head to the river below, eyes half lidded. "It's a sign...from Becca."

"I-I've always thought so."

"It is." Turning to look at her again, he smiled. "She just told me." His eyes closed, mouth set at half a smile.

Shoulders shaking, she knit her fingers together with his.

"Hear that?" Earl's eyes opened, a look of wonder brightening his face as he stared into a realm unseen. "It's her, she's singing…can y'hear?"

"I'm trying…" Naomi strained her ears to the silence and prayed. *Not yet. Please, Lord. Not yet.* Forehead to her hands, her shoulders wracked in silent sobs of one robbed, too soon, of the love of her life. *We need more time…is there ever enough time?*

No sound, no answer but his ragged breath.

She couldn't breathe. She couldn't think, for all of the roaring silence. Naomi pressed a paper-dry kiss to his forehead then stood and backed away from him. Everything about her was dry. Parched. Her soul, her mouth, her throat. She'd left the glass on the counter. Ice. *I'll get him some crushed ice, for his lips.* She muscled through the crowded emptiness into the kitchen but hesitated at the porch view.

Beyond the flowerbox window, the kids and their beaus sat out on the screened in porch talking in hushed tones.

Eden and Luke, side by side in the wicker swing, their index fingers hooked. Finally a pair. Lilah turned side to side in her swivel chair like a six-year-old, toes on the ground while Pastor Jake rubbed her shoulders and stared out toward the falls. The four of them, a newly arranged bouquet of blossoming love.

Soon this river place would be full of weddings and babies. Of laughter and life. And, if Lilah and Jake figured out what to do with each other, her little runaway could be a pastor's wife. The very notion burbled a laugh into her throat and a new waterfall of tears. Laughter. Anguish. Without sound, could one tell the difference?

She returned to Earl's side.

His head faced in the direction of the river, his body lay still. Unmoving. A look at his calm face, and she knew. His body a shell, her husband was no longer there.

The glass tumbled from her grasp to the rag rug. Ice skittered across the hardwood floor. Silence swelled with the scream that welled from her soul as she brushed over his chest, his arms, and his face with futile fingers. Still warm, but gone. Hollow. Empty. This vessel that held the soul she loved, would love, until the day she died.

"Why didn't you wait for me to come back? I wanted to hold your hand...to say g-goodbye..." But nothing mattered.

Her husband was finally free.

# 46

The misty, morning painted the Arkansas sky a dull white. The cicadas echoed in a rhythmic hum. No sounds of traffic. Even the river seemed to have gone quiet to mourn the passing of Earl Dale.

Lilah walked up the long, winding road from the chapel to the top of the hill, Jake's sermon ringing in her ears.

A good man. A quiet man. The foundation of his family. Of the town. Jake retold stories that brought folks to laughter, to tears, though not one of them experienced or heard first hand. The Earl Dale that Jake met was nothing like the man he'd known. "Obituaries are rarely that way." He'd told her the night before. At his father's mega church, often the pastor never even meets or knows parishioners first hand. Close to God, but not so much to each other. "Not like here," he'd said. Was he intending to stay?

On either side of the grassy path, centuries-old headstones bowed their heads in moss-covered disarray. Leaning oaks wove through the ghostly crowd, with exposed, knotted roots. Grave markers told the final tale of families, generations gone. Of children buried too young. Soldiers returned from war, taken before their parents. Her own mother laid to rest, there, at the crest of the hill.

She headed toward the spot marked for her grandfather's earthly remains. Where Astroturf topped the freshly dug plot, and where the three distinct rows of white folding chairs waited under a tasteful canopy, along with countless wreaths and hapless sprays of memorial flowers.

And the brass handled casket.

So wrong...Papaw shouldn't be here—he should be scattered in the river. But Nana'd put her foot down. They were going to rest forever together on the hilltop, just as they'd planned.

She paused at the crunch of approaching footsteps and turned toward the sound. The lanky glassmaker shuffled his way up the path, then froze under her gaze.

"You following me, Guthrie?"

"Not intentionally...uh...Lilah." He tried out a grin at using her name, but seemed to think better of it. Instead, he dragged the cap off his head, held it wadded and bunched at his middle. "That was a right pretty sermon your man gave."

Lilah nodded. "Jake's got a way with words."

"Why aren't you in that big black car with your'n? Your grandma and sister?"

"I needed some air." Tipping her gaze to the limousine, she shook her head. "Walk with me the rest of the way?"

"Oh, I don't think—"

"Please." She looked up into Guthrie's haunted eyes. "I could use the company."

Together, father and daughter stepped up the winding path, side by side, separated by the gulf of time and a host of unanswered questions neither one of them considered asking.

Lilah hesitated at the rise, frowned at the folding chairs lined up and waiting for her, for Eden, for Nana.

At last, she found her voice.

"P-papaw always said he knew more f-folks here than in town." Like a dam overfull, her grief finally spilled over. Tears of loss and longing for a time she'd run from. For all she'd missed. Her steps halted, she fisted her hands to welling eyes. "I shouldn't have run. I should have stayed."

"Don't." Guthrie pressed a clean handkerchief to her hand, gave her shoulder a hesitant pat. "You can't get the time back, so no sense in trying."

"I left Eden." She dragged the mascara-darkened cloth under her eyes and blinked up at the scattered cotton sky. "I left all of them, chasing the wrong guy. The wrong idea."

He nodded, eyes wide in a knowing stare. "Often wondered how that worked out for you."

"I failed at that, same as with everything else." Her breath stuttered out. "All I can do is sling hash, cast a line. All of that, thanks to Papaw."

Guthrie focused on her. "Think those things aren't worth doing?"

She couldn't help but study Guthrie's features. This time, he did not look away. His eyes, the same color as hers. She recognized herself in his shape of face, like looking in a distorted mirror. At once, she saw her reflection in his strong jaw-line. Even the shape and mannerism of Eden's in his calloused thumb, worrying each fingertip. Lilah found the part of herself that never fit in the Dale mold, here, in this man. She slow blinked and turned back to the gathering crowd. "Not sure I'm ready for a father-daughter talk, yet."

"No. Not the time or place." He un-pocketed and pressed a hand to hers, pressing something small, cold in her palm. A silver key.

She blinked up at her biological father. "Is this—"

"You take that now. That river place's all I've got to give you." he pressed lips together. "I get the feelin' Eden's happier in town."

Laughter mixed with tears as Lilah nodded. "You've pegged her right."

"Well, then. See you up there."

Guthrie continued up the path without looking to see if she followed, while Lilah rolled the key to the river house over in her palm, at last in charge of her own destiny.

# 47

"When will you be back?" Lilah hated the way her words rung with desperation as Jake checked his watch. Time wasn't on her side this morning.

"Scott Emerson's giving the sermon this week. If it goes well, he'll be there the following, too."

"If it goes well. You mean you're done here?"

He lifted, dropped his shoulders. "Mammoth's a small part of a big engine, Lilah. There are steps, measures. We have to be accountable as a church."

"So that means running back and forth to California on your father's whim?"

The church hadn't run him out on the news of his family, his deception, they'd embraced him. Did she even know who he really was anymore?

When he spoke, it was the measured words of her pastor, not the man she'd fallen in love with. "They want to hear our story out there. The Steadmans need a vacation, anyway. What a testimony they have."

"And I can't stow away in your suitcase?" She toed his duffle bag, heart welling at his responding laugh.

"Maybe next time. It's still a little complicated back there—"

"Because of your ex." She managed.

"And yours."

"Right."

The words ran out as the limo-taxi appeared.

"Looks as if dear old dad shelled out the big bucks. You flying first class, too?" At his responding silence, she gawped. "You are! Wow. Big time pastor hidden in the middle of nowhere."

"Not so hidden anymore." He held a wait-a-sec finger to the driver, and then clasped her hands. "If I could bring you with me I would."

"Just promise to take Tom and Earnestine to Disneyland. They'll get a kick out of the roller coasters. Send me pictures. Texts. Emails."

"I promise." His smile went serious, and in a flash his mouth found hers. No tentative, treading water, but hungry, needing her, wanting more with strong hands weaving through her hair, on her shoulders.

She returned every unspoken word, every shaking emotion as she clung tight, mouth inhaling sweetness, light, and somehow understanding all he couldn't, wouldn't say. Her head filled with a rush of love and panic. Wrapped in his arms, heart to heart, she wanted so much, all at once. To show him how much she'd miss him, to beg him to stay, to make him want to come back. To tell him how she really felt. And when he pressed an aching kiss to her forehead, she knew this might be not the beginning, but the end.

A honk from the driver broke the spell, and as his tail lights disappeared around the bend to the falls, doubt dug its ugly place into her heart.

Even if he could come back, did he want to?

~*~

After a week of closure, Eden and Luke announced they'd be married before summer was out. Why wait when they'd wasted so much time already?

Lilah accepted the news and their insistence that she stay on at the house, but vacated for the new couple, anyway. "You guys need your alone time."

"What I need is a chaperone, twenty-four-seven." Eden popped her gum with a grin. "You sure you want to go out there by yourself?" Eden looked visibly relieved, smiling a bit too wide as she helped Lilah pack her duffle.

She'd admitted her plan of returning to the river place.

"You tell Jake?" Eden dragged the top issue off a stack of bride magazines heavy with advertisements for trending gowns, ring-sets and honeymoon destinations.

"He'll be fine. Who knows if he's even coming back." Lilah swallowed the notion she should tell him her plans. She didn't owe Jake explanations. He, of all people, should understand. "And I...I need some time before...before things get any more serious."

"Really?" Eden arched her eyebrows. "Why?"

"It's not like I've known him since we were kids." Lilah cinched the duffle's sides together, zipping it closed. "What if he's a rebound guy? What if I screw things up again? What if—"

"I get it. Take your time. Make sure it's right." Eden waved the rest of her worries away, her diamond engagement ring sparking a rainbow of light. "You tell Nana you're going?"

At that, Lilah felt her blood cool. "I told her. She didn't like it, but didn't try to stop me."

"So that's what you two were yelling about last night." Eden cast a cool gaze at the understatement as she flipped another page. "I guess you know what you're doing."

"Yeah. Just like always." Lilah stuffed the little convertible with clothes, towels, shopped out the Ultimart for cleaning products, and headed to the river house. Away.

It was too much to be near Jake now. She couldn't think, couldn't breathe, couldn't process all the rifts in her world with him around. She might never fully understand all of the hurts left behind. She tried each and every day to heal the open wounds. Injured by a father who'd remained unknown, and by her grandmother, the only mother she'd ever known, who'd kept him away. And now, just when she was ready to accept him into her life, he'd vanished once again.

Lilah rolled up, parked in the weed-cleared space and observed the single wide trailer with an appraising eye. Outside would need a good washing. The porch sagged, but was sturdy. Inside, she blinked at the dust motes in the thin-curtained light, and sighed at wood-paneled walls and the ancient checkered couch.

Guthrie kept the place neat, but it was at least ten years past a good clean. Corners filled with cobwebs, spider webs, and worse. She threw open a window to let out the stale odor it might take weeks to get rid of.

She set to scrubbing the aged river house, a surrogate therapist ready to help her work out her issues. Lilah pounded the brunt of her anger out on dingy, ragged rugs from the cabin floor, now hung on a clothesline strung up between pines. She harnessed her hurt sanding dings out of scarred chairs, washing, bleaching lace curtains until they hung white, smelling fresh along the front windows. Her soul finally cleansed by letting the humid, late summer Ozark air filter through the long closed up house.

Hands white, pruned from mop water, the kitchen and bathroom counters sparkled. Walls scrubbed, smelling of pine and bleach, brought wallpaper back to its former glory, which unfortunately revealed the mauve and teal of the early-eighties decorator palette. She took one look around and decided the place needed updating. But really? It wasn't hers to change.

Taking her daily walk down the rutted, red dirt driveway, she angled to the row of mailboxes. No-seeums buzzed along with cicadas under the canopy of oaks. She maintained the simple act of retrieving mail out of habit, though nothing ever came except ads and junk.

Still, it was a connection to the outside world, a chance to wave "hey" to the neighbors. To see horses prancing in the Taylor fields, sauntering past the sagging red barn. She clicked to them, scratched behind the ears of an old roan, and let it blow grass from her palm. The mare set off back to its grazing. Tomorrow, she'd bring an apple.

Lilah sifted the stack of mail as she hoofed it uphill to the river house. She had daylight to burn today. She flipped over a coupon flyer and saw the yellow, manila envelope addressed to her. Inside, a letter from some lawyer in Plain View. A quick scan set her jaw hinging open as she read of property and transfer of ownership from Samuel Guthrie to Delilah and Eden Dale. Though the papers waited at the Thayer bank, this place was for all purposes, theirs.

She returned to the neglected back porch and sat to take in the expansive view. The river cut through the Ozark hills, rambling over the stepped falls with a chute that whip-tailed around the little island. There, a father and son fished off the sandy bank while a little girl scrabbled on hands and knees, hunting something at the water's edge.

The breeze in her face, she flipped through the Ultimart flyer. The ad beckoned with brightly colored Adirondack deck chairs. The deck could use a couple of those. Maybe some lights strung in the trees, or some outdoor lamps. Summer was just getting started.

She turned the page, seeing a sale on bedding and a two-for-one deal on paint. Why stop at the deck? If this place was theirs...shouldn't she do her best to make it a home?

# 48

The Thayer Ultimart was a sad comparison to its west coast counterparts. Less than half the size, serving as grocery store, nursery, electronics outlet, fashion mall, and pharmacy, it was a lot to pack into a tiny space that shared its parking lot with the squat, dark brick of Thayer's National Bank building. There, her sister waited on a bench, filing her nails, dressed in her day-off clothes of work out shorts and a bright orange, loose t-shirt.

Two birds, one stone.

"How're wedding plans going?" Lilah slammed her car door, making a red-dust streak on the paint.

"Stand still." She rushed Lilah into a bear hug, but paused at Lilah's palm out request to admire the engagement ring. "I want the party of the century, and Luke wants to run off to Vegas." Eden's eyes went wide as Lilah stiffened. "Not that there's anything wrong with—ah, shoot. We just can't agree on the details."

Lilah observed Eden's band of platinum, infused with a forest of tiny diamonds, the fat, round crystal-clear rock at its center. "He knows you so well. You two'll figure it out."

Eden nodded, wiping away a wash of tears. "Let's do this thing."

Together, they stepped to the double glass doors and pressed them open to the lobby.

An air-conditioned blast greeted them, as did the chirpy bank teller with the sandy-blond bob. Lilah drew a mint from the table and spun it open as Eden explained they had an appointment with the manager. Moments later, Beverly Abernathy had them in her office, seated in two leather chairs, promising to be back with water and their papers.

Lilah flipped through last month's *Field and Stream*, while Eden perused the pictures behind Beverly's desk. A snapshot of a fat baby on a pink blanket, drooling a toothless grin. The next frame showed the same child, now about age five, with curly blond hair, laughing, gray eyes, and a blue cotton candy crusted smile.

"Mr. Guthrie was here about an hour ago. He has business down in Joplin, but he said he'd...well. He'd like to see you girls soon."

They nodded, but Lilah wondered what Guthrie would want or need in Joplin. Family, maybe? There was still so much about her birth father that she didn't know. Odd, to think there was a whole side of their family that remained a mystery.

A figure at the door had them both look up.

Nana breezed in, her hair freshly fluffed from the Thayer salon with white curls arranged to perfection, dressed in her smart blue suit.

"Hey." Lilah dropped the magazine and stood, drinking in her grandmother's subtle beauty. She didn't sense a bit of chill in those sky blue eyes.

Nana wrapped her up in a full hug. "Missed you, my girl."

"I didn't know you were coming."

"I wasn't sure you two'd want me here...but, well." She glanced over her shoulder at the busy bankers. "I figured…"

"We want you. Come on in." Lilah gave up her seat and then, after a moment's hesitation, perched on the chair arm like she used to. Nana's hand to her back, they settled into their newfound truce. Her grandmother looked serene, at peace. "So what's the news?"

"We're just waiting."

The booming laugh from the next office could only be Tom Steadman. "When did they get back?"

"Day before yesterday—he even passed out Mickey Mouse ears to everyone at the diner." Eden showed hers in her purse. "Property sold, so he came back to buy papers."

Nana drummed the chair arm. "Bought themselves an RV. They're gonna go get lost in America."

Questions wove, but Lilah refused to ask. Did Jake come back with them? She spun to see Mr. Steadman, hands stuffed full of paperwork, standing at the counter chatting up the teller. Lilah watched as he said goodbye, then exited into the sultry Missouri heat, no weight of his shattered home about those easy steps.

She remembered how he and his wife held each other, the only thing that truly mattered when all else was lost. Love. Family. Small towns. Where you knew everybody, and everybody's business, and when someone asked you how you were, you cared enough to find out the answer.

"Don't you all look a picture?" Beverly breezed in, shot a sunny smile to the trio of Dale women, and set out water bottles for all. "Mrs. Dale, we sure do miss Earl. He was one of the best."

Nana nodded, folding her hands.

Lilah covered them, and Eden topped the pile.

A moment of silence, then Beverly continued with the business at hand. "The river property—thanks to Mr. Guthrie—is now deeded back over to the Dales."

"About that." Eden tapped her teeth. "Nana and I've been talking about that one."

"What Eden's trying to say is—" Nana cleared her throat, she turned to her wayward granddaughter. "Honey, I know what that place means to you. It should be just yours."

"But the papers said—" Lilah dry-swallowed at the thought. Revamping the river house, the landing, and the slope, the dock, and the hilltop singlewide—so much to do, and all of it, hers to decide?

"Papers say something else now." Eden sat up straighter. "Don't go thinking you don't have to save a room for me, when Luke and I want to visit."

"I've got the house." Nana sighed. "Eden has her cottage. We thought you needed a place to call your own—such as it is."

Lilah stared at the blur of papers that Beverly offered forth to sign. Her name, and initials on the signature lines. The pressing of fingerprints to notarize the change of ownership. At last, it was done.

Hugs all around, Lilah inhaled the buoyant feeling, anchored by all that remained undone.

"One more thing." Nana wrapped her arms around her girls. "Your Papaw wanted you each to have a little something. We're paying for Eden's wedding—something we waited a lot longer than we thought we ever would."

Lilah stiffened at the words. Eden's wedding shone a light on her own failure in the marriage department. For that matter, the fact that neither one of them even mentioned Jake, was proof positive she'd failed in that relationship, as well.

Nana held her all the closer. "Your sister's getting married. And, we'll celebrate proper—all of us. Together." Nana turned from Eden to face Lilah, full. "And as for you, sweet Delilah Dale, when you choose the right man, we'll do the same. In the meantime, let's outfit your new home, right special." Nana pressed a kiss to her forehead as only a mother can do, then closed Papaw's Chevy keys into her hand. "And get you a decent truck to get you out that'a'way."

"Nana, I—"

"Just remember how much you're loved, sweet girl." Tears pricked sky-blue eyes, full of love. Her voice heavy with emotion. "Now let's go shopping."

# 49

Over a month later, she'd filled the river place with everything from housewares to patio furniture, to a truck full of Nana's hand-me-downs. Lilah transformed the cliff-top single-wide into a very pretty little home.

She'd have everyone out for Independence Day. A big party. So big, no one would notice if Jake came or not. They were in some polar standoff, delaying the inevitable, maybe. She loved him, he loved the church, and she was not the kind of woman he needed on his arm.

Her cellphone was full of texts and pictures from Eden's latest gown-hunting jaunt, but not a word from her so-called boyfriend. Even the word seemed silly at this age. Perhaps it was good. They both needed time to think, to sort things out about what came next for them. She'd made her play and was digging in outside of Hardy, and he, well, he was bound to pull up stakes soon and head back to the coast.

Still, the river ran as she plucked another bunch of yarrow and Queen Anne's lace from the wildflower garden. Thick air blanketed the oak scrubbed hilltops, the sky dog-days hot, white, and heavy, but there was a hole in her soul that even wildflowers in mason jars couldn't fill.

Lilah trundled down the stone steps to the secret launch and plopped onto the damp grass. She dragged a bare toe across the muddy bank and drew her name like a child, a flourish underneath, followed by a question mark.

A breeze tugged her hair, the only answer. A kingfisher splashed into the river and then flapped away with an echoing call.

When the great heron floated down from the treetops to take its place, she froze to watch. The big bird stepped on stilted legs, cautious, searching, through the reeds, fishing for dinner as she mentally compared it to its glass twin, now resting in the kitchen window of her river house.

Papaw's memories were part of the river now. The way it rippled in the sunlight. He was in the thrilling tug of a fish on her line, and the voice in her head while she reeled it to shore.

And, all this beauty was a waste without anyone but her to witness it. Last person she'd shared it with was Jake, who'd kissed her in the sun-dappled shade. If only she weren't so stubborn, so afraid. She'd rush back and tell him—

"*Lilah...*" The wind whispered her name from the cottonwoods.

Ears perked.

Darting birds chattered, zipping tree top to tree top. A trout broke the surface of the water, while the heron stood perfectly still, waiting in the reeds.

Was she hearing things?

In full season, the river would be noise and laughter, skiffs, canoes, and inner-tubes. No sound, but in the rattling cattails. She was alone with the chirping frogs, a low buzz of dragon flies. In the distance, a train whistle, the slow-chug of the six fifteen on its way to Jonesboro.

At the sound of the approaching engine, the heron raised its long neck, flexed its wings, and launched upriver.

She watched its departing form lift into the M shape of a child's drawing, its reflection wavering on the water as the big bird rounded the bend just as a lone canoer paddled into sight.

She returned her gaze to the chained skiff, hooked on the rough planks of Papaw's fish-dressing table with silver fish scales forever embedded on its surface. The wood, weathered, twisted, and broken.

*Have to hire a carpenter to fix those,* she mused. Steps to the river dock and the others back up to her house all needed resetting. Those and countless other tasks remained on her to-do list. Wasn't it funny that the constant maintenance Nana hated about this place was what Lilah loved about it most of all?

The mewing caught her attention. Another batch of kittens? She knelt to peer under the shadow of the upside down boat. There, in the dim light, a stray black and white adolescent kitty stretched its claws and yawned. "Here, kitty. I won't hurtch'a." She beckoned.

The creature took one step. Two. A third, and then rubbed its chin on her outstretched hand. Its purr kicked up over the lapping water.

She cradled the purring creature, stared into its green, blinking eyes, and sat back on the dock. Her right foot dangled in cool water. With her back to the river, she cuddled the foundling and realized just how lonely she really was. "Where's your mama?"

"Looks like you're it." Jake's voice startled her from behind, and she whipped around. "If you're up for the job." He paddled up to the dock.

Lilah adjusted the little cat along her arm. "What

are you doing here?"

"Came to see my girl." Grabbing the dock pylon, Jake wrapped his tie rope and knelt-stood in the boat, his hands gripping the sides of the wobbly vessel.

"You can't get out that way, Jake." Lilah warned, stepping to help him a split-second too late. The canoe bobbled, careening crazily under his weight.

"How does one get out of a canoe, anyw—" He overcompensated, leaning away from the water against the capsizing boat.

*Sploosh!*

Kitten claws out and hissing, the black and white creature pushed out of her grasp and retreated to safety underneath the upside-down rowboat.

Lilah glanced from it to Jake's waterlogged form as he stood, drenched in knee deep water. A cloud of silt murked the clear pool around him. "That's one way to do it."

"I like to make an entrance." He tossed back dripping hair and shook his head like a dog, then grabbed the canoe's bow-rope and sloshed up the sloping edge.

Hand outstretched, Lilah helped him onto the bank. "Where'd you come from, anyway?"

"Maya's renting canoes out of Seven Falls." He tied the rope to a knotted root. "I stopped in to check on her, and she convinced me it was a good idea. Thought it would be romantic."

"She's a good kid." She could see the kitten's form huddled against the far wall of the boat. "Any word on her father?"

"They all cleared out until next year, if they come back at all. Maya wants to stay, though. She's working on her GED." Jake pulled a soggy handkerchief from a back pocket, wrung it out, and returned it. "Trying to lend some guidance. Get her to services once in a while."

She knew that look in his eyes. He was trying to see why she'd missed a month of Sundays, as well. He repeated the motion with his t-shirt, and water rained around his sandaled feet.

Why'd it plunge so deep at the very mention? She dropped to her knees at the base of the tree, jockeying over the roots, "Here, kitty, kitty." She reached as far under as she dared.

Jake dropped to one knee by her side, dripping a puddle from his sodden clothes. "Sorry I scared your cat."

"Not your fault." Her mouth twitched a smile. "Have a nice swim?"

"Wasn't exactly what I had in mind." He dusted off his shorts. "Should have worn my suit."

With a moment's coaxing, she gathered the black and white fur-ball and tucked it back in the crook of her arm. "Come on. I'll get you a towel."

"In a minute." He stepped to her, touched her cheek with damp fingertips. The sinews of his neck tightened, no sign of a bruise at his jaw. His mouth unreadable, gaze questioning, but Jake pressed no further. His gray t-shirt pasted to his chest, and he gave a shiver. "I missed you."

"Have you?" She blinked and looked down to her bare feet. Any attempts to keep it light were weighted by memory. "You didn't call."

"Neither did you."

A standoff, then. Fine. Two could play at that game. Far as she could tell, they were both losing. But she remembered the languid, healing waters of his kisses, the warmth of his skin. Her heart surged with need to hold him close even as her stubborn head mapped out a chessboard of possible moves. But did she want him for the right reasons?

"I've missed you..." His voice remained silver-smooth as she shot a wry grin.

"I've been a little busy..."

Jake brought her hand to his mouth. Warm lips pressed on her hand, light as a firefly. "Diner's not the same without you in the kitchen. Eden's specials are nowhere near as interesting as yours."

"I'm sure the rest of the town's missing my pico de gallo, too." Lilah's spine did a shiver-shake, and she shrugged to cover it. She gave the purring kitten's chin a scratch with her index finger.

"Don't make excuses." He stepped closer still. "You've been hiding."

"Like you haven't?" She jutted her chin, but her heart was slamming. "Pastor Gibson?"

His face went hang-dog. "Some folks like that we're out here. Hoping Dad'll come out for a guest speaker now that I'm not hiding anymore. But you're still hiding. Aren't you."

The kitten glanced up in question, and then closed its eyes and purr-snored.

Lilah kissed its head. "I don't need to hide."

"That's the truth." Jake's mouth angled toward hers, inches, centimeters, millimeters, yet remained a million miles away. As if their souls were mingling in an electric dance. His green-eyed gaze, soft, patient as he waited for her, just as he'd waited a month for her to sort things out, for her to close the distance.

She tipped her attention heavenward, through the twist-trunked trees. *Lord, if I kiss him now, its forever, doesn't he deserve someone better? Someone...*

A branch, newly ripped off, showed a broad section of trunk she'd never noticed. There, a carving, until now, obscured by time and overgrowth. "What's that?"

She pushed the wet cat into his arms and hauled herself up the first branch, then the second, attention on her target.

"What?" Jake watched her climb, head cocked in obvious confusion. "What do you see?"

"Up there." She strained to see, traced the rough bark carving. "Someone's initials. S plus R. In a heart." The bitter sweetness of her parents' love wrapped around her, born in secret and over too soon. "Sam plus Rebecca. They were just kids." She sniffed a pensive laugh. "He really did love her, didn't he?"

"Yeah. That's what he says."

"You've talked to him?" Lilah jumped back down to the earth.

"Sure." He handed her back the stray, stepped confidently to the stairs, and took them two at a time in front of her. "Can I get that towel?"

"Jake!" She trotted after him to the top of the ridge. "Tell me what you mean."

"Guthrie's replacing the stained glass window— it's a new design, but it fits."

"He's working for you?"

"Volunteering." Jake pressed a smile. "Went to Joplin to collect recyclable glass. He's starting next week. You really should come back..."

"Jake, I—"

"To see him, I mean." He walked into the house ahead of her. A slow whistle of approval blew through his lips as he turned a slow circle in the small living room. "You've been busy."

She set the cat in the chair, and it snugged into the draped quilt. Because her hands were vacant, she grabbed a rag-woven throw pillow, fluffed it, and tossed it to the edge of the couch. Shoulder to doorframe, Lilah re-admired her handiwork through his eyes.

White paint dressed up the old table and chairs. She'd antiqued Nana's wicker rocking chair, a crackle-coat that showed through with original wood. Clean sunlight filtered from open windows, and the six-candle shabby chic chandelier, bought at an antique store in Hardy, hung in place of the dated chain lamp. Everywhere, pale greens and whites in various patterns, neither too feminine nor too masculine. Mason jars, the color of Jake's ocean eyes, sat on every window sill and table, blooming with wildflowers.

"Wow." By the appraising look on Jake's face, he meant it. "Eden's place is so...Eden. But this is all you."

"Just a little elbow grease." She shrugged, standing a little straighter at his compliment in spite of herself. She opened the fridge, grabbed the milk carton with a slosh, and poured a saucer full.

Jake leaned against the kitchen counter and selected a green apple from the bowl, next to her Bible, and crunched a bite. His attention lingered on the page.

Heart pounding, she remembered the phrase she'd outlined that morning.

His smile curled as he read, swallowed. Nothing smug about it, just satisfied. "This'll make a great getaway."

She set the saucer to scrubbed linoleum, and the

cat happily lapped it up. "I was thinking it was more, home."

"Long way to drive for your diner shift." He took a fistful of nuts from the bowl on the counter. "I've missed your cooking," he said with a crunch.

"I needed some time off." The floor rattled underneath her as she stepped over to a hallway closet and freed a fluffy sage-green towel.

With one statement, he'd deflated her notion that this could be a year-round home. He was right. Winters out here would be unbearable. Ice, snow, and weather would wash out the rutted road. Propane would be scarce. Life in the backwoods of the Ozarks wasn't for sissies or city folk.

Jake's heavy steps reverberated across floor as he followed. He accepted the towel and scrubbed a corner at his damp hair. Now finished with its milk, the cat gave a thoughtful paw-lick.

He reached for her with confident, warm hands, setting them firmly on her hips. "You call this home, but do you even know what that means?"

"I'm doing my best to find out." Lilah faced Jake, square-on.

"You're not gonna find it here. All this place has for you is memories. Even with a fresh coat of paint and a furry houseguest." His gaze warmed her, head to heels. Even while he searched her eyes, she knew he saw straight into her soul. "I came back and you weren't there. Mammoth isn't the same without you. Please come home with me."

"Do we know each other well enough for you to ask me that?" She held her ground, verbally, even as her heart melted for him.

"I know you, Lilah." He cupped the back of her

neck, stroking her curls with his work-roughened palm.

"What about my past? What about yours? Your father...surely, he wouldn't approve." She backed a step away, shaking her head.

Jake's lips pressed into a thin, unreadable line. In one swift motion, he held the towel around her waist before she could escape and roped her against him. Trapped.

"But..."

"It doesn't matter." Jake's mouth lowered to hers, intoxicating, drowning her in a rush of sudden longing, an undertow he created, only now allowed to surface by his shaking restraint.

Her lips warmed by his touch. They held on to one another, drawing warmth, life, and light. Breath to breath, she allowed the silent moment to linger.

When she opened her eyes at last, she drank in the questions in his brow, the solid feel of his arms around her. It proved he would accept nothing but complete surrender, her complete and total trust in him.

His rich, resonant voice wasn't preaching now, but pleading. "I'm not perfect, Lilah. And, neither are you. But we're perfect for each other."

Before she could think, he dipped his mouth to hers, her hands looped around his neck, her senses filling again as they swayed to music only their souls could hear.

"OK..." She gave in as he let her up for air. Hands to his chest, she held him back, feeing the measured beats of the heart that had captured hers. "You win."

"I win?" He blinked in foggy confusion.

"I fell in love with you. Jake. Jacob. Whoever you are, whatever you want to call yourself." Laughter, relief, surrender mixed in her words as she confessed with total certainty, vulnerability, exposed. "You made me fall in love with you. Are you happy now?"

"This isn't a game, Lilah." His eyes pleaded, mouth tugging into a wide smile. "Please. Don't say it unless you mean it."

"Fair enough." Lilah's thoughts drifted to their beautiful, inevitable future. Jake offered healing waters and she accepted them, indeed, offered her own in return. "So what do we do now?"

A cellphone full of her twin sister's wedding questions and demands showed there was more to think about than her own happiness. "This is Eden's time. She deserves all the attention and a fairytale wedding."

Confusion looped his brow as he heard her out.

"I do love you, Jake." She smiled. "But we need to keep it under wraps for now. At least until after."

"Always looking out for your little sister. So, November?"

She nodded. Holding her ground while he blew a whistle. "You got something else to do, but wait for me, Pastor Gibson?"

"I'm just thinking it might be a nice little surprise to have Dad come out, maybe conduct the ceremony himself. Think Eden'd get a kick out of that?"

"Have Pastor Bill officiate her wedding?" Lilah laughed and draped her arms around his shoulders. "She'll be over the moon!"

"Let's save that for a wedding present, hmm?" he squeezed her close, words whispered to her neck. Safe, warm, and together at last. "Our little secret?"

"I love you, Jacob Gibson."

"Delilah Dale..." Her name on his lips, his hands

wove through her hair, she allowed herself to be drawn in as his mouth claimed hers, her heart, and sealed it. "I love you with all that I am, and all that I have…and it's not even close to enough."

Hand in hand, they returned to the riverbank to cast their lines, without caring if they got a bite.

Thank you for purchasing this White Rose Publishing title. For other inspirational stories, please visit our on-line bookstore at www.pelicanbookgroup.com.

For questions or more information, contact us at customer@pelicanbookgroup.com.

White Rose Publishing
*Where Faith is the Cornerstone of Love*™
an imprint of Pelican Ventures Book Group
www.PelicanBookGroup.com

Connect with Us
www.facebook.com/Pelicanbookgroup
www.twitter.com/pelicanbookgrp

To receive news and specials, subscribe to our bulletin
http://pelink.us/bulletin

May God's glory shine through
this inspirational work of fiction.

AMDG